When professional organizer Maggie McDonald finds a body in a snowdrift outside her friend's ski cabin, she must plow through the clues to find a cold-blooded killer . . .

Lake Tahoe in February is beautiful, but Maggie can't see a thing as she drives through a blinding blizzard with her friend Tess Olmos and their dogs, golden retriever Belle and German shepherd Mozart. Maggie has offered her professional decluttering skills to help Tess tidy up her late husband's cabin in preparation to sell. She also plans to get in some skiing when her husband Max and their boys join them later in the week.

What she doesn't plan on is finding a boot in a snowdrift attached to a corpse. The frozen stiff turns out to be Tess's neighbor, Dev Bailey, who disappeared two months ago. His widow Leslie expresses grief, but Maggie can't help but wonder if it's a snow job. As more suspects start to pile up, things go downhill fast, and Maggie must keep her cool to solve the murder before the killer takes a powder . . .

The Maggie McDonald Mystery series by Mary Feliz

Snowed Under

Maggie McDonald Mystery Series

Mary Feliz

LYRICAL UNDERGROUND
Kensington Publishing Corp.
www.kensingtonbooks.com

LYRICAL UNDERGROUND BOOKS are published by Kensington Publishing Corp.
119 West 40th Street
New York, NY 10018

All Kensington titles, imprints, and distributed lines are available at special quantity discounts for bulk purchases for sales promotion, premiums, fundraising, educational, or institutional use.

Special book excerpts or customized printings can also be created to fit specific needs. For details, write or phone the office of the Kensington Sales Manager: Kensington Publishing Corp., 119 West 40th Street, New York, NY 10018. Attn. Sales Department. Phone: 1-800-221-2647.

Lyrical Underground and Lyrical Underground logo Reg. US Pat. & TM Off.

First Electronic Edition: June 2020
ISBN-13: 978-1-5161-0528-1 (ebook)
ISBN-10: 1-5161-0528-1 (ebook)

First Print Edition: June 2020
ISBN-13: 978-1-5161-0531-1
ISBN-10: 1-5161-0531-1

Printed in the United States of America

For my family

Acknowledgments

Thanks, first and always, to my family. It's tough to share living quarters with an author, but you've always supported me, even when my job seemed unfathomably strange.

Thanks, too, to everyone at Kensington and Lyrical, including those I've not yet met, who have worked to put Maggie's stories into the hands of readers. To Dru Ann, Lori, and other bloggers who connect books to bibliophiles and have a special affection for the cozy comfort of traditional mysteries. To everyone in Sisters in Crime, a fabulous organization welcoming women and men of every color, nationality, gender, sexual preference, ability, and disability. They listen. They act. They teach. They learn. They care.

I so appreciate the warm smiles of the team at Peet's Mountain View on cold pre-dawn writing mornings. They know my order better than I do!

Thanks to the Snows for letting the Olmos family borrow their ski cabin for the duration of the narrative. Maggie and I remodeled it a bit, adding a bedroom wing upstairs. I'm sorry about the damage to the garage door and all the clutter we put in the closets.

Thanks to Gwen, whose Adirondack cabin helped furnish the bunk room.

Thanks, Wombats and the Sunday morning Farmer's Market crew. Without friends like you, Maggie would be a not-very-interesting hermit.

I'm so grateful for the editing skills of Jennifer Fisher and the sharp-eyed proofreading provided by Amanda Terry.

Thanks to you for buying, borrowing, or listening to this book. A manuscript only becomes a novel when it touches a reader.

Finally, if you can read this book, please thank a teacher. If you were able to find this book, please thank a librarian or bookstore owner. Without the members of all these professions, I would not be able to do what I do.

A Note on Chapter Headings

Each chapter in the Maggie McDonald Mystery series begins with an excerpt from Maggie's notebook. In previous books, these snippets revealed Maggie's approach to keeping chaos to a minimum in her own life and the homes and workspaces of her clients.

In this book, Maggie shares quotes she's amassed on organizing and planning comprising thousands of years of wisdom from an array of religions, professions, continents, cultures, and countries.

To Maggie, this collective thinking reveals the relentless and universal human struggle to curtail clutter and confusion. It demonstrates that planning, simplifying, organizing, and clearing out are central to the human experience. It may be one area in which we are all more alike than we are different.

Chapter 1

Chaos is inherent in all compounded things. Strive on with diligence.

—Buddha
Lived in Nepal between 6th and 4th centuries BCE

Wednesday, February 17, Late evening

The scene was like every description of a near-death experience I'd ever heard.

I drove through the darkness toward a white light on California's Interstate 80, east over the Donner Pass toward Lake Tahoe.

Banks of plowed snow towered above the freeway, obliterating what would have been gorgeous mountain vistas if there had been any visibility. What the newscasters had calmly predicted as "winter storm conditions" howled around us, buffeting the car and overpowering my headlights, defroster, and windshield wipers.

For miles, I'd searched for a rest area where I could unclench my hands from the steering wheel, clear ice from the windshield, and take care of more basic human needs. But snow obscured the exit signs and wind erased tire tracks as soon as they formed. My golden retriever, Belle, huffed warm wet breath in my ear. Her pal Mozart panted beside her. My friend Tess Olmos dozed in the passenger seat.

I didn't dare pull over, in case what I took for a safe shoulder turned into a thousand-foot descent into oblivion. In weather like this, we'd plummet to the ground and wouldn't be found until spring.

"Turn here," Tess said.

"Where?" My view out the front windscreen was no different than it had been for the last three hours—remarkably similar to the static on midcentury televisions.

"Here. Stop. The exit."

I pulled the car slowly to the right, squinting to distinguish something—anything—that would tell me we'd reached the turnoff for Highway 89 in Truckee, the gateway to North Lake Tahoe's world-class ski resorts. The swirling whiteness took on a salmon-colored tinge as I drove beneath sodium vapor lights marking the main road that led toward Tess's family ski cabin.

"Turn. Right. Right. Right. No, not so much."

The rhythmic thump of my tire chains slowed as I crept forward. "Do you want to drive, Tess? You know these roads."

"You're doing great. Besides, the shoulders aren't plowed. If we pull into a parking lot we're apt to get stuck." I wasn't convinced. Tess's voice sounded strained, as though she spoke through clenched teeth. "It's only a few more miles."

"Which should take a mere two or three hours at this rate." My fingers ached from tightly gripping the wheel. What would normally have been a four-hour drive from Orchard View and the San Francisco Bay Area had taken nearly twice that long thanks to the heavy rain turned blizzard that had blown through hours earlier than anyone expected.

We weren't stupid, Tess and I. We'd been watching the weather report for days and left early to beat the weather. The storm had other plans.

My eyes burned, my knotted shoulders felt like hardened concrete, and my nerves frayed. I took a deep breath and tried to relax. The good news was there was little traffic. The bad news was that there were no tire tracks to follow. Snow plows worked overtime to keep the main arteries open, but secondary roads hadn't seen removal equipment for hours. It was only Tess's familiarity with the route that kept my tires on the pavement instead of spinning off the road. I inched from one reflective snow stake to the next.

"Okay, there on the left," Tess said. "Leave the car in front of the garage for tonight."

I looked out at a blank canvas. "I'd be happy to do that if I could *see* the garage."

"It's right there." Tess pointed into the nothingness. "Wait." She scrambled in her purse, pulled out a garage door opener, and pointed it past me. I heard a muffled grinding and thought I detected a slight lessening of the whitewashed darkness. "Rats. The door is caked with ice and snow. It can't clear the doorframe." She pushed the button on the clicker again. The grinding stopped.

"We can't just leave the car in the road. What if a snowplow comes along?" My voice broke from exhaustion and I struggled to keep from taking out my frustration on my best friend.

"Inch forward," she said, as though I had a choice in the matter. "We'll park at the end of the road. It's not strictly legal, but we'll move it as soon as we can. There's a turnaround circle. You should see the lights over the mail center and bear boxes."

"Bear boxes?"

"Bear-proof dumpsters. Here. Stop."

I couldn't distinguish any landmarks in the static whiteness.

"The rest of the hill has some drainage issues. It gets icy all the way to the bottom. The lights are out, but you're good here. Pull to the right as far as you can. There are drifts of plowed snow between the road and the rocks."

"Comforting," I said, not meaning it. I pressed gently on the brake. The car slewed to the right as though it had heard and obeyed Tess's instructions.

"Good enough. We'll take the dogs and leave everything else. I'll give you a toothbrush and something to sleep in. It's going to be hard enough to trudge back uphill to the house in this wind without loading ourselves up with stuff." She grabbed two leashes and handed me one. I stashed a bottle of wine in my jacket.

"Mozart knows where the house is," Tess said, rubbing the ears of her German shepherd, a bomb-sniffing special forces marine reassigned to life as a devoted family pet. She hugged the dog and whispered in his ear. "I'm not sure whether I'm leashing you so I don't lose you or so you don't leave me behind. We'll need your help to find our way back to the house." Mozart wagged his tail.

Belle woofed politely to remind me she was waiting. Then she woofed again in either impatience or encouragement. Or both. I clipped the leash to her collar.

"Ready?" Tess asked.

"Do I have a choice?"

"Not if you want heat, a hot toddy, and a bathroom."

I straightened my shoulders, zipped my parka, and pulled my knitted pink hat down over my ears. Snow or ice pellets pricked my cheeks like needles.

If Tess said anything more, her words were lost in the howling wind. The frigid air stuck the insides of my nostrils together and made it difficult to breathe. If I thought Belle could hear me, I'd have ordered her to heel. I hoped she wasn't so eager to follow Mozart that she'd pull me too quickly over treacherous ground. The only good thing I could say for the storm was that the thick snow might cushion a fall. A broken limb was the last thing any of us needed.

If the day had gone according to plan, we'd already be several hours into our project for the week, clearing out generations of clutter in the Olmos family's ski cabin, preparing it for a quick sale that would help finance a career change for Tess and college tuition for her son Teddy.

With my initial timetable long abandoned and a complete inability to spot a single landmark in the storm, I heaped my trust on Mozart and Tess, ducked my head, and put one foot in front of the other. Two steps forward, one ungainly wobble, and a slip back down the hill. Wash, rinse, repeat.

When we reached our destination, we banged on the door though we knew no one was home to hear us or welcome us into long-sought warmth and comfort. We pounded to break up ice that had frozen in the jambs and sealed it shut. In the end, it took the weight of both of us to free it. Overbalanced, we nearly landed in a squirmy pile on the entryway floor.

My teeth chattered. I was frozen clear through to my bones. "How far is it between here and the car?"

"Hundred yards, give or take."

"Uphill. Seemed like miles." An unpleasant whiny tone tinged my words.

"Food, fire, a little booze. We'll both feel better."

I trudged down the chilly hall, desperately seeking a perch that wasn't vibrating and shuddering like snow-chain covered tires on rutted pavement.

"That's the garage," said Tess from the staircase. "Reverse floor plan. Kitchen and living room are up here."

* * * *

Upstairs, we shed our coats. I plunked down the wine bottle I'd smuggled under my jacket. Tess swatted at my arm. "Thank goodness you didn't fall on that and slice yourself open. There's no way we'd get back on the road tonight to get you stitched up."

She pulled crackers and cheese from fridge and cupboard while I searched for mugs.

"I'll make you Patrick's grandmother's recipe," Tess said, pulling honey and bourbon from a cabinet. "Lemon, honey, and a bit of ginger. Cures colds, warms a chill, and is good for what ails you, even if nothing ails you."

I fed the dogs and filled their water dish, then arrayed snacks on a plate.

"Can you turn up the thermostat?" Tess asked, pointing toward a living room wall, speaking around cracker crumbs, and brushing more from her fleece sweater. "I called ahead to take some of the chill off, but I don't think it's crested sixty degrees."

"You called ahead?"

"One of those fancy-pants tech gadgets that talks to my cell phone. Comes in handy when you're managing a second home and want to keep the pipes from freezing."

I took Tess at her word though I'd never owned a second home. I nudged the thermostat up and then scurried to the fireplace and phoned Max and the boys to tell them we'd arrived safely. They didn't answer, and the connection seemed iffy, so I texted the message, sparing them the scary details of our trip.

I knelt to open the flue and light an already-laid fire. As meager flames struggled to gain strength against the cold, I gathered our damp coats, hats, and mittens and draped them over the hearth-side drying rack.

Torn between planting my backside against the fire screen and being swallowed by a voluminous sectional, I chose the couch. On three sides it surrounded an enormous square coffee table under which both dogs had already retreated. The homey sound of a boiling kettle sang out. Tess joined me soon afterwards with a tray of steaming mugs and the snacks.

"I don't want to move from this spot," I told her, grasping a mug in both hands and letting the steam waft over my face and warm my nose.

"I hear you. Our guests often crash here after a day of skiing. Sometimes I wonder why we bothered with bedrooms at all. But—"

"No. Just no. Tell me there's no but. *But* can't be good. I don't want to know."

"*But* in weather like this, chances are the electricity will go out. We'll need to stoke the fire through the night to keep the pipes from freezing."

"Sleep here and throw a log on the fire every few hours? That's doable."

"First we need to bring wood up from the garage, let it warm by the fire, and set our phones to wake us. If the alarm goes off and the power's still on, we'll just roll over and go back to our dreams."

I sank into the sofa cushions. "Toddies first, right?"

The room went dark as if Tess's warning of an outage had made it so. We sat in the eerie glow of the fire, listening to the gusts outside. In the absence of refrigerator, furnace, and other modern noises, the wind noise grew more threatening.

The night ahead loomed long, cold, and dark.

Chapter 2

Life is really simple, but we insist on making it complicated.
—**Confucius**, Chinese philosopher. 551-479 BCE

Thursday, February 18, Morning

I awoke to the sounds of the microwave beeping, the refrigerator motor firing up, and the feel of warm dog breath on my face.

"G'morning to you, too," I told Belle, pushing her head away and struggling to extricate myself from the deep cushions. I cursed my recent absence from my Pilates class at the Mountain View YMCA. Stronger core muscles would have helped.

I tossed a log on the fire and noted that Tess, at some point, had escaped the sofa, presumably to find a real bed. I let her sleep and then began the multi-stage process of outfitting myself, layer by layer, for the weather outside.

I leashed up the dogs, left the front door off the latch, and stepped gingerly off the front stoop, gripping the railing until I could determine the slip factor of the ground underfoot. My first steps, in the shade of the house, were promising. There were two conditions I feared more than any others—a thin layer of melted water over ice, and a dusting of powder disguising slick terrain. So far, so good. I squinted into the sun reflecting off the fresh snow and patted my pockets for the sunglasses I'd left behind. Next time I ventured outdoors, I'd remember to bring them.

The air was still cold, but much warmer than it had been the night before, and the wind had died overnight. I unhooked the dogs' leashes and followed them as they bounded over the drifts like puppies with a new toy. We retraced our steps downhill to the car, where I brushed nearly a foot of snow from the roof and windshield. I stopped and leaned against the hood, watching the dogs and resting, out of breath after what amounted to light exercise. My body struggled to adapt to the altitude and the fact that it took me five or six breaths to take in the same amount of oxygen I could capture in four inhalations at home, closer to sea level. The dogs' antics had already furrowed the terrain in the turnaround area of the cul-de-sac. In the center of the road, we pushed through knee-high snow with a few areas nearly blown clear by the overnight gale. Everywhere else, nearly four feet of snow softened every surface, making it appear that the bear boxes, mail station, and vegetation had been covered with a thick puffy duvet. I grabbed a bag of groceries from the car and whistled to the dogs. The rest of our luggage could wait until Tess helped me drive the car back to the cabin. I needed her knowledge of the landscape to help keep my wheels on the snow-covered road, away from concealed rocks, and out of hidden gullies. I wondered what other creatures lay just out of sight. Hibernating bears? Tiny voles and mice? Snowshoe rabbits? Mountain lions? I shuddered and glanced over my shoulder. I had that tense feeling between my shoulder blades that meant someone or something was watching me or I'd spent too long yesterday at the wheel.

The last time I'd been to Tess's cabin had been during a summer heat wave, back before the recent death of her husband, Patrick. It had been the height of the tourist season. Every house was full of guests. Any self-respecting bear would have stayed far away from the noise. But now, I saw only one house other than Tess's with a plume of smoke escaping its chimney. The nearest house to the left looked long abandoned and in need of care. Icicle spears stretched from the roofline to the ground.

How many neighbors did Tess have in the winter months? Were the rest of the houses owner-occupied, vacant, or rented?

I trudged back up the hill toward coffee. I'd drag Tess out of bed if I had to. We had a long list of chores we needed to finish this week so that we could spend the weekend skiing. My husband Max, our children David and Brian, and Tess's son Teddy were joining us Friday night. After that, with the contents of the ski cabin discarded, donated, or stored, Tess would bring in painters and repair people to get the house spruced up to sell.

It was her late husband who'd loved the mountains. Tess and Teddy were beach people. Without Patrick, the ski cabin had lost its luster—

Panic derailed my thoughts as my foot found a slick spot in the road. I gasped, fought for balance, and windmilled my arms. Without my noticing, the sun had warmed the neighborhood to just above freezing. Icicles dripped from the eaves of all the houses. Rivulets of water carved their way through the drifts. After I'd regained my balance I shuffled my feet to keep from catching a heel on a patch of ice. I hoped some of the snow would survive the thaw. I'd been so focused on yesterday's driving conditions that it hadn't occurred to me to check the forecast regarding weekend ski conditions.

* * * *

Back inside the cabin I stomped snow off my boots and left them near the door. The dogs dashed up the stairs, leaving a trail of melting clumps behind them. I dodged the damp spots in my stocking feet and inhaled the aroma of hot coffee and cinnamon. Either Tess was up or she had the friendliest most hospitable ghost in the world.

"Morning, sleepyhead," I said to Tess as she poured coffee and pulled fragrant cinnamon buns from the oven.

"Thanks for taking the dogs. Is your car okay?"

"Yup. I don't think we'll need to shovel it out at all. Snow's melting fast."

Tess wrinkled her nose and peered out the window. "I was afraid of that."

"Most of the lifts will still be in operation this weekend, right? Even if we don't get more snow?"

Tess plucked a bun directly from the pan and transferred it to a plate, leaving a trail of icing drops that she cleaned up with her finger. "I think so. I'm not worried about that so much as the possibility of flooding."

"At this time of year?" I associated flooding with the spring snowmelt rather than a brief winter thaw.

"Maybe." She took her coffee mug to the window and stared out. "Could you hear the creek when you were out with the dogs?"

"I didn't think to notice."

"It's probably not a problem. When we have a quick thaw and the ground is still too frozen to absorb water, run-off creates flash flooding. The ice on ponds and lakes will be soft but concealed by the new layer of snow. We'll stick to the trails if we do any hiking. Falling through ice is a nasty but avoidable tragedy."

"We won't have time or energy for outdoorsy exercise. Not until after we make a dent in the clutter."

Tess returned to the table. I'd already demolished my cinnamon roll and was cleaning the icing off my plate. I was tempted to scarf hers if she didn't eat it soon.

"Do you have a strategy?" Tess asked. "I want to go through the closets and drawers and donate any clothes that Teddy's outgrown or that are so old-fashioned no one would be caught dead in them. I'm certain some of Patrick's grandmother's ski gear is still in the attic. I don't want to even think about the basement and garage."

"But didn't you and Patrick remodel just a few years ago? You didn't clear out stuff then?"

Tess shook her head. "We were focused on speed, so we just boxed up everything and labeled it. Pretty haphazardly." She scrunched up her face. "We're going to have to go through everything all over again."

"Are you selling the place furnished? Do we need to hang onto linens and housewares?"

"Yup. I can take the kitchen. There's a lot of whittling down I need to do. One set of pots, dishes, and bedding should be fine."

"The beds all look made. Can the rest of the sheets be donated?"

"I'll need to check first. Some of the patchwork quilts have sentimental value."

"Show me a bedroom we won't use this weekend. I'll make one pile of stuff I'm pretty sure you won't want, and another of things you'll need to approve more carefully. After you've given them a once over, I'll pack them up and we can take a load to your local charity after the snow plow comes through."

Tess tilted her head and saluted. "So orders the professional organizer."

"Trust me. It will go faster that way."

"I'll start in the basement. Some of the old skis may be museum quality, but most of them are just junk."

"Four piles," I told her. "Garbage, recycling, donate, keep." Tess plugged in her phone, cranked up the sound on a Motown playlist, and we set to work.

We labored steadily for two hours until Tess brought me a second cup of coffee. Cobwebs draped her hair and dark circles ringed her bloodshot eyes. Streaks in the dust on her cheeks told me she'd been crying.

"It's a tough job," I said. "All those memories."

She sneezed, then sipped her coffee as she stared out the window. "I met Patrick in high school," she said. "Spent weekends up here with his family, and then college weekends skiing with our friends. We were married here. Honeymooned. Vacationed with Teddy as a baby. Every dust bunny is whining sentimentally at me, begging me to save it."

I thought for a moment before replying. Tess was my friend, but she was also my client. I'm a professional organizer. Clearing out, down-sizing, and reorganizing are my superpowers. I help clients blast through these crisis moments to get the job done.

But Tess and Teddy had lost Patrick eighteen months earlier. They were still fragile. Maybe it was too soon. "Are you sure you're ready to sell?"

Tess sighed. "I was so sure up until this morning. Teddy and I need the money to make our dreams come true. College and possibly graduate school for Teddy, and a career change for me."

Since Patrick's murder, Tess had lost interest in her lucrative job as one of Silicon Valley's top Realtors. After we uncovered the clues that led us to the creep who'd killed her husband, Tess had declared her intention to enroll in the local community college and pursue a career in law or law enforcement. Her initial plan was to become a criminalist, analyzing forensic evidence from crime scenes, but she was keeping an open mind. She'd approach the future one or two classes at a time and revise her plans as needed and as her interests developed.

I put down my coffee mug and wrapped my arm around her shoulder. "Everyone says to wait a year or two, or even more, before making big decisions. It's only been eighteen months—you're still well within that time window."

She shook her head vehemently, tickling my face with her long velvety black hair. "No, I need to do this."

"How 'bout this, then. We'll do what we can for now. Hit the high spots. Get rid of the baby stuff along with everything broken and worn beyond repair. We'll reevaluate the long-term scheme on Sunday. You'll know more by then about how you feel and how Teddy's handling it all, okay?"

She wiped her eyes and sniffed. "I guess."

"Whether you decide to go ahead with the sale or not, this place could do with a good clear away and cleaning. Nothing we do this week will be wasted, no matter what you ultimately decide."

"It's a plan," Tess said, squaring her shoulders and trying to smile. "But I still would like to finish up this weekend."

"Did you bring your magic wand?"

Tess gave me a friendly shove. I stood up, brushing my grimy hands on my dusty jeans.

"Are you up for a break?" I asked. "I want to move my car. I could use your knowledge of any hazards that the snow is hiding. You know, attack-trained boulders, car-swallowing sinkholes, that kind of thing."

Tess stood, leaned forward, and finger-brushed her hair. She gathered its weight into a ponytail and snapped a hair tie around it. "And after that, lunch. I'm always starving in the mountains."

* * * *

We took the dogs and shovels just in case. Snow melting and settling, combined with drifts sliding off cabin roofs and down the hill, had increased the density of the mounds surrounding the car. Mozart and Belle had a quick sniff around, focusing on the bear boxes with their odors of garbage and visiting critters, both wild and domestic.

I took one side of the car and Tess took the other, digging out the tires. The weight of the snow and the altitude made me breathless in a hurry. I stood, set down the shovel, and stretched my back.

"How you doin'—" I started to ask Tess, when my feet slipped out from under me. My head slammed against a rock or still-icy snowdrift, and I scrambled to regain my balance. But the more I struggled the faster I slid. Hidden under the drifts was a thin stream of snow melt over a slab of ice. I yelped and screamed as I careened down the steep slope of the turnout area, fighting to keep my head uphill. My jeans were quickly soaked. I was freezing.

Grabbing for something, anything I could use to slow my fall, I lost my mittens and scraped my knuckles until I took hold of a jeans-clad leg just behind my head on the right. Tess had apparently fallen victim to the same combination of physics laws that had sent me flying, and we'd both ended up in a jumble at the foot of the hill. "Neither one of us gets any points for grace and coordination," I said.

"What's that?" Tess stood up behind me on the left. "I was laughing too hard to hear what you said. If I weren't such a klutz with my phone's camera it would already be on YouTube."

I stared at Tess's legs covered in stylish black corduroy pants and bright red snow boots that were significantly grippier than my footwear. I followed the legs up her body to her face, and shuddered.

"Oh my God," Tess screamed in alarm, falling to her knees at my side. "Are you injured? I'm so sorry. I shouldn't have laughed. Where does it hurt?"

"If you're there," I said slowly. "Whose jeans was I holding on to?" I shuddered again, too creeped out to turn my head and see for myself.

Tess drew back. Her eyes grew wide. I hesitated, but then glanced behind me. Like Tess, I stared at the black winter boot and sodden clothing on the leg that emerged from the partially melted snowdrift.

Chapter 3

How many things I have no need of!
—**Socrates**, Greek philosopher. 470-399 BCE

Thursday, February 18, Near noon

I scrambled back, putting as much room as I could between myself and the offending boot. I wiped my hands on my jeans, leaving swaths of blood from my injured knuckles. I repeated the motions, but my hands felt no less tainted by their proximity to a dead body.

"Was he there last night?" Tess whispered, eyeing the boot as though she expected it to wake up and attack her. "Tell me we didn't walk over or on him last night."

I covered my mouth and fought my growing horror. "Did I hit the guy with the car? Did we knock him down and then leave him behind to freeze? I couldn't hear a thing in that wind."

"Wouldn't the dogs have smelled him? Warned us a stranger was near? Tried to greet him?" Tess shook her head. "No. No. He couldn't have been here last night. Not like this."

"Then how long has he been there? His leg is frozen. Stiff. He must have been deep under the snow. I guess it thawed just enough this morning to unearth him." I glanced around the cul-de-sac, my heart racing. Whether it was from panic or the altitude, I couldn't say.

Belle bounded toward me and play bowed, assuming I was up for a fun new game. Mozart lifted his leg against the snowdrift encasing the frozen body.

"No!" Tess shouted, a moment too late. "It's a crime scene!" She was a natural for a law-enforcement career, or she would be once she got her timing down. She scrambled to her feet, grabbed the end of Mozart's leash, and reached out a hand to help me up.

"Should we call—" My words were cut short by a screech of metal on metal, followed by a weird crashing sound I couldn't identify.

On my feet, but feeling a little wobbly, I glanced up the hill. In the nearest house, across the street from the neglected one I'd noticed earlier, a woman leaned out of an open second-story window. She knocked a broom handle against icicles as long and as thick as my arm. Attached to the roof, the frozen spikes loomed over the window like lethal monster teeth. Freed, they slammed into the snow drifts and quickly disappeared.

Tess patted my arm. "It's okay," she said. "It's my neighbor, Elisabeth Roche."

"Hey, Elisabeth," she shouted, waving. "It's Tess. Tess Olmos from across the street."

The seventy-something woman with gray hair and a pinched face squinted toward us. "Whose car is that? Do they have a permit?"

"It's my car, Mrs. Roche," I said, smiling and stepping forward. "We were about to move it. Couldn't get it into the garage last night. Door was frozen." My explanation wasn't precisely accurate, but I didn't think it mattered. I'd identified the offending driver and promised to move the car immediately.

"Don't delay. We can't have it blocking the mailboxes, the dumpster, or the path of the snow plow. And leash those dogs." She continued to fuss. "People don't think. The rules are there for a reason." She poked a few more icicles, breaking them off with a shattering crack.

Her face disappeared into the dark recesses of the house and she slammed the window shut, knocking down a few more deadly ice spears. But not before I heard the telltale yapping of a tiny and very annoyed dog.

"Chihuahua mix," said Tess. "Duke. He thinks he's a Great Dane, but he uses a litter box in the winter. He'd get lost in all this snow if he didn't freeze first."

I glanced at the foot of the man who had apparently been lost and frozen in the snow. My stomach lurched. I swallowed hard. "I guess I should move my car."

"Crime scene."

"Right. Do you have your phone?"

"Back at the house."

"Should one of us stay here and guard the…boot? The body, I mean?" Both dogs had figured out that we weren't in the mood to play. Instead, Belle sat on my foot and leaned into my leg, her eyes on mine, begging me to tell her what was wrong and how she could help. Mozart guarded Tess, his ears and the fur along his spine at high alert.

"There's no one here to protect it from," Tess said, frowning. "And Mozart's already tampered with the scene. Let's go back, call the police, and wait in comfort. I'm guessing Elisabeth will confront anyone who sets a foot wrong out here."

I pulled my keys from my pocket and stepped toward the car but then stopped as Tess's words sunk in. "I guess you're right. We should leave it. They'll need the car to figure out whether I hit him."

"And you're soaked to the skin. If we stay out here any longer, thaw or no thaw, we'll be frozen as stiff as he is." Tess tilted her head toward the booted foot and tugged on my arm, urging me back toward the cabin.

Once there, Tess called the local police then hustled me into a hot shower. "I'll leave warm sweats, socks, and slippers just outside the door," she said. "Take as long as you need. Dispatch said they're swamped with storm-related disasters, but they'd get to us as soon as they could. My guess is that means dinner time. Nothing happens fast in the mountains."

Shivering from much more than the cold, I let the water wash over me until I was warm, my fingers were pruney, and my skin finally felt almost clean.

We pulled together what we'd hoped would be a comforting lunch, but we both just picked at the grilled cheese sandwiches and chicken soup. Tess had foregone a shower but changed into dry sweats over a thick cotton turtleneck. Tess's oversized sweats were her signature red. Mine were a faded forest green. We were unseasonably festive.

Tess glanced out the window and her back stiffened. "It's Elisabeth. Coming this way. Quick. Downstairs. No, never mind, I'll do it. Stash the plates in the dishwasher and conceal the evidence of lunch. We don't want her to settle in for a meal."

Tess grabbed an overgrown and seedy-looking potted spider plant that must have been overlooked when she'd prepped the house for the winter. She closed the dog gate at the top of the stairs, and descended in her ungainly fleece boots. I leaned over the railing, ignoring her instructions so I could see what, exactly, was so urgent. She plunked the ugly, dying plant on the flat-topped newel post at the bottom of the staircase and dashed to the closet directly across the small foyer from the entrance. With a sharp exhalation that told me her burden was heavy, she lifted a full-length over-the-door hanging mirror from the inside surface of the door. Stepping back, she transferred it to the hallway side. Closing the door gently, she glanced at her reflection, straightened her hair and her sweatshirt and then turned when the doorbell rang. I lifted my eyebrows. My friend had gone round the bend.

"Tess, honey, it's Elisabeth," called the neighbor from the other side of the front door. "I brought you some cookies. We need to talk. About the rules, you know. I'm the association president now." Through the sidelights of the front door, I could see her face draw close to the glass, eyes squinted, lips pursed. Like a rat devouring a seed, her entire face seemed pointed and puckered with the permanent lines of a lifelong smoker.

Tess sighed. "Brace yourself, Maggie," she said, then opened the door. "Elisabeth..."

"Oh. I'm glad I caught you." Elisabeth stomped her boots on the stoop and handed Tess a foil-covered plate. "We need to talk."

Tess's shoulders hunched up near her ears as she took the plate. "I guess you'd better come in." She stepped back far enough so that Elisabeth could enter, but not enough to be genuinely welcoming. She stood between her unexpected guest and the staircase.

"It's about your dogs." Elisabeth glared at Mozart and Belle who stood at the top of the stairs. "They were out of your control down there in the turnaround. The evidence is in the snow." Her face looked as though she'd smelled a foul odor. She straightened her back and lifted her chin, bringing her height to what couldn't be much more than five feet. "Dogs must be leashed and under the owner's control at all times." She sniffed. "It's the rule."

"Yes, of course, Elisabeth. It's important," Tess said.

"There's no excuse."

Tess nodded. "Won't happen again."

It wasn't like my friend to so quickly placate a neighborhood tyrant, making me wonder again about Tess's agenda. But before I could form a question, two large black or dark green SUVs barreled past the house with their lights flashing. I peered out the front window toward the turnaround area of the cul-de-sac. One vehicle stopped dangerously close to my car while the other pulled up near the mailboxes.

"Oh dear," Elisabeth said. "We haven't had the police in our little neighborhood in weeks. It wasn't me, you know. I didn't call them. I mean, you were breaking the rules with the dogs and the illegally parked car, but the police? That would be overkill."

"I phoned them." Tess fessed up. "I need to get down there. Would you like us to walk you back to your house? We found a dead body down there. It's enough to make anyone nervous."

Elisabeth gasped. Her hand fluttered in front of her face. "What? In *our* neighborhood?"

"We did."

After waiting for Tess and me as we layered our snow gear on over our sweats, Elisabeth joined us as we all trudged, with the dogs, toward her house near the end of the road. We'd only taken a few steps but could already hear Duke the Chihuahua yipping from inside Elisabeth's house. He vehemently protested being left behind.

"I'm sorry to be such a stickler for the rules," Elisabeth said. "It's my Duke. I'm protective. The Baileys' dog, that Winston, he's always getting out and harassing my baby. I just won't have it. And if you and your friend had seen that devil Winston off leash, and thought it was okay to let your own beasts run free—"

"Winston," said Tess, interrupting. "Such a sweet old Labrador. Mozart adores him."

Tess's glowing endorsement of Winston seemed to rile Elisabeth, but before she could respond, we heard another vehicle approaching. We drew the dogs close and flattened our bodies against the drifts that narrowed the icy road. We wanted to keep out of the way and avoid forcing any driver to slam on the brakes. An unplanned skid could take out all three of us and the dogs.

"It's Leslie Bailey," Tess said. "With Winston." I detected a note of glee at the mention of the Labrador's name. Was my typically peace-loving friend spoiling for a fight?

The dark green SUV pulled slowly to a stop. The driver lowered the window. "Tess! I'm so glad to see you," said a thirty-something woman I took to be Leslie. She leaned her head out the window. Her short, expensively coiffed brown hair moved in the light breeze, and she looked far more polished than anyone else I'd seen at the ski resorts on this trip or any other. "I had no idea you'd be up this week. We have to get together."

We have to get together. In California's unwritten dialect it translated to: "I haven't seen you in ages, and I really don't care, but I don't want you to think I'm rude or unfriendly."

"Meet my friend Maggie," Tess said, turning and waving her hand to urge me forward. "She's helping me clear out the house. I'm getting ready to sell."

Leslie pouted. "Sell? You can't. I mean, I understand. I'm so sorry for your loss. Dear sweet Patrick. But that house has been in his family for generations. It was the first one on the street." Leslie's words tumbled out all in a jumble with one word squished right up against the next.

Tess spoke when Leslie paused for a breath. "We'll see. This is just the first step."

"What's with the cops? Is it safe to pick up the mail?" Leslie pointed toward the end of the street, where officers had placed a barrier across the road, limiting access to the turnaround area. A young officer who looked no more than twelve years old held a clipboard and guarded the barricade.

Tess hesitated and Elisabeth broke in. "It's a *body*," she hissed. "A *dead* body. Tess found it. The police need to talk to her." Somehow, though her words were benign, Elisabeth made it sound as though Tess was a murder suspect. I was used to drama queens. There's at least one in every neighborhood. But Elisabeth was in a class by herself.

Leslie's face blanched under her makeup. "I'll just put my car away and be down to join you."

"You don't have to. We'll let you know. Or the police will." Tess said quickly. There was a subtext I was missing.

"I have to." Leslie rolled up the window, checked to make sure we were well out of the way, and pulled her car into what must have been a driveway next to Elisabeth's house. At first, I thought the two women must live together, but then Leslie drove past Elisabeth's. I spotted the roof of a mansion-sized edifice looming among the trees behind the homes that fronted on the street.

"Do you think...?" asked Elisabeth.

Tess shook her head. "No. The poor thing." She turned toward me to explain. "Leslie's husband has been missing since just after Christmas. They have two small children. He went out one night with Winston and the garbage. The dog came back, trailing his leash, and no one has seen Dev since."

"That's horrible! Should we wait for her?" I wasn't eager to confront the dead body again.

"We'll go ahead," Tess said. "Leslie may decide to stay put. If the body we found turns out to be Dev she'll learn the truth soon enough."

Tears pricked at my eyes at the brittle sound in Tess's voice. Eighteen months earlier, Tess had gotten word that her missing husband had been murdered. She knew the horror that might await Leslie. One look at Tess's pale and sweating face told me she was reliving the experience. I grasped her arm. I didn't know if it helped Tess, but it was the only thing I could do. Tess stepped away from me, all business. "Let's get this over with." She tilted her head toward an older police officer who walked toward us with the limping gate of someone who needed a knee replacement. He towered over us, somewhere around six feet six inches, and was dressed head to toe in black. His Mountie-type hat held a large silver badge that glinted in the sunlight. "That's Quinn Petit. Winter Harbor police chief. Good people. We can trust him."

Chapter 4

In order to seek one's own direction, one must simplify the mechanics of
ordinary, everyday life.
—**Plato**, Greek philosopher. 428-348 BCE

Thursday, February 18, Afternoon

Chief Petit tipped his hat and stopped about three feet away from us.
It seemed like a practiced gesture that made it easier for people to avoid
craning their necks to look up at him. I wondered if he had a different
approach when addressing bad guys. Two steps forward, he would loom
over us and seem much more intimidating.

"Afternoon, ladies," he said. "It's good to see you, Mrs. Roche. Do you
need to look after that very unhappy dog I hear?" We all took a moment
to listen to Duke's insistent and incessant yapping. I'm a big-dog fan, but
I don't have anything against little ones, provided they're well-trained and
secure enough to avoid constant high-pitched communication.

"Oh no, Chief Petit, Quinn, I want to help." Elisabeth's cheeks turned
pink and she fluttered her eyelashes as she stepped forward.

Quinn turned toward Tess. "I understand you found the body?"

"It was my friend Maggie McDonald."

I held out my hand. Quinn shook it with a firm but comfortable grip.

I knew that anyone with legal training would have suggested I wait
for Quinn to ask me questions, which I should answer with a brisk *yes* or
no, volunteering nothing. But my curiosity was stronger than my patience

and forbearance. And with several friends in the Orchard View police department back home, I trusted and liked people in law enforcement. "What can you tell us?" I asked. "Did I hit him with my car last night? We couldn't see anything. I parked there because we couldn't get Tess's garage door open. We didn't see anyone. I didn't hear anyone. But the wind was loud. *So* loud." I tightened my grip on Tess's arm feeling a little wobbly as I revealed my dark fear that I'd killed or wounded the man and left him to freeze in the blizzard.

"Mrs. McDonald, we'll need to wait for the medical examiner to thaw him out and let us know more," Quinn's voice was gravelly, but gentle and kind. "But if that white vehicle is yours, there's no mark on it. I don't see how you could have hit him hard enough to hurt him without it leaving some kind of a mark on the car."

I let go of a breath I hadn't known I was holding. "Maggie, please. Thank you. I know I hit something, but it could have just been the snowbank. I was so afraid..."

"And all the snow last night could have cushioned the impact so that it left no mark on the car. Course, like I said, the medical examiner will tell us for sure. After fifty years in law enforcement, I know more than most, but I'm no physician."

"Is it Dev?" Tess asked. "He went missing—"

"I know the story," Quinn said. "We investigated his disappearance and haven't stopped looking for clues to his whereabouts." He paused and looked us over closely. "Can I trust you to do the right thing?"

"Whatever do you mean?" asked Elisabeth in a tone that was halfway between indignant at the suggestion that she couldn't be trusted and flattered by the fact that he'd paid such careful attention to us.

"Rumors fly around these resort communities as though driven by gale-force winds." He removed his hat and smoothed his mostly bald head. "Say nothing about this to anyone. *We* need to be the ones to inform the family." He pointed to the officers poking at the snowdrifts behind my car.

"Do you want us there when you talk to Leslie?" Tess asked. "When you tell her? It's him, isn't it? It's Dev." Her voice broke.

"Looks that way. Clothes match the description of the ones he was wearing when he disappeared. And the ID in his wallet—"

Elisabeth gasped and grabbed Tess's other arm. "He's been here all along? Right here with us? Did we pass him every time we took out our trash or picked up the mail? Are we that clueless? That thoughtless? Oh, poor Leslie. Poor dear Leslie."

"Poor Dev," said Tess.

Though I felt sorry for everyone concerned, I didn't know Dev or Leslie Bailey, and my thoughts leaned in a more practical direction. "Chief Petit," I said. Unsure how to address him, I opted for a level of formality that was unusual in California. "Do you need my car or would it be better if I got it out of your way? I could drive Tess and Elisabeth back up the road..."

"We'll need to bring out some heavy snow removal equipment so we can preserve any evidence that's hidden in the drifts," he said. "Moving your car would help, thank you." He turned toward Elisabeth and Tess, his expression soft. "The sun sets early this time of year and it gets cold fast. Y'all get home and warm. One of my team will be by to question you later this evening." The chief spoke with a hint of a southern accent, and I wondered how long ago he'd moved here—how long he'd worked in the Tahoe basin.

Elisabeth moved like a poorly programmed automaton, but she allowed us to guide her into the car and then into her house. We left Belle and Mozart in the car. Tess fed Duke while I led Elisabeth to a chair in her cozy front sitting room and lit her gas fire. She stared into the flames and said nothing.

"If you need anything, Elisabeth, we're just across the street," Tess said, handing her a mug of tea. "You call and I'll come running."

Elisabeth shook her head and was silent. Though I understood shock and had previous experience with the body blow delivered by an unexpected death, Elisabeth's stunned speechless reaction seemed a tad extreme. But Tess didn't seem surprised. She clasped Elisabeth on the shoulder. "You take care now," she said. "Maybe a hot bath?" Elisabeth nodded.

"Do you want Duke in the kitchen or out here with you?" Tess asked. Elisabeth patted her lap. I walked to the swinging door to the kitchen, pushed it open, and Duke barreled through, barely touching the floor as he launched himself toward Elisabeth. He landed in her lap, snuffled her neck with his tiny nose, and sat gazing into her eyes. She stroked his back.

"You've got exactly what you need now," I said. "There's nothing like the comfort and unconditional love of a dog."

Elisabeth nodded and her eyes twinkled. "Even a little stinker like Duke."

* * * *

After we'd tucked in Elisabeth, Tess and I pulled the car up outside her cabin and finally unloaded the groceries, clothing, and other gear we'd brought with us. "Watch your footing," Tess warned. "We're at the top of the rise here. It's all downhill to the main road on the north side of the house, and a steep slope down to the mailboxes to the south." With my newly adopted shuffling gait, I avoided any missteps. We emptied the car quickly and were ready to settle ourselves the same way we'd tucked in Elisabeth. Tess and I sat in front of the fire with blankets, tea, and the dogs. We sipped silently as we processed all that had occurred and pondered how the day's discoveries would impact us and the little mountain community.

"Doesn't look like we're going to get much more done today," Tess said.

"Some things are more important than being organized," I said. "Give it time. How are you holding up? Flashbacks? Aftershocks?"

Tess thought for a moment, taking stock. "I think I'm okay. I feel for Leslie though. I guess this has made me realize how far I've come since Patrick's death, even though it seems like I've got a long, long way to go."

"Grief takes its own time. Would distraction help? Gossip?"

"Heck yeah," said Tess, scrunching down under her blanket to get comfortable. "Dish."

"What were you doing earlier with the mirror and that near-death plant?" I was tempted to ask Tess about Leslie too. How did she manage to look so cosmopolitan in a world where fleece-lined jeans, plaid flannel shirts, insulated boots, and puffy jackets ruled the day? Was she the grieving widow or a likely suspect in Dev's death? But I was afraid those questions might hit too close to the bone...or the heart. Tess had been a suspect in Patrick's death, an accusation that had made her grief even harder to bear.

Tess snorted. "That was me at my most petty. Sorry you had to see it. I'll do better."

"But why?"

"Elisabeth is a sweet lady and a good neighbor, most of the time. But she's easiest in small doses. She has a habit of overstaying her welcome."

"But, the plant?"

Tess looked sheepish, like a little kid who'd been discovered in a lie. "It's going to sound even more ridiculous when I try to explain. It doesn't reflect well on me at all. Here goes...she's really into feng shui. Wants me to hire her to help stage houses and won't take no for an answer. That's what the mirror and plant were all about. Passive aggressive feng shui. Mirrors reflect energy. Dead plants represent death. Together, they should repel visitors."

"So, instead of telling Elisabeth you were really busy and had to get back to work you tried to get the plant and the mirror to take care of your problem for you?"

Tess sighed and looked toward the ceiling. "I told you I'm not proud of my behavior. I'll work on it. Try to be a grownup."

I wasn't sure how to respond to that, so I said nothing. Nobody's perfect. We all do dumb things we wish we hadn't. But then I shifted gears. "Feng shui, huh? I should talk to her. There's a lot of overlap between feng shui and what I do. Reducing clutter is big in both. I don't much like dead plants, either."

"I'll toss the plant tomorrow," said Tess. "My actions were stupid and childish."

I changed the subject. "What's the rest of her story?"

Tess sipped her tea and stared out the window toward Elisabeth's house. "She's an interior decorator. I think at one time she was mayor of some small South Bay town. She gets stuff done, so she's a great asset to the community, particularly to those of us who are only here on the weekends. There's no job she won't undertake for the good of the neighborhood, though she does everything her own way."

"And the dogs? She loves that little Duke but seemed terrified of Belle and Mozart." At the sound of their names, the dogs thumped their tails under the coffee table.

"She got it into her head that Winston, the Baileys' Labrador, eats Chihuahuas like Duke for breakfast. There's a local legend that she stole an airsoft gun from some kid who was up here for the summer and used it to shoot kids and dogs she doesn't like."

"The neighborhood witch? There's one in every town."

"Yup. Teddy won't eat any food she brings over. I don't think he really believes she'd poison him but he wouldn't walk on her side of the street until he was eleven." Teddy was now sixteen, halfway between the ages of my two boys, Brian and David.

"She's a good decorator. I may get her to stage this place for me if we run out of time. She knows better than to make a family vacation home a showplace that requires a lot of fussy upkeep."

"Married?"

Tess stood up and reached her hand out for my mug. "More tea?"

I handed over my cup. From the kitchen, Tess continued Elisabeth's story. "She was married to a landscaper. I don't know whether she still is. Rumor has it that Duke relieved himself on Mr. Frederick J. Roche's roses one too many times, and Freddie made Elisabeth choose between him and Duke. No one's seen the man since."

"So disappearing husbands are nothing new around here. What's the story on Dev?"

"Poor Leslie. Two little kids. Harry and Naomi, I think. They're preschoolers somewhere around three and maybe almost five. Dev's teenaged sister Amrita has been living with them since late last spring and drives the kids around."

"But what's Dev's story? I mean, is he the kind of guy that someone would murder while he was walking the dog?"

"Total mensch. Accountant. Or was. I wonder what will happen to his clients? He did taxes for seniors at reduced rates. Coached basketball. Drove the ski team. Everyone's favorite neighbor."

"It must have been an accident."

Tess toyed with the wedding ring she still wore on her left hand. "Probably. No one would attempt suicide by throwing himself headfirst into a snowdrift. But it doesn't matter how he died. You can't worry about this, Maggie. No investigating. We have too much work to do and today has been a total waste."

"We can get back to decluttering after dinner. Want me to throw a meal together?"

Before Tess could answer, the doorbell rang. The dogs nearly upended the coffee table scrabbling out from under it to pelt down the stairs. The drooping spider plant committed suicide on the foyer tiles, covering the entryway in potting soil.

Chapter 5

The more possessions, the more worry.
—**Hillel**, Jewish leader. 110 BCE–10 CE

Thursday, February 18, Evening

I joined Tess as she answered the door. Chief Quinn Petit entered the house consumed with easygoing laughter over the antics that are inevitable when two large dogs and three people try to occupy the same small place.

Tess led him up the stairs and offered coffee and a sandwich. Our friends in the Orchard View police had taught us that when cops investigate an unexplained death, sleep and regular meals take a back seat. Quinn took her up on the offer. I stayed downstairs to sweep up the dirt and give the tragic spider plant an ignominious burial upside down in a plastic wheeled bin in Tess's adjoining garage.

When I joined Tess and Quinn upstairs, the chief sat at Tess's dining table with Belle glued to his leg. He scratched her ears. So far, I liked this guy.

"So what have we learned?" I asked, pulling another chair up to the table.

"Sandwich, Maggie?" Tess asked.

"Split one?"

"*What have we learned* is my line," said Quinn. "I want to go over your story again. Tell me how you found Dev Bailey and what happened last night when you parked the car."

Tess brought three plates to the table with thick ham and cheese sandwiches on artisan rye. "First tell us how Leslie is. Does she need someone to stay with her?"

Quinn shook his head. "One of my sergeants will stay with her tonight. She has some family driving up from the Bay Area." He glanced out the window. "Weather report's calling for more snow. We'll check on her again tomorrow, but if snow keeps her family away, I'm sure she'd appreciate a neighborly visit." Quinn picked up the sandwich, took one bite, made appreciative noises. He sighed as if reluctant to halt the meal, but then pushed his plate away and pulled out a dog-eared notebook and stubby pencil.

"Old-school, eh?" I said. "Just like our friend Jason Mueller in Orchard View."

"Good skier and a great cop," said Quinn, scanning several pages of notes. "Patrick introduced us a few years ago. Stubby pencils rule. Fits my pocket. Never runs out of batteries."

Neither Tess nor I spoke as he gathered his thoughts. In the silence, I could hear a clock tick, the fire hiss, and Mozart snore.

Quinn cleared his throat and looked up. "This isn't an interrogation. I just want to talk over some of the things we've already learned and get your take on them, Tess. You've got the pulse of the neighborhood better than I do."

"That's partially true," Tess said. "But I don't live here full time. You'll want to talk to Elisabeth, Leslie, and the Zimmers—they're in the duplex—second home on the left as you turn into our road. But you already know that."

Quinn raised his eyebrows. "The Zimmers." I had the sense that he was familiar with the neighbors, but wanted to hear Tess's take on them without saying anything that might influence her response.

"Grandfather, father, and son. They've always been friendly, though Jens, the granddad, can be kind of gruff. They've got the big rental shop in the resort. Skis in the winter, bicycles in the summer."

"No mom or grandmother?"

Tess shook her head. "Not as far as I know. Now that you mention it, I don't really know whether Han is actually Klaus's biological son. I assume so, but he could be a nephew."

"Han, like Han Solo?"

Tess smiled. "It was Hans with an 's' at the end until the first time he watched *Star Wars*." She pulled a slice of ham from her sandwich and rolled it up. "You'll get a better sense of their family dynamics if you talk to them directly."

Quinn doodled on his pad. I strained to see what he was doing. It looked like some kind of map, but I couldn't be sure.

"Who lives on the other side of the street?" I asked. "Elisabeth's side."

Quinn ducked his chin and looked a little embarrassed. "I live across from the Zimmers, with one house between me and Elisabeth's."

"You knew this?" I asked Tess. From the conversation so far, I'd assumed the neighbors were all strangers to Quinn.

"Of course," Tess said. "It's hard to hide someone the size of Quinn. He's lived here for ages."

Quinn leaped to his own defense. "The nature of life around here is that Tess sees an entirely different kind of neighborhood on her weekend and summer jaunts than I do living here full time. I expect we notice different things."

Tess nodded. "How long has the house across from Elisabeth's been empty? The Wilsons'?"

Quinn shrugged. "The son owns it now. William. His wife had a baby around Halloween. Tough pregnancy. Haven't seen 'em in ages. The parents, old Mr. and Mrs. Wilson, used to have a handyman look after the place, but it doesn't look like much caretaking has been going on recently. Young family. Second home. One income while the infant is tiny. Not surprised they're trying to economize." Quinn grabbed another bite of his sandwich, sipped from his coffee mug, then shook his head. "California real-estate costs."

"How's Elisabeth doing?" I asked. "She seemed shell-shocked after we found Dev."

"She's doing better," Quinn said. "But you might want to check in on her later. Let me know if she remembers anything relevant. She's been reticent to share much about the neighbors."

Tess scoffed. "That's odd. She watches all the comings and goings like a tabloid reporter. Her dining table has a great view of the mailboxes—the neighborhood meeting place. And she loves to keep track of the young people."

"Who else lives on the street?" I asked, trying to build a map in my mind. My fingers itched to get hold of my habitual note-taking supplies—a yellow legal pad and fine-tipped felt marker.

"Siobhan Lake lives between Quinn and Elisabeth," Tess said. "She owns Flour Power, a bakery and sandwich place at the ski resort, near the Zimmers' rental shop. It's one of the few businesses open year-round. Popular with locals and tourists."

"I understand she's starting a catering operation," Quinn said. "Know anything about that?"

"First I've heard of it," Tess said. "Is she doing picnics and meetings or more formal things like weddings?"

Quinn made a note with his pencil. "I'll have to check."

"Does it matter?" I asked.

"Probably not," Quinn said. "But the lines between police work, nosiness, and neighborly interest are blurred around here. The more background and history I can scoop up on my usual rounds, the better." He closed the notebook and slid the pencil through the wire loops of the binding. "Helps me spot and solve problems when they're still small."

Tess sipped her coffee and stared out the window, twirling the end of a lock of hair. She turned to face Quinn, looking sheepish. "My time recollections following Patrick's death are muddled."

"If the timing is important, I'm sure we can pin it down," said the Chief. "What do you remember from the time that Dev disappeared?"

"Elisabeth has been filling me in on the phone. She was worried about Dev. Said she suspected he wasn't the straight shooter everyone thought."

Quinn reopened his notebook and flipped back to the beginning. "She'd asked me to keep an eye on him," he said. "She intimated that he had more money to throw around than he could earn as an accountant, particularly since he charged reduced rates for locals and senior citizens." He smiled. "She kept saying 'Follow the money' in a hushed voice, like she was on the trail of a crime lord."

Tess scoffed. "Drama queen. But that doesn't mean she isn't sharp. And observant. Ask Leslie and the Zimmers," Tess said. "Dev comes from a big family of developers in Los Angeles. Real estate investments." She shrugged. "I didn't really pay much attention at the time. Patrick had just died. I had other things on my mind." She continued twirling her hair around her index finger. "I had the sense Elisabeth had already aired her concerns with the rest of the neighborhood. I've never thought Dev had a dark side. He's a conservationist and was at odds with the big resort developers, but that doesn't mean much. Every political issue around here comes down to a faceoff between the folks who want to expand the tax base and those that want to quash growth to protect natural resources."

Quinn jotted notes. "There was a big flap about rebuilding the mailbox structure after it collapsed between Christmas and New Year's. What do you know about that?"

Tess pressed her lips together and tilted her head. "It's been rickety for years. But no one ever wanted to spend the money to shore it up. Patrick and I talked about paying for it ourselves, but that's a bad precedent to set in a homeowners' association." She frowned. "But wasn't it flattened in the wind storm we had in late November? Before Dev went missing?" She cleared her throat and leaned on her elbows. "I've said for years that we needed to fix the drainage down there and build a more protective structure, but you full-timers overruled me."

Quinn looked from his notes. "What was the issue? Was it contentious?"

"You were here," Tess said.

Quinn shook his head. "Humor me. As police chief, I try to stay out of any political battles. In a community this small, it seems everything is political."

"We've had problems for years with the mailboxes freezing shut and with slick black ice forming in front of them," Tess said. "We had to shovel out after every storm so the postal carrier could get to the boxes. It was a pain. Not to mention that the tiny overhang dripped ice water down your neck if you checked for a delivery in the rain."

"So where was the conflict?" I asked.

"Money," Tess said. "I don't know what happened after the old structure fell apart, 'cause I haven't been up here in months. But for nearly a decade Patrick lobbied for a new drainage system to keep the water from collecting down there and freezing. The new roof keeps rain off the boxes, but doesn't prevent run-off from collecting at the bottom of the hill." Tess pulled the crusts off the remains of her barely touched sandwich. It worried me. She usually had a healthy appetite but still hadn't regained the weight she'd lost following Patrick's death.

"I do know that the full-timers wanted something new built right away without the expensive use of heavy equipment," Tess explained. "Drainage would have to wait until after the spring thaw. I could see their point."

"Anything else?" Quinn asked.

"How did he die?" Tess shivered and hugged her upper arms. Mozart stirred under the table.

"We'll know more later. Looks like a head wound, but it's too soon to say whether he bonked it in a fall or if he was hit with the classic blunt object." He closed his notebook, stashed it in his shirt pocket, and polished off the rest of his sandwich. "Thanks for this," he said. "I was running on empty."

"Call me if other questions come up." Tess pushed her chair back from the table. "And stop in if you need more refueling. I like to stay on law enforcement's good side." She swept some crumbs from the table to the floor. Mozart vacuumed them up with his tongue.

Quinn turned to me. "How 'bout you, ma'am? You're the outsider here. Any special insight into anyone's behavior?"

I shook my head. "Sorry. Tess and I are just here to work on clearing out the house to sell. We're not making much progress I'm afraid."

Quinn frowned and lifted his hat from the table. "You're leaving us?" he asked Tess. "We'll be sorry to lose you. And Teddy. Good kid." He petted Belle behind the ears, pretended not to notice that Tess's eyes had grown damp, and moved his dishes to the kitchen counter near the sink. "I'll see myself out. Stay safe." He plopped his black trooper hat atop his remaining silver hair, and in three quick strides was at the top of staircase. The dogs followed, but Tess and I remained seated and silent, listening to the front door open and close, and to the sound of his engine revving as he drove away.

"Ready to sort through some more closets?" I asked, not particularly interested in the project myself, but feeling the need to stay on task and set a good example for my client.

Tess pursed her lips. "Let's go check on Elisabeth. Something's bothering me about that mailbox structure rebuild."

Chapter 6

An object in possession seldom retains the same charms it had when it was longed for.
—**Pliny the Younger**, Roman lawyer. 61-113

Thursday, February 18, Evening

We crossed the icy street to Elisabeth's, choosing our footing carefully. This time, we'd left Belle and Mozart behind. There was no sense in taking them to Elisabeth's house and riling up little Duke again.

Tess filled me in on what was bugging her. "Elisabeth said something to Quinn along the lines of 'follow the money,'" she said. "Last spring, when I suggested we resolve the drainage problem and redesign the mailbox structure, the Zimmers, the Baileys, and Elisabeth all agreed the work needed to be done, but they didn't want to spend the money. Yet, in December, after the structure collapsed, they wanted it rebuilt as quickly as possible, without even addressing the drainage issues."

"Okay," I said, to let Tess know I was paying attention. And I *was* following along, mostly, though I didn't yet understand where she was going with this line of argument. Drainage improvements were needed, but the money wasn't there, so the homeowners' association put it off. The delay later created an emergency situation that needed to be resolved quickly. To me, it sounded like a scenario that was being played out in communities across the country.

Tess pulled a flashlight from her pocket and turned it on. There were no streetlights. The temperature had dropped and our boots squeaked on the refrozen snow. "They said the budget wouldn't stretch to more than a basic rebuild."

I nodded, forgetting that Tess couldn't see me in the dark. I slipped on a slick patch of ice and grabbed Tess's arm. There was a knack to walking in a winter climate that I'd never quite mastered.

Tess didn't miss a step. "But the structure that's down there is three times the size of the old one. The roof is bigger, the beams are heavier, and it's got expensive reflective paint and blindingly bright LED solar-powered motion-sensor lights."

"So you think they were sandbagging when they claimed the budget was an issue?" I wondered why I hadn't seen the lights when we first parked the car in the turnaround and why they weren't on now. Even during an outage, solar lights should come on. But I'd already demonstrated I knew nothing about living in the snowy mountains. My shoes were wrong and I could barely walk without taking a tumble. So I didn't ask.

"Don't you? If they had extra money to spend, why not address the more serious issue of drainage? And if the association was broke, why build such an elaborate structure? It makes no sense."

"What are you saying?"

Tess threw up her hands. "Isn't it obvious? Someone on the homeowners' association board must have had some reason they didn't want to disturb the ground down there by digging a drainage trench. A reason that had nothing to do with time or money."

"You think they're hiding something?"

"Don't you?"

"Like what? Someone stashed Dev's body in a trench and just pulled it out now? Who? And why? They could have dumped the body in the woods and left it to the animals. You're making it too complicated. Every community has people who create roadblocks to change. Replacing an existing structure is always easier to accomplish than something as boring as drainage. It's like plumbing. No one wants to think about it."

Tess stopped in the road in front of Elisabeth's house. "We should have brought cookies or soup or something," she said.

I was having a little trouble keeping up with the roller coaster that was Tess's brain this evening. First, she'd suggested her neighbors formed a murderous conspiracy to kill and bury Dev. Then, they were supposed to have avoided digging a trench that might reveal where they stashed the body. Next, with hardly a breath in between the statements, they're the sort of people who might be miffed if we dropped in without bringing cookies.

"It's not okay to pop by and check on her? Maybe say we're going to the store if she needs anything?"

Tess looked skeptical about this apparent breach of the neighborhood's unwritten visiting code, but she continued up the walkway and knocked gently on the door. I wasn't sure it was loud enough for Elisabeth to hear, but Duke announced our arrival with shrill barks. How one tiny dog could make so much noise was beyond me.

"I'm so glad to see you," Elisabeth said as she invited us inside. "I was going to call. It seems extra dark and lonely out there tonight."

Tess's efforts to be more adult and neighborly toward Elisabeth had elicited a similar response from the other woman. All traces of Elisabeth's earlier scolding and judgmental behavior seemed to have vanished.

"Have you noticed the lights are out over the mailboxes?" I asked.

Elisabeth frowned and shook her head. "Vandals. Ryan Stillwell fixes the wires whenever he notices. Sometimes they appear to have been cut by a human pest, other times it looks like some rodent chewed the wires. Either way, we haven't been able to stop it."

"How's Leslie?" Though I wondered who Ryan was and how he was connected to Elisabeth and the rest of the community, I was more worried about the newly bereaved wife and mother.

"I haven't seen her. The police have come and gone. I phoned Leslie earlier. Her sister-in-law Amrita picked the kids up from school. I should bring them something, but I'll wait until tomorrow after the sun softens up the ice and their driveway isn't quite so treacherous. Breaking my hip wouldn't be helpful to anyone."

"Amrita, Dev's much younger sister, lives with the Baileys and acts as a sort-of nanny to the two kids," Tess whispered the details to me as Elisabeth ushered us into her front room and invited us to sit on her cheerful red sofa.

"Can I get you something?" she asked.

"We'll only be a minute," Tess said. "Unless there's something you need?"

"I stocked up before the storm."

Elisabeth sat in what must have been her favorite chair. It was the same place we'd left her earlier in the day. Duke jumped onto her lap and was finally quiet.

Tess leaned forward. "I wanted to ask you something…"

Her voice trailed off and Elisabeth filled the silence. "About Dev? The police already—"

"No, no. That's between you and Quinn. I wanted to ask about the mailboxes. The structure went up quickly."

"Looks nice, doesn't it?" Elisabeth sat up straight and proud. "I managed the project. Left to the others it would have dragged on until spring."

"Winter projects are so hard. I know you all wanted to wrap it up in a hurry. It makes sense that you didn't want to do anything as invasive as trenching and laying drains, I guess, even though it would have been less expensive to take care of all aspects of the project in one fell swoop." Tess took a breath and cleared her throat. "But weren't you concerned about the budget? Did you get a special deal? The rebuild looks like it's way beyond the scope of the original project."

"We wanted something that would withstand the next storm, and we couldn't trench with the ground frozen—not without paying through the nose," said Elisabeth, bristling.

"What about the lights?" Tess pressed for more information. "Did one of the neighbors donate the money for that? There were no lights on the old structure. Did you need to get a special permit to expand the project? Everyone said that extra permits for the drains would delay the project."

Elisabeth's cheeks flushed. She picked at a stray thread on the arm of her chair.

"Elisabeth?" Tess asked.

"You know how it is. It happens with every building project. They expand."

"Yes, but last summer you were adamant about containing costs."

Elisabeth smoothed the fabric of the chair arm. "What are you suggesting?" she asked, without looking up.

"Nothing." Tess waited.

"The builders had rebuilt several similar structures. We went with the design they said worked best."

"And that included the lights?"

Elisabeth nodded. "The initial investment was more than we'd planned, but the safety aspect made it worth it. And since they're solar powered, the energy costs won't break the bank going forward."

Elisabeth's explanation made sense to me. Tess must have felt the same way. She leaned back in her chair, shifting gears. "Your house has a great view of the area where we found Dev," Tess said. "What do you think happened to him?"

Elisabeth froze. Her flushed face drained of color and her eyes widened. Tess prompted. "Did you tell Quinn what you thought?"

Elisabeth shook her head, opened her mouth to speak, and shut it before saying anything. She pressed her lips tightly together. Duke whined and then growled at Tess.

"*Shhh,*" Elisabeth said, stroking Duke until he calmed down.

"Would you like me to leave?" I asked, thinking she was reticent to share her suppositions with a stranger.

Elisabeth turned toward me as though she'd forgotten I was there. "No," she said. "You're fine. I'm not sure I want to tell *anyone*. It's terrible." I held my breath.

Elisabeth covered her face with her hands. "It's just that..." A small cry escaped before she continued. "I think I killed him. Dev's dead because of me."

Tess rushed to Elisabeth's side, sat on the ottoman in front of her chair, and took her hand, stroking her arm softly. "Tell me what happened."

"Dev and I don't get along, dear. You know that. It's because of their dog, Winston. He's vicious."

I listened quietly, not wanting to interrupt Elisabeth's confession, but I remembered Tess saying that Winston was an old softie and a beloved friend of Mozart.

"I'd heard the rumors," Elisabeth said, breathing heavily every few words as though it was difficult to force the words out. "The neighbors were all saying that I'd stolen some visitor's airsoft gun—you know what I mean? One of those plastic BB-guns that look like real weapons." She shuddered. I shared her apprehension. I'd had some bad experiences with toys that resembled assault rifles.

"It wasn't true," Elisabeth said. "I'd never steal from a child or anyone else. But after I heard the neighbors talking, I bought a used one from that sporting goods store in Truckee. I bought it on a whim, when I was passing by a window display. I don't know what I was thinking, but I wasn't planning to *fire it*. Certainly not at one of the neighbor kids."

I couldn't guess where Elisabeth was going with her story. Had she shot at Dev and believed one of the little plastic BBs had killed him? Surely not. I knew the blasts could hurt and probably maim someone who took a pellet in the eye. But as far as I'd heard, the weapons were only deadly when terrified cops mistook them for real guns.

"Did you shoot him?" Tess asked.

Elisabeth shook her head so emphatically that Duke jumped off her lap and disappeared into the kitchen. "Not on purpose. But Dev had let Winston off his leash, even after I'd told him over and over about the rules. That dog was barking and jumping up and snapping at poor Duke." Telling the story had brought back some of Elisabeth's outrage. Her words were sharp and crisp. But then she paused, took a deep breath, and looked chagrined. "I pointed the gun at Winston though. I could tell by Dev's face that he thought the gun was real and that I was going to shoot his dog." She blushed. "As if I'd do something like that. To an animal. Even a brute like Winston."

"What happened then?" Tess prompted.

"The gun went off by itself. I was holding onto Duke and he was squirming. I must have pulled the trigger by mistake. It was an *accident.*" Elisabeth stopped to catch her breath. She pulled her hand out of Tess's grasp and clutched her elbows. She whispered the rest of the story. "It was super slick underfoot. When he pushed Winston out of the way, Dev overbalanced and went down hard on the ice." She shook her head. "At the time, I was so angry over Dev's willful flouting of the rules, Winston's harassment of Duke, and Dev's assumption that I would shoot someone's pet..." Her voice broke and a small sob escaped. She looked at the floor. "I didn't—I didn't stay to see if he was okay. What if he got knocked out and froze to death? It snowed hard that night. More than a foot. Much more. What if he had one of those brain injuries that seems okay at first but then kills? What if the drifts covered Dev and someone ran over him?" Her words became faster and more shrill as she confronted the possibilities. She looked up at Tess and started to cry. Ugly half-gasping tears that left her face blotchy.

"Oh, Elisabeth," Tess said. She looked at me and then back at Elisabeth. The poor woman had carried her burden of guilt for months. "Let's think about this logically. If Dev hadn't been able to get up, he'd have called someone to help him. Winston ran home alone that night. Even if Dev had hit his head hard enough to knock himself out, surely Amrita and Leslie would have looked for him in all the obvious places."

Elisabeth cried louder. "It gets worse. That was the night it was so windy. The night the mailbox structure blew down. But...it didn't blow down. It had help. I'd driven to pick up the mail that night. With the wind howling at blizzard speeds, I didn't want to walk. I was expecting a check and I didn't want to leave it in the box overnight. Everything would have been fine if I'd left Duke at home, but he does so love to go for rides in the car."

Tess took Elisabeth's hand again, and leaned forward both to hear her soft words better and to encourage her. "When was this? I thought the mailbox structure blew down after Thanksgiving."

Elisabeth shook her head. "No dear, it was between Christmas and New Year. The same night that Dev went missing, I'm sure of it." She took a deep breath and plowed on. "Duke wanted to defend me from Winston. He's such a little gentleman." Elisabeth smiled at the thought and looked up at Tess and I, and then toward the kitchen. "I grabbed him again when he was about to launch himself out of the car."

I struggled to visualize what had happened. "So that was after the gun went off and Dev fell?" I asked.

"Yes, I told you." Elisabeth sounded frustrated even though she'd left out a few of the key details we needed to understand how the events had played out and why she was so concerned. "Dev and Winston and Duke and I were all at the mailboxes together. Then we tangled, the gun went off, and Dev went down." She paused, then continued. "Like I said, my temper exploded, and I stomped back to the car in a huff. Dev was on the ground and Winston had escaped. I rolled up the window, put the car in gear and sped off without sparing a thought for whether I was endangering my neighbor or his devil dog."

Elisabeth stopped for a moment.

"Should we take a break?" I asked.

"I need to get this out," said Elisabeth. She took a deep breath in through her nose and out through her mouth. "I heard a big thump, like I'd clipped one of the supports on the mail structure…or hit something else, like Dev or Winston." Her cries began again in earnest and Tess turned to look helplessly at me.

"I'll get some water," I said, hoping my pal would consider it helpful.

Chapter 7

Be like a tree and let the dead leaves drop.
—**Jalalud'in Rumi**, Persian poet and Sufi cleric. 1207-1273

Thursday, February 18, Evening

When I returned and handed her the glass, Elisabeth took a few long slow gulps.

"This has been eating at you," Tess said. "You're worried that you contributed to Dev's death. But we don't even know whether he died the night he went missing, or weeks later. The postmortem will tell us more. Were there any marks on your car?"

"I was afraid to look. I took the car to the Easy Wash in town the next day. I've got a few dings in my bumper, but I don't know when they got there. It's ten years old. It's indestructible, but that's the thing." Elisabeth took another sip of water and swallowed hard. "What if I damaged one of the support posts and it came down on Dev while he was lying there—"

"They would have found him under the fallen beams in the morning when they cleaned up the wreckage," Tess said.

Elisabeth looked up with a hopeful expression. "They *would* have. Oh Tess, I'm so glad I told you. I've been feeling so guilty. I couldn't eat or sleep for worrying."

"And if you'd hurt Dev with your car and he wasn't under the beams, they still would have found him that night. I'm sure Leslie would have checked on him. You probably weren't the only neighbor to pick up your mail that night, either."

"Did you glance out the window later?" I asked. "Call to check on him?"

"I did both," Elisabeth said. "I couldn't see much through the falling snow and no one answered at the Baileys' house."

"Dev's family was probably out looking for him," I said. "And if he'd still been there in front of the mailboxes, they would have found him. You have *nothing* to worry about."

Elisabeth wiped her eyes and started to speak, but Tess interrupted. "You still need to tell Quinn what happened. While you weren't responsible for his death, your story about what happened the night he disappeared might fill in the official timeline or explain odd things in the postmortem, like a bump on the head or whatever," she said with a heavy sigh. "We're still left with one big problem."

I held my breath waiting for Tess to finish her thought. After an excruciating pause, she did. "We still don't know who or what killed Dev or when it happened. Did he disappear that night but die later? Or did he die that night and someone hid the body for weeks? How long had he been stashed in the drift before Maggie found him? Where was Dev, alive or dead, after you spoke to him at the mailboxes that night?"

I gasped. Even though Tess's statement was accurate, even though I knew that I was the person to discover Dev's body, I'd told myself that Tess and I found him together—with help from the dogs. I wasn't sure why, but it sounded so much worse to say that I, and I alone, had uncovered a body.

* * * *

We stayed a few more minutes until Elisabeth seemed calmer. When we stepped outside, the wind was up, sending gritty granules of refrozen snow skittering along the drifts and into the air. I covered my face with my mittens in an effort to protect it from what felt like tiny darts.

I dropped my arms at the sound of an engine revving. Tess pulled me to the side of the road, scrambling up a small mountain of plowed snow. I tripped, slamming my forehead against the rock-hard frozen drift, then picked myself up and followed my friend, taking her extended hand. Tess pulled me up out of the road to stand beside her. I touched my face and looked at my hand. Blood. Lots of it.

The engine sounds grew louder. Frantic honking drowned them out. An old blue truck with dim and wobbly headlights crested the hill, careened across the road, and slammed straight into my car, pushing it through Tess's closed garage door.

Typically, in an emergency, I'm the one barking orders, staccato fashion. Not this time.

Tess jumped down from the drift and raced toward the crashed truck. I don't remember calling to her for help, but I felt abandoned atop the slippery drift. Tess rushed back and took my hand without flinching at the blood, helping me climb down the drift and then along the icy road to her front door. "Get inside," she said. "There are ice packs in the freezer. Don't worry about the carpets or towels. Just get ice on that cut." She gave me a gentle push. "I need to check on the driver."

"Mr. Zimmer," she called out. "Jens? Are you okay? What happened?"

Feeling woozy, I sank to the ground, then scrambled backward to sit on the step.

Jens, a compact older man in a worn brown corduroy parka, emerged from his truck, rubbing his face. "I'm a tough old codger," he said. "Cracked my nose on the steering wheel. Anyone hurt? Brakes went out. Tried to stop the truck by pointing it uphill, but it didn't slow." He kicked at a tire. "I saw you two in my headlamps and pointed the hood straight at this car here." He patted the side of my car and squinted at the damage. "Sorry about that." He shook his head. "But cars and garage doors can be replaced. That's what insurance is for. I don't want to think about what could have happened if I'd hit you and your little friend."

Tess was saying something, but I couldn't identify her words. She guided Mr. Zimmer back toward me. He skidded to a stop and stared at me. "Is that blood? Tess, do something. Does she need stitches?" He looked frantically up and down the street. "Someone's got to get these vehicles off the roadway before somebody slams into them. What a mess." Mr. Zimmer seemed to be dodging any responsibility for the mess or for cleaning it up.

Tess helped me up. "This is my friend Maggie. I need to get her inside. Do you know if Alison and Ben are home? You should both be checked out."

Alison Romo, I later learned, was a neighbor sharing a house with Ben Huertas. She was a physician's assistant at the urgent care clinic at the resort. Ben was an emergency medical technician and the designated EMT on his ski patrol crew.

Both of them had heard the crash and came running, showing up just after Tess mentioned their names. They stood in the doorway firing questions moments after Tess brought me inside. I couldn't follow the conversation. My forehead throbbed. If anyone needed answers from me, Tess provided them.

A teenaged boy appeared at some point, still shrugging into his coat. Unless he was taking it off. A middle-aged man, rugged looking with wind-burned skin, arrived, and seemed to be related to the boy. With Mozart and Belle clamoring for attention and reassurance, communication was impossible. The room seemed to lack the normal concentration of oxygen. I crumpled to the floor.

I woke to the sound of Alison barking orders as she cradled my head. "If you're standing, go upstairs." No one argued. A sudden silence was followed by muffled footsteps on the carpeted stairs. "Ben, check out Jens and get some ice on his nose," Alison said.

"Suture kit?" asked a voice I assumed was Ben's.

"Jens first. Make sure there's nothing more than the obvious."

"Call for a bus?"

"Hold off. We'll get them to the unit faster in our car."

"Tess?" My voice quavered. I felt abandoned for the second time this evening. And I was scared. Too much was happening too fast. I'd watched medical dramas on television. I knew Ben and Alison were talking about calling an ambulance. As far as I knew, Mr. Zimmer and I were the only people who'd been injured. Ben must have thought at least one of us warranted a trip to the hospital. I wasn't proud of the fact that I was hoping it was Mr. Zimmer.

Alison called for Tess to provide moral support then patched me up and slapped an icepack over the bandage. She sat back on her heels. "Think you can make it up the stairs?" she asked after shining lights in my eyes and instructing me to touch my fingers to my nose. "This tile floor is ice cold."

She and Tess helped me to my feet and up the stairs.

"We're not going to get any work done tonight," I told Tess.

"What was your first clue?"

The rest of the group had taken up positions at the dining table. Ben went through the flashlight and nose-touching neurological check-up routine with Jens, then had him perform some other tricks like pressing his hands against one another and standing on one foot. Without his heavy winter coat, the old man appeared less hunched and younger than I'd originally thought. In fact, he was athletic and fit for any age, let alone a man in his late sixties.

"Stop fussing," he said gruffly, waving off Ben's hands and pushing him away. "Call the snow plow guy to tow my truck and that gal's SUV-minivan thing. Check the garage door. If it's not structurally sound, we'll put 'em up for the night and sort all this out in the morning." He paused. "Guess we'll have to do that anyway. Insurance."

"Where do you want Maggie?" Tess asked Alison as I wobbled next to her. "Do you have a twin bed?"

"Only bunks."

"Get towels over that recliner then."

Recliners had always reminded me of dental chairs, and all my fears associated with a dental procedures piled on to my already shaky psyche. Tess gripped me firmly. Alison took my hands, pivoted, and lowered me into the chair without letting go. "Maggie, your neuro tests look good. All the swelling is on the outside of your head." She must have felt my increased heart rate. "Look at me."

When my eyes met hers she said slowly. "That's good news. Breathe with me. Three counts in and three counts out." I followed instructions and her example. As my heart rate slowed, Alison continued. "You need four or five sutures. We can take you to the emergency room in Truckee if you want. Or I can stitch you up right here. Your choice."

I looked to Tess for guidance. "No brainer," she said. "Do it here. No waiting and straight into bed immediately afterwards."

"Sounds like the Wild West," I said. "Sure you don't want me on the kitchen table?" I was making a joke about old-timey surgery scenes, but no one laughed.

Ben and Alison prepared a small table with blue drapes and sterilized metal equipment. I didn't examine their work too closely. Instead, I closed my eyes and focused on the sound of a tow motor and heavy chains clanking on the street in front of the house.

Tess rigged up a piercingly bright light. "It's my sewing lamp," she said. "So Alison can do her best embroidery on your forehead."

"That's one of the things you'll want to pack up to take home," I told Tess. "You won't want that cluttering up the cabin when it's staged for a sale."

"I'll have it bronzed and give it to you as a trophy." Tess patted my hand. "Does it hurt?"

I focused on the sounds of the tow truck taking away my relatively new car and didn't answer. I felt unreasonably sad.

Alison warned me I'd feel a small pinch. I tightened the seal on my already closed eyes, gripped the arms of the recliner, and pressed my heels against the footrest as I concentrated on keeping my head still. Though I knew she was using a syringe to inject a numbing fluid into my wound, it felt as though she was using a tiny flamethrower to weld my gash closed.

"Let me tell you about our neighbor Ryan Stillwell," said Ben, in a rumbling bass voice that sounded as though it belonged to a man twice his size. I knew he was only trying to distract me but it was working. Folks had mentioned Ryan a couple of times without giving him a last name or explaining who he was. I kept meaning to ask for more information about where he fit in, but hadn't found an opportunity to wedge a question in between the crises that had beset us. In any case, I appreciated Ben's efforts. I felt as comforted as a small child being told a bedtime story.

"He's the dude towing your car," Ben said. "Also drives the snow plow and is a decent mechanic and carpenter. Works as a caretaker at some of the empty homes, checking heat and security. Sounds like a handyman, right? But don't call him that. He's more of a Renaissance man. He can do anything. He may actually be a wizard." Ben paused for breath and Tess took up the tale.

"He's cobbled together a decent living out of all that gig work," she said. "Mostly because he's reliable and communicates well. The neighborhood is lucky to have him." Her grip on my hand tightened.

"First stitch," Alison said.

I felt a little tug but no pain. Tess continued. "I've tried to hire him away," she said. "I could have used him in my realty business. He's got great organizational skills and an eye for detail. A self-starter."

"Sounds like the kind of help I could use in my work," I said. I must have tried to raise my eyebrows, even though I could only feel them on one side.

"Hold still," ordered Alison.

Tess carried on. "Dev was always after him to go back to school and get his degree or a mechanic's certification. But Ryan wouldn't have it. Claimed he was happy doing what he was doing and had no ambition."

Ben tilted his head. "I don't think it was that. He was in my class in school. Never could sit still. Desk and locker were always a mess. Dude was a clown. Always joking around, ya know."

"Until the accident," Alison said.

"A tragedy," Tess agreed.

I furrowed my brow, earning me another scolding from Alison. "Unless you want to look like Frankenstein's monster, *don't move.*"

"It was after high school graduation," Tess said. "He and his friends had too much to drink. Ryan was driving. Too fast. With a bunch of his pals in the back of his pickup. They came around that big curve on Highway 89 before you get to Tahoe City. Ryan slammed on the brakes to avoid a kid on a bicycle."

"Hurt?" I asked, keeping my face devoid of expression and earning a smile of encouragement from Alison.

"The cyclist was fine." Ben picked up the story. "But one of the older kids fell out the back. Everyone laughed and carried on until they realized he was unresponsive. Ryan's cousin. They grew up like twins, weeks apart in age. Ambulance got to him quickly but he didn't make it. Could have hit his head a dozen different ways and survived, but he collided with a slab of granite at the wrong angle."

Ben *tsked*. "Ryan's blood alcohol level wasn't over the limit, but he was still underage, so he was technically driving under the influence. He lost his license and got a suspended sentence with two years of community service. He'd had a football scholarship at UC Davis but needed to complete his service first. Davis withdrew his funding."

Alison added to the narrative. "Ryan's a great guy, but he's kinda stuck, like he's sentenced himself to never doing more than a paid version of that community service the judge gave him." She frowned, but then shook her head and chuckled. "Still can't sit without moving though. Knees are always jiggling. Hands banging on every surface like drummer."

The story was tragic, but I didn't have my usual capacity for compassion. I found myself worrying about the safety of the vehicles Ryan was towing.

A sharp pain above my eyebrow made me clench my teeth and hiss.

Chapter 8

Let not our souls be busy inns...but quiet homes...where the needful cares of life are wisely ordered and put away.
—**Julian(a) of Norwich**, British theologian and mystic. 1342-1416

Thursday, February 18, Evening

Alison stopped stitching. "Sorry," she said. "I'll need to numb you up a bit more."

I made a face.

Alison patted my arm. "It won't hurt as much this time, tough kid." She turned her back on me and busied herself with the contents of her med kit.

Ben jumped into the breach to distract me. "Your car may need some similar mending. Rest easy. It's in good hands. The best. Dude's proud of his work and won't let anything bad happen to your baby. Guy named Koko." I pictured a gorilla with a small kitten and wondered if Alison had injected some kind of systemic pain killer in addition to the local anesthetic that blocked feeling around the wound.

My head and my car were just two casualties of what seemed like a grand and complex scheme to derail the schedule Tess and I had devised for the week. So far, we'd mostly moved backward. Had we stayed home we'd be further ahead on the project.

Now, we needed to add getting my car fixed to our mix of chores. I took a shallow cleansing breath to avoid disturbing Alison's deft fingers and tried to focus on a more positive topic. Max and the kids would be up for the weekend.

The boys had surpassed my skiing ability in the last few years but deigned to keep me company on a couple of runs a day. In my mind, I replayed happy memories of previous ski trips, dating from the days when David was a toddler wearing a helmet so large it made him look like a mobile mushroom.

By the time Ryan had finished moving the vehicles and joined the crowd in Tess's living room, I'd heard the rest of his life story. Alison tied the last knot on my wound, which was tiny compared to the enormous bandage she'd pressed gently to my forehead. I touched it in the mirror Alison provided.

"I could have used a smaller bandage," she said. "But I was afraid that the tape would pull out all your eyebrows when you tried to remove it. Keep it dry and covered, and find someone to take the stitches out in three to five days. If you're still up here, Ben or I can do it for you. Let us know if it starts to look infected or your head goes wonky."

Ben grinned. "*Wonky.* Technical term for anything that might indicate you took a harder hit than we thought. Blurred vision, impaired balance, dropping things, confusion—that kinda thing. I'll shoot you an email later with the signs to watch for. If you were in the hospital we'd give you reams of paper to sign absolving us of every medical crime known to lawyers. But what's a few stitches between friends?" He patted my knee and stood, continuing to chat as he gathered up all the drapes, wrappings, and other detritus of the procedure in a bright red plastic bag marked "BIOHAZARD."

"You were tough," Ben told me. "You should have heard the carrying on a few weeks ago. Police brought in six big guys they'd picked up when they broke up a fight. These were scary dudes with gang tats. You'd think they'd be tough, right?"

I made a noise to show I was listening, though I was halfway between being alert and being asleep.

"You'd be wrong. Oh my god, the whining! We wanted to give them all general anesthesia."

"But that would have been unethical," Alison said.

"Right. But we did give them all mild sedatives. Quieted them down and made them friendlier," said Ben.

"We'll have to ask Quinn what he can tell us about those guys," Alison said. "I never found out what the fight was about or what kind of crimes they'd been arrested for, but they looked like they'd be capable of almost anything—assault, burglary, trafficking. I hated the way they looked at Rachel—a young medical assistant who works with us on the late shift." She shuddered, remembering.

Ben patted my shoulder, but not in an icky way, and nodded to Tess. "We're seeing a lot more of the aftermath of serious crime in our ER lately. Shootings, beatings, injuries from exploding meth labs. This is not the sleepy little resort town it once was. Watch out for each other and lock up everything, you hear?"

"I had no idea it was getting that serious," Tess said. "Maybe this really is a good time to sell and get out of the area." She promised we'd be careful and made a half-hearted effort to *shoo* me off to bed and encourage the neighbors to head home. But I was reluctant to move and the locals seemed pleased to have an excuse to gather. Someone made popcorn. Tess pulled blocks of cheese from the fridge and crackers from the cupboard. Jens Zimmer pulled out a pocket knife, opened it, and was peeling and slicing local organic apples that disappeared as fast as he put them on a plate. I assumed he'd brought the apples, but had no idea when he'd had the time.

I scanned the crowd and tried to figure out what percentage of the neighborhood was assembled in the living room. Who was missing? The Baileys, of course, Elisabeth, and the detective, Quinn Petit. I asked Tess if I'd left anyone out, and she glanced around the room. "Siobhan Lake. I told you about her. Lives between Elisabeth and Quinn. Runs a bakery in the village called Flour Power. I'll take you there tomorrow. You'll like her. She's our kind of people. Smart. Witty. Community oriented."

"Anyone else?"

Tess wrinkled her nose. "Walter Raleigh. He lives and works by himself in the huge house at the very end of the road where it meets Olympic Drive."

"Seriously? Like *Sir* Walter Raleigh?"

Tess shrugged. "His parents must have had a warped sense of humor, or they were unusually cruel."

"What do we know about him? Is he as nice as the rest of your friends? I can't see any of them being responsible for Dev's death."

Tess pulled a rolling ottoman next to the recliner and perched on top of it. "You're incorrigible," she said. "Can you turn off the investigative reporter in you for just one night? So you can concentrate on healing?"

I shook my head, which hurt more than I thought it should. "In a word, no," I said. "We came up here to clean out the clutter amassed by generations of Patrick's family members and get your house ready to sell," I reminded her unnecessarily. "We're making no inroads into the amount of work that's left to do. None." My voice rose in volume and tension. "You've said you need to maximize your profits from the sale if you and Teddy are going to realize your dreams. But an unsolved murder is going to tank the selling price."

I stopped and replayed what I'd said. Tess knew all that without my telling her. She was a savvy real estate agent and I was harping incessantly about our project. But we weren't all that different, she and I, which was why we'd become such good friends. If I was obsessing about these issues, she was too.

She nodded. "You're right. But we need to leave the investigating to the police. Quinn is good at his job. He knows everyone around here, including the people who live way back in the woods in the shadows of the mountains—the people the rest of us never see."

Tess made it sound as though the woods were full of creatures from Middle Earth, both the good ones and the evil.

The doorbell rang, forestalling the speech I was about to make to Tess. Belle and Mozart barked and pelted down the stairs, nearly leapfrogging each other in their eagerness to greet the newcomer.

Tess peered out the front window. "Police car. Must be Quinn."

"It must be and it is," said Quinn, who'd let himself in. He crested the top of the stairs with Mozart and Belle following close on his heels. "Do you know you left your door both unlocked and ajar? With an unexplained death in the neighborhood? Is that wise?"

If I'd been standing, I would have kicked at the rug and dropped my gaze, embarrassed at our failure to adhere to the most basic home safety rules. But Tess laughed. "Who would break in? Most of the neighborhood is already on this side of the door."

Jens Zimmer separated himself from the crowd noshing around the table and stepped forward to shake Quinn's hand. "So, is Elisabeth the killer?" he asked. "She and Dev hated each other. Are your men taking her away in cuffs as we speak?" I couldn't tell whether or not he was kidding, but there was a nasty cutting edge to his voice that made me wince.

Quinn removed his trooper hat and spun the brim through his fingers. "Why bother asking?" he said, smiling to take the sting out of his words. "You know I can't comment on an ongoing investigation. At this point, everyone is a suspect." He waited a beat or two. "Especially someone like you, Jens, who can't get along with anyone for more than a few minutes."

Jens laughed as though he may have had too many glasses of wine, and I wondered whether he'd been under the influence when he crashed into my car. Or whether, as he'd claimed, he'd made a sober and reasonable choice in an impossible situation. That question was one I could leave to the police, who would undoubtedly test his breath.

"You been drinking, Jens?" Quinn asked, gesturing toward the wine glass in the older man's hand. "Guess there's no point in a breath test now."

Jens recoiled. "What are you saying?" he asked in a voice that was louder than necessary. "I'm not drunk and I never drive if I've had so much as a sip. You know that. No way anyone in my family gets behind the wheel when they're impaired." Jens's grandson Han flushed, and I didn't know either of them well enough to determine whether it was in embarrassment over his grandfather's outburst, or if he'd skated too close to the edge of the law a time or two and felt guilty.

"Relax," said Quinn, patting Jens on the shoulder. "If you hadn't had a glass of wine, I would have done a breath test so you could pass it along to your insurance company. And to quell any gossip. No point, now, but I believe you." He ran his hand over his forehead and turned toward me, "Jens here gives annual lectures at the local schools under the auspices of Mothers Against Drunk Driving. Most folks around here wouldn't drink and drive for fear of facing the wrath of Jens, let alone a DUI. When we have a problem 'round here, it's almost always visitors."

"Natives know that drink and winter driving conditions don't mix," Jens said. "For Pete's sake, the resort runs its shuttle in even the worst storms. No excuse for anyone to get behind the wheel when they've been drinking."

"You're preachin' to the choir, Jens," Quinn said. "Preachin' to the choir."

"Any news on what happened to Dev?" asked Ryan, in a voice that carried across the room in one of the inevitable lulls that occur at any large gathering. The murmur of other conversations remained silenced as everyone waited for the answer.

"Not yet," Quinn said. "I'll let you all know as much as I can. In the meantime, I urge you all not to speculate. Contact me or my officers if you think of anything that's happened 'round here that might have some bearing on the investigation, no matter how inconsequential."

"Oh, man," said Klaus. "Next you're going to tell us not to leave town. But if you're not here to update us on Dev, why *are* you here?"

"Never want to miss a party." Quinn's statement was met with great hilarity, but I didn't know enough about the neighborhood dynamics to understand why the statement was funny. Was the tall officer a known party animal or was he a notorious hermit who avoided local gatherings? I'd have to ask Tess later.

After the laughter abated, he added, "I wanted to check on the injured, but I also needed to make sure you all heard that the forecast has changed. Two Pacific storms that were expected to go around the area are now going to collide right on top of us in the early hours of the morning. Top up your emergency supplies and make whatever preparations you need. Check on each other. There's nothing any of us need to do that can't wait a few days. Nothing." Quinn made eye contact with each of us.

I glanced out the window. The snow had started already.

One look at the snow flurries swirling in the updraft close to the building and most of the guests gathered up their coats and said goodnight. Quinn lingered. "We need to talk," he said.

Chapter 9

Simplicity is the ultimate sophistication.
—**Leonardo da Vinci**, Italian polymath. 1452-1519

Thursday, February 18, Evening

"Are you sure you're okay?" Quinn asked me after everyone else had left. "I'd feel better if you saw a doctor. My department car can get through almost anything. I popped my snow blade on the front before I came out. Let's get you to the hospital before the storm gets any worse."

"I'm fine," I said. "The worst is the damage to my ego. I'm a Flatlander through and through. Walking on ice is a skill I may never master."

"Did either of you smell alcohol on Jens's breath immediately after the accident? Did you get close enough so you would have smelled it?" Tess and I shook our heads.

"Was he confused in any way?"

"What's this about?" Tess asked.

"Just a hunch. I got a complaint from Sam Stillwell. Know him?"

"The name sounds familiar but I can't place it."

"Runs the hotdog and pretzel stand next to Siobhan's bakery. A few weeks ago, Jens got into it with one of his customers. Sam called me to help defuse the situation, but by the time I got there, they'd moved on." Quinn picked up a few of the plates remaining on the table, took them over to the sink, and started loading the dishwasher. "Last week, Jens left his groceries behind at the store and said someone had stolen his truck, but it was right where he usually parks it. I wondered if you'd seen any confusion like that."

"You're thinking dementia of some kind?

"Not sure. Stillwell suspects Jens is mixed up in some criminal activity and is faking his confusion to avoid being questioned. But Sam is not our most reliable community member." Quinn frowned. "Don't mention this to Jens. I'll have a word with Klaus, see if maybe it's time for Alison to take a look at the old guy, see if we need to talk about revoking his license."

I frowned. "He seemed pretty together to me, but I don't have any frame of reference. Is he still working?"

Tess nodded. "He's a renowned workaholic. Hasn't missed a day of work in like...ever."

"Maybe it's just getting to be too much," Quinn said. "A few days off wouldn't hurt."

"Good luck with that." Tess finished clearing the table and wiped it down with a wet cloth. "What kind of crimes could he be involved in, anyway? Isn't crime a young man's game?"

Quinn shrugged. "You never know. We've got ongoing trouble with break-ins, drugs, and smuggling. And we're seeing an uptick in sex trafficking that's really disturbing."

"I've known Jens for years," Tess said. "The behavior Stillwell described isn't like him, but neither is the idea that he'd be involved in anything illegal. It makes no sense."

"I'll look into it," Quinn said, speaking firmly and communicating clearly that this particular topic was closed.

But Tess wasn't finished. "Can you tell us anything about Dev?"

"Nice try." He added soap to the dishwasher and started it up. Tess had said the neighbors were close and often hosted potluck parties in each other's homes, or in the turnaround circle in the summer. I wondered if Quinn's familiarity and ease with Tess's kitchen was the result of years of neighborly festivities or whether there was a past relationship between them that I didn't know about. But then I felt ridiculous. Tess and her late husband Patrick had met in high school and dated through college before their marriage. Besides the fact that the marriage had seemed strong, they were both unfailingly loyal. There was no room in Tess's life or history for another man.

Quinn must have read my thoughts. "When I first moved up here from New Orleans," he said, "The house I was renting burnt to the ground. Patrick and Tess took me in and I lived here for almost two years."

"Little more than a year." Tess corrected him. "You peeled out of here after Teddy was born. No stomach for a crying baby."

"I was working nights."

"You were." Tess wrung out the cloth she'd used to wipe the table and draped it over the dish rack.

Quinn sat at the table. "I need to make sure my team is ready for the storm, but I need to tell you both one thing about Dev."

Tess and I leaned forward.

"I don't yet have the official report from the medical examiner, but it's looking like Dev had a fairly severe head wound, and that he was hurt somewhere other than where we found him. I wanted to reassure you both that it's unlikely you had anything to do with his death."

I let out a deep breath and then caught it again. "But still. We must have walked right past his body in the storm that night."

"We all might have walked past him every time we picked up our mail," Quinn said, his face looking pained. "But we won't know for sure until I get the official word from the doc."

He thanked Tess and told her he'd take a look at the garage door before he left. He'd verify that it was relatively wind and weather tight. "You'll have enough to dig out after this next series of storms without having to unearth a car that's inside your garage."

"You're expecting it to be that bad?" Tess asked.

Quinn plopped his trooper hat securely on his head and pulled on the brim. "Or worse."

As soon as Quinn left, I phoned Max and the boys to make sure they'd taken note of the revised forecast and adjusted their plans accordingly. Reluctantly, I told them about my mishap and new scar.

"Be careful," Max said. "Maybe you both should come home now, before the storm. We'll reschedule the ski weekend and carve out time for you and Tess to work on her house."

"We may have to make another trip up anyway. It's been slow going."

"A few bumps in the road have never stopped you before, but...Mags," a pleading tone had entered his voice. "Even forgetting about the storm, is it safe for you two to be up there? Someone killed Dev, or left him for dead. It could be anyone in the neighborhood, or someone you haven't met who's keeping a lower profile—a serial killer."

"The neighbors all seem nice and look out for each other. Alison stitched me up, right in Tess's living room."

"Glad she was there to help, but you wouldn't have needed medical attention if one of the other neighbors hadn't had a problem with his truck. How do we know he didn't try to mow you down deliberately?"

Max's over-protective and alarmist concerns about Jens Zimmer's motives, and his fears about a lurking threat to our safety were, to be fair, based on our family's past history. For whatever reason, we'd run into more than our share of homicidal neighbors since our move to the Silicon Valley enclave of Orchard View a few years earlier.

"Past performance is not indicative of future results," I reminded him, quoting an obnoxious radio ad for a dubious investment scheme.

Max scoffed. "Fair enough but be careful. I'll keep an eye on the storm. If it veers off by tomorrow morning, we'll come up. The car is packed."

"Folks up here are taking it pretty seriously. It's already snowing and the plows are out." I could hear their powerful engines and scraping blades keeping the main artery clear on Highway 89. Ryan had already made a few passes on the main road through the neighborhood, around the turning circle near the mailboxes, and on the Bailey's driveway. "Tess and I are going to need earplugs to get any sleep."

"Keep your phone charged up as long as you can and stay safe." Max said before we wrapped up the call with our customary endearments. I missed him, but I knew he'd have fun with our two boys and Tess's Teddy, even if they weren't able to come up skiing.

Just before we ended the call, Max cleared his throat. "Mags, you know I trust your judgment, right?"

"Of course."

"And your ability to accomplish any task you undertake?"

"Especially when you have my back," I said. There were lots of ways to say I love you, and expressing concerns about my safety was one of Max's favorite ways.

"I didn't want you to interpret my worry as a crisis of confidence."

"I love you too," I said. Max laughed and we ended the call on that note.

The doorbell rang.

The power went out.

In the silence that followed, we could hear the gusting wind slam icy pellets of snow against the front windows. The direction and speed of the wind combined perfectly to vibrate the weather stripping under the storm door downstairs. It moaned loudly, as though in great pain.

Before either of us could answer the door, it opened. The wind slammed it against the wall. "Sorry about that!" called the visitor. "It's super gusty. Tore the door right out of my hands."

Tess leaned over the stairway railing. "Siobhan! Come on up."

I joined Tess at the railing and she introduced me to her friend the bakery chef. As with everyone else I'd met from the neighborhood, Siobhan was dressed in thick layers, making it impossible to guess what she looked like. Tess must have identified her from her parka.

Peering at her from above foreshortened my perspective, but Siobhan appeared shorter than average. Her voice was light and airy, bringing to mind a fairy or woodland creature. When she pushed back the plush-trimmed hood on her jacket and pulled off her knit cap, she revealed a pixie haircut that glowed gold, even in the unlit entryway.

"I can't stay," she said, holding up an enormous white paper shopping bag with twisted paper handles. "I'm dropping off care packages." Tess met her halfway up the stairs and took the bag from her. "I closed Flour Power early while my staff and I could still get home. We'd baked way more than we sold and didn't want it to go to waste. "Everyone on the cul-de-sac is getting a thermos of coffee, one of soup, a loaf of bread, and an assortment of pastries and cookies."

"Can we pay you for it?" Tess asked, opening the bag and sticking her nose inside. "It smells wonderful."

"You know how it works." Siobhan's expression was that of a patient teacher of a slow student. "I do a favor for you, you do a favor for someone else, everyone wins."

The pixie was back down the steps and zipping her storm gear before Tess replied, "That's very generous. Thank you."

"Return the thermal containers to the bakery after the storm." Siobhan shouted the words over her shoulder and above the sound of the gale as she stepped outside. Tess caught the door before it could slam into the wall again. She pushed firmly against it, forcing it closed, and then locked it before the wind could rip it from her hands once more.

She called up the stairs to me. "I'll grab some more wood before I come up. We're going to have to stoke the fire all night."

While Tess fetched logs and kindling, I adjusted the faucets in the bathrooms and kitchen so they'd trickle slowly through the night. It was standard practice for preventing frozen pipes, but it pained me to turn the tap. After so many years of drought, we Californians don't waste water lightly. My hand hovered over the fixture longer than was strictly necessary.

Tess caught up with me in the kitchen and nodded her approval. "Great. Can you open the cupboard doors under the sinks, too? Warm air from the room will help save the pipes."

By the time we'd finished our storm preparations, we settled into the couches in front of the fire with Siobhan's hot soup. Tess lit candles on the fireplace mantle and handed me a flashlight. "Keep it handy."

We listened to the weather report on the radio. The forecast was for a brutal three-day storm, followed by a week of spectacular ski conditions. We'd timed our visit wrong, but for the moment we were warm and content. Belle settled herself between the coffee table and the sofa. I stroked her ears and she sighed happily. Mozart's ears and nose twitched, listening to the storm and noting changes in the cocktail of fragrances in the air that only a dog could detect. "Settle," Tess said quietly. He tilted his head and raised one ear, then sighed and rested his head on his paws.

She set a wind-up alarm clock to wake us in two hours to stoke the fire. "Tradition," Tess explained. "It's my mother-in-law's winter storm alarm clock. Doesn't seem right to use the timer on my phone."

"Her traditions didn't include a generator?"

"Nope. Most of the people who live up here full-time have them, but we never did. Patrick's mom liked to keep things simple. A generator always seemed more of a pain than it would be worth for a weekend and vacation place."

Normally, I would have found the timepiece's relentless ticking annoying, but among the sounds of the wind, the shuddering of the walls in the gusts, and the growl of the snowplows, it offered a predictable and comforting counterpoint.

"Do we need to worry about Elisabeth?" I asked.

"She has extra food. She said so."

"I meant, do you think she could be the killer?"

Tess scoffed. "She gets upset when plants and mirrors are in the wrong place. And when dogs are off leash. I think she'd take the rules against homicide pretty seriously."

I wasn't quite as sure, but Tess had known Elisabeth far longer than I had. "She's alone," I said. "Do you think she's at risk from the killer?"

Tess shook her head. "Go to sleep, Maggie. You're safe. Elisabeth's safe. No one, not even a homicidal maniac, is going to be outside tonight." A gust threw icy snow against the front window, then prowled around the outside of the house as if searching for a way in.

I checked the Doppler radar on the weather app on my phone. "This is still just the first storm," I told Tess. "The second one is coming up from the south."

"The worst always seems to hit at three in the morning. Get some sleep now while you can."

The wind picked up and I dreamed of trains—old-time steam engines that travelled through snow sheds that covered the tracks and sheltered the trains at the highest elevations. The moaning storm door became the trains' whistles. Engineers worried about having enough fuel to make it through the mountains without stranding the passengers. Bandits lurked around every curve.

I stirred briefly when Belle joined me on the sofa, dedicating herself to warming my feet.

Before the alarm went off, I jolted awake, disturbed by a loud noise. Open drapes at the front window revealed a scene from a science fiction classic. Amber lights strobed on the road and back in the woods beyond Elisabeth's house. Something growled so deeply it shook the ground beneath us. Explosions rattled the windows. The dogs whined.

Aliens had landed.

Chapter 10

Who covets more, is evermore a slave.
—**Robert Herrick**, British writer and cleric. 1591-1674

Friday, February 19, Early morning

Tess could have won an international sleep competition. I gripped the edge of the sofa as though I was adrift upon seas so stormy that I might be tossed overboard. My friend snoozed on, buried in blankets. Mozart ducked his cold snout under her covers. Tess yelped.

"What's going on?" I asked. "Do you hear those explosions? Is it terrorists? Are we at war?"

"Snow plow." Tess stumbled to the window. "And automated avalanche control." She rubbed icy condensation off the glass with the sleeve of her sweatshirt. "Snowcats are grooming the service trails. I'm surprised the drivers can see well enough to work, but I guess they want to get ahead of the drifts."

Outside, someone revved a badly tuned engine. It coughed and caught again.

"Noah McKane," Tess said. "Ski patrol and snowcat driver. I'm surprised that pickup of his is still running. It should have given up the ghost long ago, the way he treats it. He's late for work, again."

"Have I met him?" I asked while I refreshed the weather app on my phone.

"He doesn't live in the neighborhood, so I doubt it."

"What's he doing here?"

"They're not supposed to come through this way, because it's all private property, but there's a shortcut to the snowcat barn through the Baileys' property."

I nodded, barely listening. "The revised forecast is calling for eight to ten feet before dawn. That can't be right."

Tess smiled indulgently. "Your first winter storm? I'll bet you've only been up here chasing powder *after* one of these storms, after the groomers, avalanche control, ski patrol, and the lift operators have spent the night digging everything out."

I joined her at the window. "This is a whole new world for me." I watched a snowplow clear nearly the entire width of the road in one swipe.

"When we get this much snow at once, teams of people work all night to keep up with it. Otherwise we'd be stuck for days."

I frowned. We'd been cooped up in the house for a while now, and I felt the stirrings of cabin fever. "Will it ease up enough later for us to check on Elisabeth and Leslie? For Max and the kids to come up?"

"What's your app say?"

I handed the phone to Tess. There are nuances to weather reports that only experienced locals can interpret. She glanced at the screen and scrolled, tapping and swiping through a series of emergency alerts.

"Maybe tomorrow afternoon. For now, let's bring up some more wood and fuel that fire." But then she scratched her head and pointed toward the kitchen. "Never mind. I'll get the wood. Can you check on the pipes?"

"Go outside?!" I squeaked.

"*Inside*. Find out if the water is still dripping and check that the doors on the cabinets underneath the sinks are open. You can do all that in your slippers."

Tess was my best friend. She was fearless. I felt like a fragile forest creature, trembling and yearning for a cozy protected burrow. I pulled my sweatshirt sleeves down over my hands, wrapped a blanket around me for warmth, and touched Belle's collar for comfort. She trotted with me toward the bathroom. "We'll be okay," I told her in an attempt to reassure myself.

A serious of booming avalanche-control explosions startled me. So much for the quiet rural life. This mountain resort was noisier and busier than the streets of San Francisco had been when Max and I lived there briefly after college. I shined my flashlight outside the bathroom window, which was nearly covered in lacy frozen condensation. The temperature appeared to have dipped into the teens, but it was difficult to be certain with all the snow that had accumulated on the thermometer. In any case, I knew that with the winds gusting over seventy-five miles per hour, it was treacherously cold. I shivered just thinking about it and admired the fortitude of the snowplow operators who worked through the night in terrible conditions to make the roads safer for all of us.

Tess cried out from the top of the stairs, and I ran to her aid. We watched as her entire load of logs thumped and tumbled down the steps. Mozart darted out of the way and then tried to grab one of the logs in his mouth. Tess and I came to his rescue. "You okay?" I asked.

Tess nodded. "I felt the stack going and jumped away. One of those could have easily broken a toe."

"Given our luck over the past few days, count yourself fortunate that it didn't."

But Tess was cranky from lack of sleep. She glared at me. "Just drop those logs next to the fire. We'll use them all before morning."

"Hot chocolate?" I asked.

"The pilot light will be out. Matches are on the shelf over the stove top."

Tess's late husband Peter had insisted on the propane stove. On previous visits, I'd been amused by what I considered a gourmet affectation. Now, I was grateful. With the power still out and Siobhan's thermos of coffee long since emptied, Peter's uncompromising insistence on a gas cooktop would provide us with much needed comfort in the form of food and drink.

* * * *

Armed with two steaming mugs and a plate of cookies, I returned to the living room. Tess had finished building up the fire, which roared and crackled in the hearth. "Good." She took one of the cobalt blue mugs, wrapped her palms around it and inhaled the steam. "I want to stay up for a bit and let the fire settle down. This is perfect."

"Do we have a plan for tomorrow?" I asked. "More storm-related survival chores I know nothing about?"

"After keeping the fire going all night and listening to those explosions, we'll sleep in as late as we can, look at the weather forecast, and take stock," she said. "If they've got power in the resort village, maybe Siobhan will refill the thermoses for us. We can grab some hot soup for lunch and get sandwiches from her for dinner."

"Will we be able to get your car out?" Patrick's mother's old Land Rover was an institution and a trip in it to the beach in the summer was an important tradition my family had taken part in more than once. Tess said she and Patrick had considered getting rid of it, but now that Teddy was driving, it made sense to hang on to it a while longer. "No chance. But we can ski cross-country to the village and catch the shuttle back. We'll have a bit of a slog uphill from the bus stop, but if I know the driver, he might take us door to door."

I hadn't cross-country skied in years, but I hoped it would be like riding a bike, something my body should remember how to do. "That would be fun," I said. "Especially if the wind dies.

Tess set down her mug and slid back under her covers. I took a last sip and followed suit. Belle curled up at my feet with her tail over her nose, but Mozart paced nervously, guarding the front room. The last sound I heard before falling into a fitful sleep was his paws on the stairs as he descended to patrol the lower hallway.

* * * *

The alarm rang twice more before dawn to remind us to refuel the fire, but the growl, rumble, and boom of the snowplows and the equipment deployed by resort maintenance crews kept us from getting any restful sleep. The heavy machines and their engine noises became dragons in my dreams and I awoke groggy and unsettled, to the sound of Tess opening the sliding door to her back deck. A pile of folded winter gear towered before me on the coffee table. Tess handed me a coffee mug. "We're out of milk," she said. "If the delivery trucks made it through, we should be able to get more in the village."

I sipped gratefully, even though my coffee drink of choice was a frothy latte with just a hint of espresso. The caffeine jolt cleared my head.

"The power is still out," Tess said. "You'll want to get dressed by the fire." She lifted her chin toward the precarious pile of clothing. "Those are an assortment of old clothes that belonged to Peter and Teddy," she said. "You'll need all of it. You won't win any fashion contests, but you'll be dry and warm."

"Thanks." I'd brought ski gear designed for schussing down sunny slopes in light winds. None of it would stand up to real winter storm conditions. "Can the dogs come?"

"Try keeping them here," she said. "They've already been out chasing each other. The snow is so deep I can only spot the tips of their tails above the maze they've packed down."

I tilted my head and raised my eyebrows.

"They'll be fine," she said. "Dogs are welcome on the shuttle."

I glanced outside. The snowfall was still heavy, but the flakes were falling vertically instead of being blown sideways and threatening to etch the window pane. The visibility was still minimal, making me feel claustrophobic and vulnerable, but the sky had brightened. If Tess said we'd be fine, we'd be fine. I flung off the covers and stood quickly, shivering. I grabbed a down vest off the top of the pile and pulled it on.

Tess laughed. "When you're ready, join me in the garage. I'll fix you up with cross-country boots, poles, and skis."

* * * *

Bundled as we were, with goggles bridging the gap between our neck gaiters and knitted beanies, it was difficult to talk on the mostly gentle downhill trek to the ski village. We weren't the first people out this morning. Someone else from the neighborhood had laid down tracks that we followed easily. Belle and Mozart alternated plowing through the drifts and leaping over them like dolphins in the surf. Their four-footed journey was faster than ours, so they'd surge ahead and then circle back, covering at least three times the ground that Tess and I did. By the time we removed our skis to trudge over the cleared pavement of the resort village, the dogs' energy was flagging. They panted, tongues lolling, but happy.

I followed Tess across icy paving stones to the main lodge. Big glass doors in front were covered with condensation. After two or three steps inside, I whipped off my knit cap, unzipped my coat, and stuffed my mittens in the pockets. Tess led me across the cavernous room rimmed with food and sportswear shops. The center, like a bustling indoor town square, was filled with people, benches, tables, and cozy chairs layered with mountains of coats and outerwear. Alison Romo waved from a large table near floor to ceiling windows overlooking a patio that was too cold, snowy, and wind-blasted for comfortable use today.

"Morning, Alison!" I said, grateful for a familiar face in a room filled with strangers. "Did your household make in through the storm okay?"

Alison swept her hand in a semicircle over the table. "Pick your spot. I expect the rest of the neighbors to show up eventually. Ben's ordering us enough food to last through tomorrow's storm."

"How's the head?" Alison asked, touching her forehead as she peered at mine.

Tess pulled Siobhan's loaned thermal containers from her backpack and set them on the table. "Brilliant marketing plan Siobhan had last night, don't you think?" she asked Alison. "I mean, it was sweet of her to bring the care packages, but we all had to bring back the coffee carafes at some point…and stock up on more Flour Power goodies at the same time."

Tess removed her jacket and added it to the pile of coats on the chair at the head of the table.

"Go order. I'll watch your stuff," Alison said. "Siobhan's running a special. Ryan gave her people a lift here in the snowplow around two a.m., and they've been working flat out since then, baking only the most popular favorites."

"Is that legal?" I asked. "Catching rides in the snowplow? And where *is* Ryan? He must have been up all night. Do they get any sort of a break in weather like this?"

Tess rolled her eyes. "Flatlander," she said.

Alison chose to answer my first question and ignore the rest. "Legal has nothing to do with it," she said, sounding angry. "It's neighborly." She leaped to grab the sliding pile of slippery outerwear and rebalance the stack.

Tess touched my arm. "Let's go order," she said quietly. I followed her, and when we were out of Alison's earshot, asked, "What's with her? Did I say something wrong?"

Tess shrugged. "I doubt anyone got much sleep last night. She and Ben may have been answering emergency calls all night. Their rig makes it through most weather, but the driving is still pretty treacherous, particularly if they're trying to save a life at the same time they're navigating the drifts."

"Now I feel awful." I replayed my words though and wasn't sure why I felt awful. Sometimes, empathy can be a bad thing.

Tess urged me toward the bakery counter. Like the other stores: ski rental, photo shop, sportswear, and a few other snack shops, the bakery opened directly onto the lounge area. All seemed to be doing a thriving business. All, that is, except for the shop to the left of Siobhan's place, which looked to offer hot dogs and soft pretzels along with ice cream and snow cones, neither of which much appealed to me, given the weather. I nodded toward the pretzel shop. "He didn't get the memo?" I asked. "Everyone else is so busy."

Tess laughed. "The lifts aren't running, so no one is on the mountain other than avalanche control and maintenance crews. Tourists staying in the village don't have anything to do except play in the snow and come in here to get warmed up. And most of the shop-owners have plans for days like this. The Zimmers use the time to rent sleds and saucers and get caught up on in-season equipment maintenance. It'll be a zoo up here as soon as this storm winds down. Local people need to get ready."

"So what's with the pretzel guy?" I tilted my head toward the rolling metal security door that covered the shop. Then I glanced around the room. Despite the fact that, like Alison, many of the locals seemed tired from hard work and lack of sleep, the atmosphere was cozy and festive. Bright flames danced above burning logs in enormous stone hearths at each end of the large room.

A center kiosk flickered with red lights indicating lift status. They were all closed. Across the room, a single ticket window was open below a sign marked "passes." No one waited in line.

Tess shrugged. "Sam Stillwell has never been known for his work ethic," she said.

Chapter 11

Truth is ever to be found in simplicity, and not in the multiplicity and confusion of things.
—**Sir Isaac Newton**, British scientist and theologian. 1642-1726

Friday, February 19, Late morning

When it was our turn at the bakery counter, I reached for a menu while inhaling the irresistible comforting fragrance of butter, flour, sugar, and spices. I wanted one of everything. "What's good?" I asked Tess. "It's hard to choose."

Siobhan, who must have been standing on a raised platform behind the counter, towered over us. She plucked the menu from my hands. "Not today," she said. "We're running specials on limited items to speed things up so we can all get home before the next wave of the storm hits. Twenty percent off if you order one of everything, pre-packed to go in a plastic wrapped cardboard box. Should feed two of you well for at least two days."

"We'll take it," Tess said. "Can we get soup and coffee to eat here?"

"Chef's choice." Siobhan made it clear that was our only choice. "Grilled cheese, tomato basil bisque, and drip coffee. Nothing fancy. Lunch for one feeds the snowplow drivers and lifties who've been working all night, so you and Maggie can probably split one." She called out over her shoulder, "One to-go box and one lunch, split."

A team of young workers performed a well-choreographed dance behind the counter. I had the sense that if one of them dropped something or missed a step, the entire operation would come to a screeching halt.

Tess nodded and handed her neighbor a credit card. "Let me get this," I said, reaching for my wallet.

"Nope," Tess said.

A young man with his long hair in a bun called Tess's name from a waist-high counter at the far end of the refrigerated glass display case over which Siobhan was taking orders. "Need any help getting this to your car?"

Tess frowned. "We came on skis today."

"Delivery then?"

"You're doing deliveries? In this weather?"

"Made a deal with the shuttle drivers—for a small extra charge, of course."

Tess relaxed. "We're taking the shuttle home, but we'll have skis to carry."

"No worries. We'll put the box on the shuttle for you. If you don't live too far from the route, they'll give you a hand at the other end."

"Seriously?" I was astonished at the level of service.

"Flatlander," Tess said again.

I rolled my eyes and sighed. I'd had about enough of the expression.

"You're not a local," the young man said, barely glancing at me. He pushed a pen and pad across the counter toward Tess. "Just in case you decide to ski back or you miss the shuttle. Jot down your address and cell phone number. Okay if we leave it on the front step? You don't want to let it sit there too long or it could draw bears."

"They don't hibernate?" I asked, surprised again.

"Never mind," Tess told the young man, handing back the completed form. "I'll explain it to her later."

She picked up the sack lunch and turned to head back to the table. The young man called after her. "If we can't get through, we'll leave it at Walter's." Tess waved her hand in what I assumed was agreement. I hoped the bakery worker got the message.

We took our lunch back to the table where Alison had been joined by Ben Huertas the EMT, and another man I'd not yet met. The newcomer looked stiff and formal in a collared shirt and tie and slippery Italian leather dress shoes. With his insulated snow pants, it was an odd look. I hoped he had a pair of warm overshoes or boots to change into before venturing back into the cold.

As we sat down, the man rose halfway out of his seat and leaned over the table with his hand outstretched. "Walter Raleigh," he said. "Real estate. I'm a token part of the neighborhood. I live at the very end of the road."

I shook his hand. "Are you the Walter who is the default receiver of our bakery box?"

Walter laughed. It was a hearty chortle that shook his shoulders and lit up his eyes, making him appear much less stiff than he'd seemed at first glance. "My house fronts the main road, so it's easy for people to drop stuff there if they can't get through to the rest of the street. UPS, FedEx, local carriers. Federal laws require the post office to take everything to the mail boxes, but for everyone else, I'm a frequent terminus in winter storms." He turned toward Tess. "I'll text you if anything lands on my doorstep."

"Thanks." Tess's response was barely intelligible as she tried to speak around a large bite of cheese sandwich. I nibbled at mine and nearly swooned. It was the pinnacle of grilled sandwich perfection, with cheese that was creamy and warm, but high in flavor and thick bread that was soft and fragrant on the inside, but crisp and buttery where it had hit the grill.

"Need smelling salts?" Tess asked.

I shook my head and peeled off the cover to a steaming bowl of creamy tomato soup laced with green strips of basil. "Tell me about the bears. In the cartoons, Yogi hibernates. I thought all bears slept through the winter."

"Not exactly," said Walter. "They retreat to their dens and are much less active in the winter months, but it's more of a doze than actual sleep. From time to time they'll stir themselves and take a little stroll looking for food. We see more of them every winter. Climate change."

"Big night for Ben last night," Alison interrupted, elbowing her roommate in the side. "Twins. Delivered in the rig."

"Yikes," said Tess. "Everyone healthy?"

Ben packed up the remains of his lunch, which was identical to ours but twice the size. "We got the mom, dad, and babies to the clinic just after the birth. Six pounds each. Boys. Tough as nails and so is the mom. Dad looked a little green around the gills. Clinic'll keep the family there until the storm blows over. No one wants to send tiny newborns home to a house where the power's off."

"Tell 'em about Ryan." Alison prompted.

"In jail," Ben said. "Being held in the murder of Dev Bailey."

Silence, followed by gasps, signaled the group's astonishment and alarm. "Arrested? Ryan? Where'd you hear that? What did he do?" We peppered Ben with questions until he pushed his chair back from the onslaught and held up his hands in surrender.

"Hold on. If you'll all just settle down, I'll tell you what I know." Ben leaned forward. "It's not much. I only heard because dispatch asked if I could take Ryan's shift. She didn't know whether she'd need substitutes for a single shift or a whole week. But we're so swamped with medical response, I said I can't moonlight until the weather improves."

Tess stood up and waved. "Quinn!" She shouted at a level a drill sergeant would have envied. I turned to look for the police chief, as did most of the people in the room. Tess walked toward Quinn, spoke to him for a moment, and then tugged on the sleeve of his jacket. As they approached, Ben stood, said his goodbyes, and invited Quinn to take his seat.

Lights flashed on above the Hot Dog and Pretzels sign. A tall gaunt man in an ill-fitting navy boiler suit unlocked the security door. With a screeching clatter that drowned out all other sounds in the big hall, he tugged on the handle and rolled the door up until it disappeared in the dark recesses of the ceiling and revealed a service counter similar to the one at the bakery next door.

"That's Ryan's cousin Sam Stillwell," Alison said. "He must know what's going on with Ryan."

"I wondered why he hadn't opened the shop yet." Walter filled a plastic tray with the remains of his lunch and several of the bowls, napkins, and cups that the rest of us were finished with. "Must have been held up by Ryan's arrest."

Alison scoffed. "It's not like he has regular hours." She scooted her chair closer to the table and confided in me. "We're not sure how he stays in business."

Walter shrugged into his coat and left. All eyes turned toward Quinn, who set down a cup of steaming coffee and a napkin-wrapped bagel. He sat, but left his coat on and his food untouched. "Guess y'all heard we pulled Ryan in. But don't go jumping to conclusions. We've got a few questions for him is all. Snowplow drivers are out in the worst weather, all over the mountain roads. See things that don't seem important at the time but which can lead to a break in the case. That's how we caught the Blizzard Burglar last winter. Tips from the all-night drivers. Bad guys think that since they can't see into the cab, the drivers can't see them. Big mistake." He took the lid off of his coffee and blew on it. I straightened my spine to peer into his cup. Black.

Quinn caught me looking and smiled, tilting his cup. "You can tell a lot about a person by the coffee he orders," he said.

"When you order your coffee black, you can blow on it without making a mess," I told him. "Me, I order a latte with extra foam."

Quinn grinned. I brushed imaginary foam from the front of my shirt.

"What else can you tell us?" Alison asked, interrupting our not-very-important discussion. "What did Ryan do? Was Dev's death an accident?"

Quinn blew on his coffee again then deflected Tess's question with another question. "You make it through the storm okay?" he asked.

"Ready for the next wave? Supposed to be worse than last night. Lower temperatures and higher winds. If there's anyone you think needs help, let my guys know."

"Have you checked on the Baileys or Elisabeth this morning?" Tess asked Quinn. She turned in her chair and looked back at the bakery. "We should pick up boxes for them too."

Quinn cleared his throat. "I visited Leslie Bailey and the kids this morning and checked in on Elisabeth at the same time. They're all doing as well as can be expected, but who wouldn't love to get a bakery box from Flour Power?" He replaced the lid on his coffee, and picked up his untouched bagel. "I'll leave the logistics to you," he said, before disappearing down a distant corridor.

"That was less than illuminating," Tess grumbled. "I wonder if Sam could tell us more."

Alison narrowed her eyes to slits and stared at the hot dog vendor. "He's creepy at the best of times. I'm not talking to him. No way. You go."

Tess glanced over her shoulder toward the shop, where hot dogs now twirled on a device that resembled a Ferris wheel. "I need to get those extra boxes from Siobhan."

I was still a little miffed by Tess's endless "Flatlander" cracks, and thought I could use a break from my new friends. "For heaven's sake!" I said. I pushed my chair from the table and the metal feet made a horrid screech on the tile floor. "I'll go."

Halfway there, Sam looked up and I shivered as though a tiny mouse with icy feet had run down my spine. Technically, he smiled, but his expression could also have been described as baring his teeth and glaring. A sneer. It wasn't the look of a shopkeeper welcoming a potential sale. I swallowed hard and straightened my icy spine to make myself as tall as possible. I could handle him.

"Afternoon," I said to Sam Stillwell in what I hoped was a friendly but confident and commanding voice. "Can I get ten warm pretzels?" I turned toward Alison and Tess and waved. They waved back. Though I knew nothing bad could happen to me in such a public place, Sam Stillwell gave me the creeps. I was glad to know my friends were literally watching my back.

"Who orders ten pretzels?" Sam asked.

"I just did," I said, though I had no idea how I'd arrived at that number. I hoped they froze well. I handed him my credit card and he rang up the order.

"Got to preheat the oven." Sam said, pushing up sleeves that didn't make it all the way to his wrists. "Take a few minutes. I could bring 'em over?" He didn't sound convinced that he could carry ten pretzels across the room, and I needed to ask him a few questions anyway.

"I'll wait."

Sam rolled his eyes. "Whatever. Suit yourself."

I watched Tess approach the bakery and heard her order two more bakery boxes. While I searched my brain for a tactful way to ask the taciturn hot dog vendor about his cousin, Sam started the conversation for me.

"You may be my only customer today. New in town?"

"I'm a friend of Tess Olmos." I tilted my head toward the table where the people from her neighborhood were sitting.

Sam looked up and narrowed his eyes. "Surprised they let you order anything from me."

"Oh?"

"Cops got my cousin in jail. They're going to try slap a murder charge on him." Sam wiped his hands on a none-too-clean apron, and I decided the pretzels might be headed for the garbage instead of the freezer. "Dev Bailey, some dude from their neighborhood, was found dead. Upside down in a snow bank."

"Seriously?"

"Yup. Quinn told me they'd probably keep Ryan over the weekend at least. Can they do that?"

"I'm not sure." I was lying. My previous experience with law enforcement told me that a suspect could be detained for forty-eight hours before being arraigned. But the courts weren't open on weekends and holidays. That meant, this close to the weekend with Presidents' Day looming on Monday, prosecutors would probably hold Ryan until Tuesday before cutting him loose or formally charging and arraigning him. But I didn't want to go into all that with Sam.

"Did he do it?" I asked without looking Sam in the eye. I never would have asked such a direct and possibly hurtful question at home in Orchard View, but Sam had a chip on his shoulder that was infectious. He challenged me and I challenged back, feeling only slightly ashamed of my childish behavior.

Sam pulled a box of premade pretzels from his freezer and placed them on a tray. "Nah. Ryan's one of those soft guys. Spots roadkill and wants to give it CPR. Wrecks his day. Couldn't drum up enough hate to kill anyone."

"Could it have been an accident? Way up in the cab of those snowplows, how easy is it to see down on the pavement? If some guy was walking too close to the road, could Ryan have hit him with the plow without knowing?" I cringed as I listened to my words. My interrogation approach was clumsier and more intense than ever.

Sam slammed the tray into the oven, nudged the door closed, and set a timer. I stepped back when he looked up. I couldn't be sure of his body language, but he seemed angry. Like everyone else, he'd spent a sleepless night. If anyone could literally spit tacks, it would be Sam.

"I wouldn't put anything past that Dev. He's a jerk."

I stared at Sam, my mouth agape. I was flabbergasted to hear such venom from someone who didn't live in the immediate neighborhood. In my experience, only familiarity and old grievances bred Sam's level of contempt for another human being. And I had a big problem with Sam's logic. Was he saying Dev was a jerk for dying? For having an accident? Sam must have read the astonishment on my face.

"I know him from the volunteer fire crew," he explained, restocking the napkins and plastic-wrapped utensils. "He's a health-food nut. Sneered when I brought leftover hot dogs for the crew. These are high quality all beef hot dogs. Kosher. I can show you the label."

"Doesn't working on the fire crew require a certain level of trust?"

"Weird, huh? He'd trust me with his life in a blaze but wouldn't do my taxes, even though he does them for all the other small vendors 'round here. And it's not like any of them are firefighters. Brothers in arms meant nothing to Dev." Sam pronounced Dev's name with three syllables and a sneer.

"Did Dev get along with Ryan?" The timer on the oven went off, saving Sam from answering. He plucked pretzels from the baking tray with tongs and plopped them in a white paper bag similar to those the bakery used for sack lunches.

"Ten pretzels," he said, shaking his head and handing the bag over the high counter. "Doubt any of Dev's friends there will eat 'em. Probably think I'd poison them."

"I'm sure you're wrong," I said, eager to ask Sam more questions, especially regarding Ryan's relationship with Dev. But Sam had other ideas. He sniffed and turned, stiff-arming the swinging door to a storage room at the back of the shop. I watched the doors flop gently back and forth for a moment, but Sam didn't reappear.

Chapter 12

For every minute spent in organizing, an hour is earned.
—**Benjamin Franklin**, American scientist and statesman. 1706-1790

Friday, February 19, Near noon

Tess called me over to the bakery counter. "Siobhan's short-staffed and swamped. Wanna pitch in for an hour before we head home?" I glanced back at the table where Alison massaged the ears of both Mozart and Belle, one hand on each head. She saw me looking and waved. "Go ahead, I'll look after them," she called out. "Glad to have an excuse to stay put."

Tess explained. "Siobhan came to the table to ask for a hand. I told her I'd help out for an hour or so and you probably would too." She paused and her face reddened. "Especially if I apologize for all the Flatlander cracks I made."

I smiled and gave her arm a gentle punch. "It was funny the first couple of times. After that? Not so much."

"Sorry."

"Forgiven."

I set the bag of pretzels down and stepped behind the bakery counter.

"Thanks so much," Siobhan said. She looked me over as if assessing whether I was strong enough to provide the help she needed. "You're going to want to shed your extra layers," she said. "The ovens make this the most tropical shop in the resort. There are hooks for your gear in the back."

I hung up my puffy vest and fleece, and returned to the front of the bakery to get instructions from a guy who looked familiar. He must have sensed my confusion.

"Han Zimmer," he said. "Our duplex is next door to your friend Tess. I met you last night."

"Right," I said, embarrassed at my memory lapse. "With your father and grandfather. They don't need you in your family's shop?"

Han shook his head. "It's a slow day with the lifts closed. I'm pitching in here for now, but I'll clock out when you and Tess leave. Give you a hand with the stuff for Elisabeth and the Baileys."

"Too much talk, not enough action," Siobhan said. "Load up all the boxes that need to go on the last shuttle, and then you can start putting everything away and clean up." She glanced at her watch, then whistled sharply to another employee. "Noah, grab a broom." She rolled her eyes and turned toward us. "We all need to get home and under wraps before the next wave of this storm hits. It's coming in fast."

She spun around to address some last-minute customers, stirring up enough air to lift some handwritten orders off the counter. Tess picked them off the floor and spiked the first two more securely. But when it came to the third, she stopped, frowning.

"What is it?" I asked.

"Not sure. What's this look like to you?" She handed me the slip of paper, and I squinted to decipher the scrawled notes.

A number that could have been a "3" or an "8" preceded a word that looked like "tier." "A wedding cake?" I asked.

"Look at the customer information."

"Is that *your* address?"

Tess laughed. "Not quite, but it makes about as much sense. It's Leslie Bailey's."

My mouth gaped open. "An anniversary cake? Ordered before Dev went missing?"

"Look at the date."

If my interpretation of the pen marks was correct, the cake had been ordered early this week—after Dev went missing but before he was found dead. "Huh?"

"Exactly."

"No." I shook my head and stepped back, protecting myself from the shock of the words Tess hadn't yet said. "Why would she need a wedding or anniversary cake? Could it be for a relative? Didn't you say her sister-in-law works for them as a nanny? Could she maybe be engaged?"

"Even if she were, they can't feel like celebrating now. Not with Dev gone."

"Maybe it's a distraction? An attempt to move forward?"

"Possibly," Tess drew the word out. "But...*eww*."

A shout from Siobhan made us stop sparring and speculating. Tess stuffed the order slip in her pocket.

Noah, Han, Tess, and I worked flat out for about forty-five minutes before a call came from the front of the lounge area. "Last shuttle leaves in twenty."

I glanced up. All the people coming in from outside were stomping snow off their boots and shaking their hats and scarves as they removed and unwound them. Flurries blew in every time the door opened.

Siobhan shooed us out quickly with the boxes to load on the shuttle. "Hop on as soon as all the boxes are aboard. One of you bring the cart back," she said. "I'll be right behind you."

Noah peeled off from the group as soon as we got outside, saying he needed extra time to dig out his truck. It took the rest of us three trips to move all the cartons. As we worked, the intensity of the wind and weather steadily increased. By the time we boarded the bus, we were covered with snow. Han ran the cart back and he and Siobhan jumped aboard just as the shuttle was pulling away from the curb.

"Hang on tight, people!" called the driver from somewhere inside his many layers. "And settle in. For those that don't know me, I'm Ed Bain. I'll getcha all home safe, but we're takin' it slow 'n easy. If folks need help, we'll stop and help out. Introduce yourselves around, we're gonna be awhile."

"I've got cookies!" said Siobhan, holding up a white bakery bag and securing her place in my heart as a kindred spirit. "Seconds. A little misshapen, a tad overcooked, but still completely edible."

She passed the bag around and most people took one. The simple gesture reminded me of a sacrament, and transformed the little neighborhood resort shuttle ride into a festive social event. Siobhan grabbed at an upright support as the back of the bus fishtailed and the driver steered into the skid. An older man with cheeks flushed from the cold and wind caught the bag as it fell, then peered inside. "No harm done," he said.

Siobhan smiled. "They were already a bit broken. Nothing to worry about."

I thought about passing around the bag of pretzels I'd picked up in my attempt to get Sam to tell me the details of his cousin's arrest. I changed my mind when I thought of how poorly their reheated and mass-produced texture would stand up against Siobhan's creations.

Han leaned forward to grab the bag as it came around and pulled out a chocolate walnut piece that was oblong instead of circular. "So, while we wait, we should talk about Ryan. I can't believe the police picked him up. Do you think he killed Dev?"

"No, never," said Tess. "Ryan is such a gentle man. He and Dev didn't have much to do with one another, anyway. What motive could Ryan have?"

Han answered with his mouth full. "Dev and my granddad sure didn't get along. If one said the sky was blue, the other would insist it was red."

"How is your granddad?" Tess asked. I knew she was following up on the suggestion last night that the older man might be showing early signs of dementia or an alcohol problem.

"Huh?" Han asked. "Fine, I guess."

"Someone last night wondered if he was a little confused."

Han chuckled. "Don't let him hear you suggest it. He's smarter than any other two people put together. Granddad'd be the first to tell you that." I wondered if that was true. He hadn't blinded me with his intelligence the day before. He'd just seemed like a normal nice man. A tad slow to take responsibility for the accident, he'd come through in the end. However, my experiences in helping older folks downsize and move had taught me that the people who defended the power of their brains the loudest were often those most in fear of losing their minds.

"What was their feud about?" Tess asked, dropping the sensitive topic and shifting gears. "Dev and your granddad."

"What was it *really* about?" Han asked. "Or what did they *say* it was about?"

"It's not the same thing?" I said.

Han ducked his chin then cleared his throat. "Not in their case. If you'd asked the old man, he would have said that Dev stuck his nose in where it didn't belong. And Dev would have said that my granddad was a lunatic who wanted everything in the neighborhood to remain as it has always been."

"A normal neighborhood conflict," I said. "Nothing to commit murder over."

"But it hit closer to home than that," Han explained. "At least it did for my granddad. He convinced himself that Dev was lobbying for me to abandon the family business, attend college, and leave home permanently."

"And was he?" Siobhan asked. "How come I've never heard this?"

"It was garbage!" Han slammed his palm against the chrome support pole and winced. "What happened was Dev gave a talk to my math class about finance and business careers. It got me thinking about ways to expand the store and bring it into the twenty-first century." Han took another huge bite of the cookie and kept talking, waving the remains of the cookie in the air. "I took an online class at the community college and got a ton of great ideas. I told Granddad we needed more demo equipment, a bar code system for quick checkouts and returns, and a website where we could take preorders from regular customers. We need to give discounts to folks who buy after renting. Group discounts. More packages with lessons and lunch. We need to advertise our summer bike rentals and organize rides so we're not so dependent on winter income." He took a breath. "Season gets shorter every year."

Han warmed to his subject. "But I didn't want us to be stumbling around in the dark. We don't have enough money to waste on mistakes. I wanted to develop a business plan with built-in measurements so we'd know more about what works and what doesn't." He sighed. "Dev and I skied at about the same level, so we talked about it sometimes on the lifts."

He grabbed another cookie with the confidence of an active young adult who doesn't need to count carbs. "I talked colleges with Dev too. I want a good business program that respects small family businesses like ours, not one that churns out accountants for the big four or bean counters for the global monster companies."

"Makes sense," I said. "And Jens had a problem with that?"

"Who knows? I couldn't get him to listen long enough to tell him my plan. He made up his own idea of what Dev and I were talking about. And he decided he hated it, even though the scheme he despised wasn't anything like the future I wanted."

"And Dev?"

Siobhan jumped in. "Dev didn't have time to dwell on issues as much as Jens does. He just knew that Jens sneered at him every time they were face to face. It's not a great way to endear yourself to your neighbors. Dev avoided him as much as possible." She paused, peered into the cookie bag, and shook it. She looked up to find we were all watching her.

"What?" she asked. "The baker can't have her own favorites? Mine is peanut butter, but they tend to stand up to rough handling better than the others, so not as many end up in the "free snacks" bin." She smiled, reached her hand into the bag, and pulled out a dark brown cookie with hashmarks that were slightly askew. "Ta da!"

I thought for a moment, eager to make sense of what we already knew. "So, Jens thought Dev was trying to destroy his family and his business. But could that have made him angry enough to kill Dev?"

Han laughed. "You're kidding, right?" He dusted cookie crumbs from the front of his coat and cleared his throat. "He still has a ton of energy when he's in the ski shop, but it's all bluster. When he's home, he doesn't stir much from his recliner." He gave me a look as if daring me to doubt his assessment or to accuse his grandfather again.

I hesitated to ask a follow-up question, but Tess jumped into the breach. "Bear with me here, Han. I don't think Jens would kill anyone either. But while we're talking about it, let's really rule him out. *Could* he have overpowered someone three decades younger? Dev wasn't a big guy."

Siobhan scoffed. "But he was a lot stronger and quicker than Jens. No way could Jens have killed him, even if they'd gotten into a fight and if Jens had landed a punch or two."

I patted my pockets for a memo pad and pen that I didn't have with me. "Okay, we'll cross Jens off the list. Who else might have killed Dev?"

"It can't be anyone we know. It's not like we're a bunch of serial killers." Han laughed nervously and rummaged in his backpack with his head down. "Couldn't it have been an accident?" He pulled a reusable water bottle from the depths of the pack and pointed the top toward the bus window. "In a whiteout like this, it'd be pretty easy for a driver to run a person off the road without even realizing it."

"Maybe that's why they've got Ryan in custody," I said. "The giant blade on those snowplows could have scooped up a pedestrian and thrown him into a drift without the driver having a clue what happened." I lowered my voice. "These shuttles have better visibility than the plows, but the way this bus keeps thumping over frozen ruts, I'm not sure we'd know if the driver hit anything, you know, like a person." I felt a little sick at the idea of a person being thrown to the ground after colliding with the bus. And then being left for dead.

Tess rubbed the back of her neck. "If we're considering a vehicle collision, we have to also look at the mail truck, the garbage collectors, a whole raft of service vehicles, like UPS, FedEx, and electricians, plumbers, and those guys. Plus all the weekenders and tourists."

"Now, see, that makes more sense," said Han. "It had to be a stranger. Someone who isn't even around here anymore. Someone like that would be impossible to track down."

"We can't really weigh stranger versus neighbor or accident versus murder versus suicide until the autopsy results are out." Siobhan said, choosing another cookie, then offering the bag to the person in the seat in front of her. "Keep passing it." She lurched forward and cracked her chin on the metal edge of the seatback in front of her as the driver slowed and the bus skidded.

A heavily wrapped passenger stood and gathered belongings with movements that suggested there was an elderly woman somewhere under all the layers. The front of her coat faced the stack of meal cartons awaiting delivery and looked dejected, though I wasn't sure exactly how a coat, scarf, and hat could appear sad.

Han leapt to his feet. "Let me get that for you, Mrs. Bitterman." I could only assume he identified her by her hat and coat. How easy would it be for someone to pretend to be someone else in a blizzard, just by wearing storm gear that was unfamiliar to friends and neighbors?

Han zipped his jacket, donned hat and mittens, and lifted the top box off the stack. I jumped off the bus and extended a hand to the roly-poly figure descending the slippery steps. The roads and walkways were treacherous.

My help was rebuffed and the figure trudged past. I shivered and hopped back aboard, taking my seat and blowing on my hands to warm them. Wind buffeted the bus.

Han followed the figure up a snow-covered walk and disappeared into the swirling snow. A few minutes later, he knocked on the window to let the driver know he'd returned. He plunged aboard, breathless. "Bitter cold out there." He forced out the words. "The wind is up. It's going to be much worse than last night."

Chapter 13

Good order is the foundation of all things.
—**Edmund Burke**, Irish statesman. 1729-1797

Friday, February 19, Afternoon

I lost track of the time as the bus inched from stop to stop and passengers took turns helping each other with the food cartons. I learned a little bit more about the other members of Dev's family.

Everyone seemed to like his wife, Leslie, daughter of a Canadian ski-resort developer who'd grown up near Whistler in British Columbia. But the consensus was that she didn't care as much for the outdoorsy life in the mountains as she did the cosmopolitan excitement and Hollywood glamour of a wealthy resort community.

"Dev's parents are big-time project managers in Los Angeles," Siobhan said. "Builders, so Leslie and Dev had that in common. I suspect Leslie would be happier living in a hotel in Los Angeles than in a ski cabin, even one as big as theirs. But Dev was an avid environmentalist. He had only contempt for the showy Southern California lifestyle."

"And his sister, the nanny?" I asked.

"Amrita?" Siobhan said. "Tess knows her better than I do."

"She's young," Tess said. "Teenager just out of high school. Still finding her way. Taking a gap year before she heads to college and graduate school. Ultimately, her parents want her to return to the life of an Orange County socialite." A note of disgust tinged Tess's voice, and she picked at a loose edge of trim on the seat upholstery. "I feel for the kid. Her parents want her to go to University of Southern California or one of the hoity-toity East Coast schools, where she'd meet movers and shakers. Amrita's more social activist than socialite, though. She'd rather go to Humboldt State and learn what she called 'practical stuff.'"

I knew Tess had nothing against any of the schools she mentioned but thought kids should choose colleges that best fit their needs. She turned toward me. "You'd like her. No nonsense. She's made the transition to our Alpine climate pretty well, but she hates having cold feet. She wears big puffy boots even in warm weather and is always complaining about getting the kids into all their layers. They seem to leave a trail of lost mittens, hats, and sweaters behind them."

"But did she and Dev get along?" I asked, knowing that tensions could run high in families. Any level of violence was possible, even between those who professed love for one another. I shuddered, thinking about the ghastly possibilities.

Siobhan held her hands in front of her, palms up, as if weighing the family dynamics. "Hard to say. Last time I saw her, she was in the bakery with friends, complaining that Dev sided with her parents when it came to her future." Siobhan massaged her hands as though they were achy. "Don't all teenagers go through that? If they want to make their dreams come true, they need to break their own trails."

"How angry was she?" I asked.

Siobhan leaned forward. "The kind of angry that burns itself out pretty quickly, I'd say. By the time I brought them their order, Amrita and her friends were giggling over a bumblebee tattoo Amrita had done on her day off. She said Dev would kill her if he found out."

I raised my eyebrows, wincing from the tug on my sutures. Siobhan shook her head. "Figure of speech. No way was that girl in fear for her life..." Her voice trailed off. I was just about to prompt her with another question when she spoke again. "...certainly not as much as she dreaded going back to Los Angeles and organizing social events for her parents."

"What about Dev himself?" I asked. "Had he been acting any differently before he disappeared? Nervous? Excited? Depressed?

Tess, Han, and Siobhan glanced at one another before Han answered. "Dev was the most chill guy I know. Nothing bothered him. Not for long, anyway. I mean, he was rabid about fighting development in the Tahoe basin. You'd think he'd consider Sir Walter a super-villain, yeah? He's the guy who's lobbying for more hotels and year-round resorts and entertainment."

"He and Dev were *friends*?" I found it hard to believe that two people with such extreme opposing objectives could be buddies.

"It was no bromance," Han said. "But Walter's family and Leslie's were close. They'd grown up together and may even have been engaged at some point. Dev respected that."

"Respected what? That his wife was chummy with her ex- or maybe not-so-ex-lover?

Han blushed and laughed uncomfortably. "I don't know about that, but Walter skied with Dev and me sometimes and I never saw him try to push Dev off a lift or anything." He glanced at the other passengers and lowered his voice and his head, whispering "Think about it. How many easy ways are there to kill someone at a ski resort? Nobody talks about it, but it's a dangerous sport. Tragic accidents happen every year."

I recoiled from Han's reference to the darker side of skiing, tempted to rethink my plan to expose my kids to such peril.

Tess sniffed. "But look at how many people hit the slopes each year. Hotdoggers and beginners who outski their ability. Old folks with heart conditions who try to ski like they did in their twenties. The chances of dying on the slopes are something like one in a million, less if you ski sensibly, take care of your gear, and wear a helmet. You could get killed crossing the street."

"And maybe Dev did," I said. The group went somber and quiet. I raced to clarify my words. "Get killed crossing the street, I mean." It only seemed to make things worse.

Siobhan rescued me. "Han's got a point, though," she said. "It'd be easy to conceal a murder as a ski accident. Easier than trying to hide a body in a snowdrift. Who does that? Do we think Dev suffered a fatal fall while checking the mail? For real?"

We were all on edge from the storm, lack of sleep, and the discovery of Dev's body. Despite that, or perhaps because of it, Siobhan's question tickled my funny bone. I wondered what the statistics were on mailbox fatalities. My snort triggered the others and soon we were all laughing uncontrollably, holding our sides.

"Listen up," called Ed the driver, keeping our mirth from escalating. "Next stop is yours, Tess. After that, Siobhan. Then I'm heading home myself and calling it a night. A nasty night."

A small pickup sped around us, honking as his lights slewed left to right. The wheels lost traction and nearly clipped the side of the bus. Ed shook his head. "Noah McKane. Must have taken the boy ages to dig out that truck. Now he's late for something. I'll be picking him out of a drift any day now."

The bus motor labored as Ed tried to force it up the incline to drop us at Tess's front door. We all leaned forward as if that would help. It didn't.

Ed had done a remarkable job, so far, getting all the passengers tucked into their homes for the night. "I don't want to turn on the radio tomorrow and hear that someone got lost between the bus stop and their front door," he said, explaining his abundance of caution. "If we need it, I got a rope we can tie to the door so we can always get back to the mother ship." He patted the dashboard fondly, as though his coach were an old beloved dog.

I zipped my coat and prepared to disembark. I picked up Belle's leash and Tess scowled. "You won't need the leash. She'll head straight for the house. The road will be icy. She'll pull and you'll fall on your head again. No more stitches on my watch."

I grabbed a support pole as the bus slid suddenly backward in a dizzying skid, ending up perpendicular to the road.

"You're not going to make it," Han called to Ed. "Drop us here. Tess and Maggie have skis. I'll make sure they're home safe."

I'd forgotten the skis. We'd stashed them in handy purpose-built holders installed on the outside of the bus. I must have made a skeptical noise, because Belle looked at me over her shoulder with her ears pricked, wagging her tail. Everyone else seemed to have great confidence in Han's proposal.

Ed straightened out the bus and rolled to a stop in the flat area at the bottom of the road, in front of the imposing gates that marked the entrance to Walter Raleigh's mansion. He turned to watch as we got ourselves organized for the trek home. "Promise me you'll stay with Walter if you have any trouble getting up the hill," Ed said. "I mean it. Last thing my old heart needs is to turn up in the morning only to find frozen people wearing your hats and scarves. In a battle between humans and a Sierra blizzard, the gale always wins."

We assured him we'd be careful and thanked him for the lift.

"I'll give you a hand with the boxes," Siobhan said to Han. "Do you want us to help you get them to Elisabeth's and the Bailey's?"

Han looked at Siobhan, who was dead on her feet, and responded with the confidence of youth. "You need to get home and warm. I'll help Tess and Maggie with the deliveries. We'll put 'em on sleds. It'll be quick." He grabbed two boxes and stepped sure-footed and calm, off the bus into the icy whiteness.

"Stay together," Ed urged and closed the doors. The engine labored, but the bus pulled away, leaving us in the dark of the bus stop—an area that should have been illuminated by the lone neighborhood streetlight. It flickered feebly every ten seconds or so.

Han glared at it. "It's always out—doesn't matter whether the weather is too hot, too cold, too wet, or too dry. Don't know whether an animal chews on the wires or the conduit's broken. Either way, it's a lemon."

Tess pulled her small flashlight from her pocket. "I'm not sure this will do much more than highlight the snowflakes, but it's something." The beam cast a comforting golden glow.

I knew I wasn't adept enough on cross-country skis to ascend the hill carrying a box and my backpack. Nor could I walk on the slippery ground juggling my skis, poles, and belongings.

"Should we leave the boxes here?" I asked, frowning at the white cardboard boxes Siobhan had unloaded from the bus and placed on a nearby bench that had nearly been submerged in drifted snow.

Tess thrust our skis upright into the drift with the tips pointing upward. "We'll leave them," she said. "Once we've delivered the boxes to Elisabeth and the Baileys it will be easy to come back and get them."

Han rummaged in his backpack, pulled out a disk the size of a hockey puck, and slapped it down next to the skis. The disk glowed red, blinking, and emitted an intermittent chirp.

"What in the world?" Tess said.

"Sales guy left them at the store as a sample," Han explained. "To replace highway safety flares and use as avalanche beacons. Should help us find the skis even if they're buried in the snow."

Good idea, I thought. The wind had come up. The temperature had plummeted and was making it difficult to breathe, let alone talk. Siobhan yawned, shivered, and stumbled. We needed to get her home. I tugged my cap down over my ears, pulled my neck gaiter up to protect my mouth and nose, adjusted my goggles, and picked up a box with both hands, struggling to get a secure grip on the awkward-sized box with my mittens.

"Onward," said Han, trudging away from Walter's place lugging the other two bakery cartons. Tess took my backpack and whistled up the dogs. "Shuffle your feet," Tess recommended. "Keep them in touch with the ground. Makes you less likely to slip."

I shuffled onward, feeling for the first time in my life that I could have used an elderly person's walker for support. I had no sense of how close we were to our destination. My vision was further hampered by the large box, and I slammed into Han when he came to a stop at his front door.

"Got a kid's sled in the garage," he said. "Wait here."

While we waited, Siobhan thanked us for our help and headed to her home and her bed. She waved her lighted cell phone from her porch to let us know she was safe.

Han returned quickly, pulling an orange molded plastic sled. "The boxes might weigh it down too much, but let's see." I was eager to unload my burden and dropped it on the sled, crumpling one corner of the carton. The sled sank into the snow.

"Take these bungies and secure the box," Han said. "More sleds coming up."

Tess and I crisscrossed elastic cords over the box, hooking the ends to the sled. When Han returned with two more sleds, we repeated the process and trudged onward at an accelerated speed as we each pulled our loads easily over the snow. At Tess's we left the dogs inside with fresh kibble and water and picked up a battery-operated lantern along with head lamps that we strapped on over our knit hats. I glanced at Tess and burst into laughter.

"You look like one of those bald yellow henchmen with overalls from that kid's movie," I told her. She responded with a stream of gibberish, then handed us each a foil-wrapped chocolate from a bulging pocket in her parka. "For fuel. I stocked up."

Han unwrapped his chocolate and popped it in his mouth. "Onward, minions," he shouted, and we set off, with Tess and I taking turns pulling the second sled, since we'd left our own carton behind at her house. First stop, Elisabeth's. Despite the heavy snowfall, the road was easy to follow, marked by berms of old plowed snow and faint tire marks. Fortified with the chocolate and cheered by the illumination, we made a swift advance. The wind was still brutal, but carried the cheerful smell of a log fire.

Chapter 14

The best-laid schemes o' mice an' men gang aft a-gley.
—**Robert Burns,** Scottish poet. 1759-1796

Friday, February 19, Afternoon

Elisabeth's front window glowed with light from the blaze in her hearth. She answered the door draped in a plaid wool blanket. Underneath she sported a puffy down vest and a dazzlingly bright cap knit in an unflattering shade of safety-orange. Duke yapped at her ankles wearing his own wool coat and slippers, struggling to maintain his dignity. I was glad we'd left Belle and Mozart behind. They might have laughed and hurt his feelings.

Elisabeth squinted and tilted her head. I turned off my headlamp. "It's Tess, Maggie, and Han," I said, realizing that, wrapped up as we were, there was no way the neighbor would know us by sight, especially with my light shining in her eyes.

"Come in, come in," she said, picking up Duke and fussing. "What on earth—?"

"We brought you supplies from Flour Power," Tess said as she detached the bungee cords and lifted the box. "Siobhan sent them. Hot coffee and soup, sandwiches, and cookies."

"Marvelous," Elisabeth chirped. "How sweet. And you three delivered it. You must join me for dinner. We'll have a party."

Han took the box from Tess. "Point me toward the kitchen." He strode down the house's central hallway without waiting for an answer.

"We'd love to stay and chat," Tess explained, shouting over Duke's incessant barking. "But it would take us too long to get out of these layers and put them back on. We've got a second box for the Baileys."

"Of course." Elisabeth clamped a hand gently around Duke's tiny snout. "And you must get home before it gets any worse." She glanced round the room. "I've some more lanterns. I'll put them in the windows to help light your way to the Baileys'. That road is dark, even on a beautiful day."

"Do you need help with anything before we head out?" Han asked.

"Nonsense," Elisabeth said. "You've already done more than enough. I'm spending the evening curled up in front of the fire with Duke. We started an audiobook this afternoon. It's a thriller. I can't wait to see how it turns out, but I can't do that until you get out of here." She flapped her hand, shooing us off.

Despite her protests, we each carried armful of logs in from her garage and stacked them in front of the fire. But then we made our escape before our clothing became soaked with sweat. Elisabeth ushered us out, warning us to be careful. Before she closed the door, she held up her cellphone. "It's all charged and I've got a backup battery," she said. "Please call me to tell me you got home safely."

"Give us at least an hour," I urged, thinking that would allow us plenty of time to stop at the Baileys and then trudge back up the hill against the wind.

Han grabbed the rope on the remaining sled, though Tess and I both offered to take turns pulling it. I stashed the other one in a snow bank, where we could pick it up on the way back.

Tess passed us more chocolates. "To keep our spirits up," she said.

Lights winked on in Elisabeth's windows. We still needed our headlamps, however, in the dark tunnel of trees that flanked the Bailey family's long driveway. I was unused to the effort required to walk through heavy snow and to the difficulty of exercising in the diminished oxygen at six thousand feet. With less oxygen in my blood, my muscles responded sluggishly to instructions from my brain. I felt even clumsier than usual. Luckily, one of the Baileys had taken the car out recently, or they'd had a visitor. We walked in the tire tracks, grateful for the relative ease of traversing the packed snow.

Ahead, the tunnel of darkness opened onto a scene that looked like a Victorian Christmas card—a peaked-roof two-story home with a broad porch and illuminated windows. I slowed to absorb the comforting image, forgetting for a moment the pain that the Bailey family had been forced to endure.

As we approached the house an explosion rent the silence and the illusion of peaceful comfort. I yelped and my feet shot out from under me. I slid on my back all the way to the Bailey's front steps, and lay there catching my breath staring up at sword-like icicles that dangled over my head.

Tess glided gracefully to my aid, grabbing hold of the stairway railing with one hand and extending the other to me. "Automated avalanche control," she said, as additional explosions echoed after the first.

"I knew that." I pretended unconvincingly, though I remembered Tess identifying similar ground-shaking booms the night before. "Or...I should have known."

Once I'd reached the safety of the broad covered porch, I patted my arms and legs, taking stock of my injuries. The slick surfaces had provided little friction and my many insulated layers of clothing had cushioned my fall. If I had any bruises, I couldn't feel them.

The door opened before we could ring the bell, and I realized we'd all been shouting to be heard over the sound of the explosions and the howling wind. We turned off our headlamps, told Leslie who we were under all our camouflaging layers, and stepped into well-lit warmth.

A young woman with cheeks red from windburn or the warmth of the fire sat on the sofa reading to two small children. Snuggled in on either side of her, the kids were nearly obscured by puffy quilts. The younger one sucked his thumb and gripped the ears of a well-loved stuffed bunny. The older one popped out of her blanket cocoon to say hello.

"I'm Naomi," said the girl I took to be about five years old. She bounced from one foot to the other and tugged on Tess's hand. "Come in. We're going to make s'mores." She pointed toward her brother on the couch. "That's Harry, the baby. And Amrita. She's Harry's nanny. I'm too big for a nanny."

Leslie Bailey took Naomi's hand. "Walk sl-o-w-ly to the kitchen and bring back the marshmallow forks." Naomi pirouetted and bounced down the hall. Leslie let out a sigh. "Sorry," she said. "The kids have been cooped up too long because of this storm."

She invited us to sit down and we demurred, saying that we'd only come to drop off the food. Amrita stood. "Put the box in the kitchen please," she said. "I've spent all day putting away casseroles that people have dropped off, but I think there's still room." Amrita's smile lit up her face, but did little to eliminate my shock over what amounted to instructions on what we could do with our gift. No thank you or appreciation was forthcoming. *These people are grieving,* I told myself. *They're entitled to a few breaches of manners.*

Leslie frowned, mirroring my confusion over her young sister-in-law's behavior. "Amrita, can you get the kids ready for bed? We'll do the s'mores after so all they need to do before crashing is brush their teeth."

Amrita sighed and picked up Harry, who I pegged at close to two years old. I smiled at him and he ducked his head into his aunt's shoulder.

Leslie waved us forward. "Can I get you anything? I'm surprised you ventured out in this storm. What's the weather like out there? I could run you back in the Jeep."

Tess unzipped her coat but left it on. "We can't stay long. The wind is coming up and the temperature's dropping. I wouldn't think about trying to get out a car, or even your Jeep, in this weather."

Han came back from the kitchen. "Is there anything we can do for you before you go? Chores?" An aging black Labrador with a graying snout roused himself from behind the sofa and came forward, tail wagging. He tucked his nose under Han's hand, and the young man knelt to rub the dog's floppy ears. "Hey, Winston. You looking after your family here?" Winston wagged his whole body then flopped to the floor and rolled over on his back inviting Han to rub his tummy.

"Vicious watch dog," I observed.

Leslie laughed. "He's being brave. Up until you arrived he had his head buried under the couch trying to escape the avalanche explosions. But he knows Han. They're old friends."

Han looked up from his attentions to the dog. "Don't let this act fool you. He's got a deep scary bark that terrifies anyone who doesn't know him."

"He's been waking us up every night for almost a week, snarling, barking, and pawing at the back door," Leslie said. "Quinn Petit took a look, but any footprints have been covered by all the recent snow. It could be a human prowler, a bear, or some other predator. So far, though, whoever or whatever it is hasn't come up on the porch or emerged from the tree line."

I shivered. I knew from my own experience what it was like to worry that strangers might be watching your house.

Leslie wrapped her sweater more tightly around her too thin body. Her face looked worn and gaunt. Tess gave her a hug and the two of them sat in matching armchairs near the fire. I wanted to give Tess time to express her condolences and offer comfort to her neighbor.

"Those are some massive icicles you've got hanging from the eaves out front," I said. "Would it help if Han and I took some broom handles to knock them down? I imagine it's hard to do with the kids, and Amrita's not quite tall enough."

Leslie sighed. "If you don't mind, that would be great. They're dangerous, but I haven't had time to do it myself, what with, well, you know." She laughed uncomfortably. "Naomi won't hold still, so I'm terrified to try to do it while she's around."

Han and I excused ourselves to knock down frozen spears that could have injured or impaled a dog or a small child, probably even a full-grown bad guy. One hard whack with the shovel or broom and they fell to the ground with a satisfying crash, sending broken chunks of ice skittering over the frozen pathway.

We each brought in another load of firewood, told Leslie to call if she needed anything, and retraced our steps. With empty sleds and the light of Elisabeth's lanterns, I expected the trudge home to be easier. I was wrong. Uphill, against the bitter wind, with exhausted legs, our forward momentum slowed to a crawl. As we neared Tess's, I remembered the skis we had yet to retrieve from the bus stop at the end of the road.

"The skis!" said Tess, echoing my thoughts.

I groaned. "I know. I'd forgotten all about them. It may take more than a few chocolates to keep my spirits up. Any chance we can leave them there? I'm pooped."

I wasn't sure anyone had heard me. My words were so muffled by my storm gear and my lungs ached from the cold and exertion.

"Maggie, look." Tess said, giving me a soft punch on the arm. Bent over and gasping for air, I shook my head. "No, really. Look," she repeated, tapping me again and pointing.

I'm sure I've seen more beautiful sights. Like the faces of my newborns, for instance, but the skis and poles, lined up neatly side by side and leaning against Tess's front door were well up on the list of the prettiest things I'd seen. Certainly, the most welcome thing I could think of tonight.

Han looked smug. He held up his phone. "I texted my dad. Asked him if he passed by the bus stop in his 4x4, he could grab the skis for us."

"And some smart kid made them easy to find with that blinky thing," I said. "Good job. And thank you. I owe you."

Han's face turned serious. "You owe me nothing. Neighbors help neighbors. That's how the world works."

"You're a wise man," I said. Tess emptied her pockets of chocolates and gave them all to Han. "Call or text us when you get home?"

"I will. Don't forget Elisabeth, either."

"We'll text her first thing. Thanks so much for all your help."

Han ducked his head and thanked us back. Tess handed him the tow ropes for the sleds. He headed down the other side of the hill, disappearing into a late afternoon that was as dark as night.

The dogs nearly bowled us over as we opened the door, sending the skis flying. We let them take care of business out in front of the house. While they were almost always in a playful mood, the biting wind penetrated their thick fur coats and they were ready to come back in before we'd returned the skis to their racks in the garage. It was all I could do to gather up another load of wood and scale the stairs, my muscles protesting with every step. A hot bath would have been heavenly, but without power, it would have to wait.

Tess brought me a glass of cool water and a pitcher she placed on the table beside it. "You're dehydrated. Finish two glasses. I'll get Siobhan's box from the garage." Tess's voice made it clear that I was not to argue. I didn't have the energy anyway. With one sip I realized how parched I was. The water was cool, clear, and fresh, but I drank it quickly without savoring it.

Tess looked relieved when she came back upstairs. She dropped the carton on the coffee table and kicked off her boots. She put her mittens, cap, and neck gaiter on the drying rack before the fire, and draped her parka over a dining room chair. But she still had layers to go. Waterproof thermal wind pants and a heavy wool sweater joined the parka. "Ugh," she said, sniffing the sweater. "These are all going to need cleaning. They're as soaked on the inside from sweat as they are on the outside from the snow."

"Elisabeth?" I reminded Tess to call.

Tess pulled out her phone, dialed, and spoke to Elisabeth with great efficiency, wasting no words. "We're safe. So is Han. You?" Tess paused. "Great. Stay warm. We'll check again in the morning."

I wondered if Tess had been lying when she said Han was safe. Her phone vibrated with a text as she put down the phone. She glanced at the screen. "What a great kid," she said. "Turned my lie into the truth. I just didn't want to worry Elisabeth and I didn't want to have to phone her back."

"The universe forgives you," I said. "We need to talk about what we've learned so far. I'm losing track of the facts."

"More water and half a sandwich."

I groaned but moved to obey. Tess fussed with the fire while I ate. "I need to tell you what Leslie said while you and Han were out knocking down icicles," she began.

I was vaguely aware of Tess talking, and later realized that she'd helped me with my parka and boots and pulled a thick comforter up around me.

If there were any explosions, snowplows, sheets of snow cascading from the roof, howling wolves, growling bears, or other soothing country noises, I missed them.

Chapter 15

None of us want to be in calm waters all our lives.
—Anne Elliott, *Persuasion*
Jane Austen, British novelist. 1775-1817

Saturday, February 20, Morning

The next thing I knew was the dim light of a stormy morning and the sound of Tess stoking the fire as though she'd stood guarding it all night long. Belle licked my face, forcing me to sit up to avoid further attention.

"I'll let them out," I said, leaning forward and groaning as muscles I didn't know I had told me how badly treated they'd been the day before.

"Ibuprofen's on the coffee table," Tess said. "More water will help too."

By the time I returned with the dogs, Tess had opened Siobhan's box and was pouring lukewarm coffee into mugs and unwrapping aluminum-foil covered cinnamon buns. Tess put one for each of us on a napkin and rewrapped the remaining two. She tucked them behind the fire screen close to the coals to warm.

"What were you saying last night about Leslie?" I asked. "Did she tell you who killed Dev?"

"She has no clue and she's terrified," Tess said. "With Winston making such a racket during the night, they're all exhausted. I told her to bring the kids up here when the weather clears. We've got a swing in the garage and Teddy's old train set. We can keep them entertained while Leslie gets some sleep. If she falls apart, the whole family will go to pieces."

"But what about Amrita? Surely she's helping out?"

"That's what I was saying last night. Leslie was near tears. She said that Amrita came to them in the fall with the promise of being a nanny and doing grocery shopping, kid schlepping, and housework. At first, it was fine. But little by little she's found ways of doing less. Or of doing things wrong or so slowly that it's easier for Leslie to do them herself."

"Is she sick? Taking drugs?" I asked. Someone else might have first guessed that Amrita was lazy or taking advantage of Leslie and Dev. But I was the mother of two energetic teenaged boys. Han, also a teen, had put in a full day of work yesterday and was responsible for the lion's share of the energy required to pull off humanitarian efforts the night before. The last thing I would suggest about any teen or twenty-something was that they were lazy.

"Leslie doesn't think so." Tess wrinkled her forehead and rubbed the back of her neck. "Amrita's made a couple of friends, also nannies. They were all hanging out together with their kids. For Naomi and Harry's protection, Leslie did some discreet background checks on the other girls. She trusts them, for the most part."

"But not Amrita? Her own sister-in-law?" I asked.

"Leslie's pregnant too. Three months."

"Talk about exhausted." I sighed, weary just remembering.

We were silent for a moment, listening to the sounds of the logs popping in the fire. Belle nudged my hand, and I stroked her ears, thinking of those early weeks during both my pregnancies when all I wanted to do was sleep.

"Did you ask about the cake order?" I said, remembering the odd receipt we'd found in the bakery.

Tess pulled the receipt from her pocket and smoothed it out on the coffee table. "I forgot all about it. I really meant to ask Siobhan. She'd know what kind of event it was for and wouldn't be embarrassed to answer."

"Good idea. But could that be an example of the kind of thing Leslie was talking about? Amrita ducking out of some of her responsibilities? I'd think that ordering a cake for a party would be something she could have easily done while the kids were in one of their lessons."

Tess rolled her eyes. "We thought our kids were overscheduled, but Naomi and Harry do gymnastics, art, music, ice skating, and skiing. Naomi attends dance classes and she's on an indoor track team in the winter."

"With all that on their plates, when would they need a nanny?" As soon as I said it, I realized unless all the activities were held in the same place, or provided transportation, it would take, at minimum, deft scheduling and carpool coordination to shuttle the children from class to class.

"That's just it," Tess said. "Leslie didn't want a nanny. They only took on Amrita because she wasn't getting along with her parents in Los Angeles. But Amrita was more interested in social justice, like Dev."

"Is she doing any of that up here? Taking classes or anything?"

Tess shook her head. "Apparently not. Dev had suggested classes at the community college or volunteering, saying that he and Leslie would make sure she had free time for anything she wanted to do. But Amrita kept putting him off."

"You think she has some other agenda?" I peered into the bakery box in search of more cinnamon rolls. No luck.

"I'm not sure," Tess said. "Leslie isn't either. But it changes the picture a little, don't you think?"

"What are you saying? You think Amrita killed her own brother? Why?"

Tess wiped icing off her face and threw the napkin in the bakery carton. "I haven't a clue."

I thought back over all we'd learned from Quinn and the other neighbors. "Do you have any paper? I need to write this all down. And draw some diagrams."

"Maggie stuff," Tess said. She opened a shallow drawer under the coffee table and pulled out a yellow legal pad and a bunch of sharpened pencils secured with a red rubber band.

I sighed in comfort. "Now we're talking. Let's get to work. What do we know?" I asked, sketching out a map of the neighborhood, including the location of the houses, mailboxes, bus stop, and bear boxes.

"Dev Bailey was last seen on December 26. He took out the garbage with Winston. The dog came back but Dev didn't." Tess put her stocking feet on the coffee table and sipped from her mug.

I marked an x on my sketch near the bear boxes—Dev's supposed destination that night. "But his family didn't report him missing until the next morning. Do you know why?"

Tess tapped her fingernails against her cup. "I seem to remember someone saying that Dev and Leslie had an argument, and Leslie figured he'd gone to catch up on work or sleep at his office. But now I can't remember who told me that or whether it's just something I assumed."

I wrote a note on my pad to check whether anyone had searched for Dev or his car that night. "Was his car gone?"

Tess sipped her warm drink. "I'm not sure," she said. "Someone must have checked, but I honestly can't remember anyone mentioning it."

"Was that normal for Leslie and Dev?"

"What do you mean?"

"Do they normally get along or are they always bickering?"

"I don't know them that well, but I'd say they're both pretty easy going. Their families have plenty of money and both Dev and Leslie work, but their hours are flexible. That takes away most of the pressures on a marriage, right?"

I raised an eyebrow.

"Arguments about time and money," Tess said. "And who's spending too much of both on something that's a low priority for the other person."

"An affair?"

"Until I found that cake receipt, I would have said no way. They appeared to enjoy their family and each other. But Leslie worked with Walter Raleigh. He's rumored to play around. And Dev? I'm not sure. He skied a lot. I guess he could have spent some of that time cheating on Leslie instead."

"With whom?"

"That's just it," Tess said. "He's a community guy—coaching, doing taxes for the elderly, helping out in the neighborhood. If he'd been stepping out on Leslie, everyone would have been talking about it. Not that he had the time to develop another relationship with his athletic activities, kid's programs, environmental efforts, and a demanding profession."

"What about vices?" I tapped my pencil against the pad.

"Like drinking?"

"Or gambling, drugs, risky behavior." I wrote risky behavior on my list and circled it.

"I don't think so, but why?"

"Any of those things can put a person in serious debt. Debt leads to secrets, illegal activities, and violence. Addicts will do anything to conceal their habits. Ben and Quinn both said they were seeing more and more big city crime problems up here, but hadn't been able to identify or bring in the ring leader. Maybe Dev was mixed up in all of that."

Tess shook her head. "I don't think so. In the summer, everyone has their windows open all the time. If the Baileys were fighting, we'd have heard it. Especially Elisabeth. And once Elisabeth hears something, everyone knows."

"If Dev was clean, what about Leslie? Or Amrita?"

"Maybe. I don't know Amrita that well. But Leslie? Uh-uh. She's not the type."

I didn't mention to Tess that there was no "type" that fell victim to addictions. The tendency crossed all racial, economic, class, and national boundaries. It was a human condition. There was no predicting who would succumb and who would escape. But Tess knew that.

I made a note on my pad. "We need to talk to Amrita and Leslie again. Separately. And check these stories."

"If the weather clears even a little bit, we can offer to shop for them. Or tidy up while Leslie naps and Amrita takes the kids. Do you really think we'll discover they have dark secrets they'd kill to hide?"

"You never know..." I waggled my eyebrows and laughed a henchman's laugh that startled the dogs. Mozart went to the top of the stairs and barked. Belle wagged her tail. "Do you two need to go out again?"

"Let them out on the back deck," Tess suggested. "They've plowed a track that will keep them from sinking too far into the snow." Because the house was built on a steep hillside, both the first and second floors had doors that opened at ground level.

While the dogs played, I refilled our water glasses and the pitcher. I was adjusting to the altitude, but not to the increased need for hydration in the dry climate. Mozart barked and scratched at the sliding door to the deck. I opened the door and both dogs pelted through, bringing clumps of snow with them. Mozart made a beeline for the stairs and flew down them, barking. A moment later, the doorbell rang.

Tess made a move to get up, but I waved her back. "You waited on me last night. It's your turn to be lazy. I'll get it."

I opened the door to what looked like the abominable snowman. A big creature of indeterminate gender loomed over me, so heavily bundled and wrapped that I couldn't have described the person under the most intense scrutiny. "Hello?" I said. "Would you like to come in?" At home, I wouldn't have immediately invited a stranger into my home. But I had a hunch that under all the layers, this person was a neighbor. The wind-chill factor was well below zero. Inviting someone in out of the cold seemed like the only humane thing to do.

The creature pulled off his hat and unwound his scarf. I relaxed. "Ryan," I said. "It's great to see you. The police cut you loose? Decided you weren't a homicidal maniac after all?"

Ryan winced. His face flushed and I regretted my words, but decided that apologizing would draw too much attention to my clumsy barb. Ryan rallied in a show of forgiveness and good humor.

"Either that or they decided that they needed me to drive the snowplow more than they needed me in a cell." As he detached himself from each layer of clothing, I took his gear from him and hung it on hooks over what was typically a hard-working heating vent. With the power off, hanging the clothes up just meant they wouldn't get any wetter as the caked-on snow melted. I shook off as much as I could. Tess had told me that the frigid air was so dry that melting snow evaporated quickly and helped humidify the air.

"Come on upstairs and tell us all about it," I said. "Have you had lunch? We were about to dive into one of Siobhan's boxes again. You can help."

"The generators were running at the snowplow barn. I took all of our thermal bottles down there and filled them up with coffee." He pulled two quart bottles from his backpack. "I'm dropping them off with all the neighbors who don't have generators."

"You're an angel," I said as I took them from him and cradled them in my arms. We were able to heat water with the gas stove, but I never say no to fresh coffee, especially when someone else has made it.

"Tell that to Quinn Petit."

"That he should accept your coffee?"

"No, that I'm an angel." Ryan grinned as we headed up to the main floor. "I'm hoping he'll have the same reaction you did. It's my defense strategy."

Upstairs, we each poured large mugs of steaming hot coffee and filled plates with lunch stuff provided by Siobhan's box of goodies.

We sat on the sofas at the coffee table, where Ryan picked up my note pad. "Looks like you two are participating in my defense," he said, glancing over my notes. "Thanks."

"Anything to add?" I asked, in between bites of sandwich.

Ryan picked up a pencil. "Can I?"

"Sure. What are you thinking?"

"From the questions they were asking me down at the station, it sounds like Dev had a severe head injury, along with broken bones and bruising. Cops think he was hit hard by something, but they're not sure what. I think they ruled out a snowplow after talking to me."

"Did the autopsy reveal other injuries?" I inhaled the steam from my coffee.

"I don't know. Maybe? They don't tell you much when you're a suspect." Ryan's face reddened and he looked at the ceiling. The shame of being suspected by the police hadn't yet left him.

I pointed at the pad in an effort to distract him. "So, add that Dev had major bruising, broken bones, and a head injury. Next time we see Quinn we'll see if we can get him to give up detailed results from the autopsy, but that's enough information to help us move forward. It tells us Dev didn't just wander off or abandon his family. Someone tried to hurt him."

"But if he was mortally injured, how did he get from the mailboxes all the way over to that drift on the opposite side of the circle?" Tess asked. "He was in the middle of a snowdrift. How did he get there without anyone seeing him? And why didn't the searchers find him? Surely they would have probed any piles of snow."

I tapped my fingers together, wanting to wrench the pad from Ryan's hands so I could doodle and make notes. "You're thinking that if he'd been downhill from the mailboxes, gravity could have put him there?"

"Gravity or snowmelt," Tess said. "But neither one works if he moved uphill. Which he apparently did."

"Was there a lot of blood in the snow where you found him?" Ryan asked.

"Nope. Which means he must not have died there." I was growing more confused by the minute. "Could he have run into a bear who was raiding the garbage? Would a swipe from a bear result in a head wound? Would it have thrown him to the ground with enough force to cause the other injuries?"

Tess shook her head. "Maybe, if it was a grizzly, but the bears we have around here are black bears. I wouldn't want to tangle with one, but I don't know anyone who's been injured. Certainly not fatally."

"I'd think a bear would leave claw marks." Ryan tapped the notepad with the pen. "And surely if Dev had been attacked by an animal, Winston wouldn't have calmly walked home. He would have barked. Dev would have called out. And the bear would have growled. One of us would have heard the commotion and come to his rescue."

"So, are we saying someone picked Dev up in a car? Someone both he and Winston trusted?" I asked.

Ryan nodded. Tess gasped. "We were up here at Thanksgiving last year. I witnessed a scene almost exactly like Ryan described. Dev was out with Winston, but Winston went home alone." Her hands covered her mouth and her eyes above them were wide and horrified.

I waited for her to say more but then prodded. "Don't leave us hanging. What happened?"

"It was Elisabeth," Tess said. "She needed help with a stuck door or something. Dev went to help but sent Winston home so he wouldn't bother Duke."

"Elisabeth's is certainly uphill from the bear boxes," I said. "But what are we saying? That little old lady killed Dev?" I'd never met Dev alive, but dead, his body had seemed enormous and fit, easily confused with that of a much younger man. Too big for the smaller woman to lug around. "She said she didn't get along with Dev. Why would he help her?"

Tess shook her head. "I'm just saying it was a similar scenario. If Dev got along with Elisabeth enough to help her with a stuck door, can we trust anything else Elisabeth said? Could she have confessed to the pellet gun incident to convince us she hadn't done something worse?"

"You know her better than I do," I thought aloud. "But I'd guess she's tougher than she looks. Even if Elisabeth killed Dev, either accidentally or on purpose, that still leaves us with one big part of the puzzle unsolved. How did his body get from where he was killed to where he was found in the snowdrift? It's not like Duke could have helped."

Chapter 16

'Tis the gift to be simple, 'tis the gift to be free
—**Joseph Brackett,** Shaker elder. 1797-1882

Saturday, February 20, Morning

My musings were interrupted by the ring of my phone. I grabbed it and moved into the hallway that led to the bedrooms. "Hey Max," I said, shivering in the chilly corridor. The fireplace's heat hadn't reached this far.

"Maggie! I've been trying to call. This connection isn't great, but at least I got through."

"Just a sec." Warmed by the sound of my husband's voice, but not quite enough, I dashed into the first bedroom on the left. I pulled the comforter off the foot of the bed and wrapped myself in it. "We're doing fine. No power, but we're sticking close to the fireplace and we've got plenty of food and at least a cord of wood in the garage."

"The storm is expected to blow through by noon tomorrow. With a couple of clear days before the next one hits."

Northern California storms were like that. Some years they lined up, miles off the coast, gaining strength before they slammed into the Bay Area one right after the other. Other years, they missed us completely.

"The storm shifted our priorities. Tess and I haven't gotten a thing done on her project to clear out the house."

"Will you stay up there longer?" Only because we'd been married for twenty years could I hear the disappointment in Max's voice.

"We've both lost our momentum. Tess may be having second thoughts about selling."

"Will you head home as soon as there's a break in the weather?"

"You and the boys don't want to come ski?"

"Of course we do. But the way the storms are lined up, I don't think it's going to be possible, unless we want to take them out of school."

"We don't."

"Well at least you haven't stumbled on a dead body."

"About that…"

"What? No. You okay? What happened? Anyone Tess knows? Are you sure you're safe?" Max fired off questions faster than I could answer them.

As soon as he took a breath, I hastened to reassure him. "We're fine. Cell phones have been working well enough for us to stay in touch with the neighbors and make sure they're safe too. The dead guy is Dev Bailey, an accountant friend and neighbor of Tess and her family."

"Kids?"

"Two little ones and another on the way."

Max said nothing. Processing. "Are they in danger?"

"The family? Local police don't seem to think so. We're keeping an eye on them. Bringing in wood and food. We'll check again later today. It's looking like the dead guy, Dev, was killed the day after Christmas. We just happened to find him recently."

"Hurricane force winds, record snow fall, arctic temperatures, power outages, injuries, and a dead body. Maggie, hon. That doesn't sound safe to me."

"Driving over Donner Pass now would be worse. Deadly. Besides, my car's in the shop and Tess's ancient Rover is snowed into the garage. Anyone who can stay home is keeping off the roads until the plows get through. One false move and cars are in the ditches. This weather is lethal for anyone stranded."

Waves of worry rolled off Max and reached me, though we were hundreds of miles apart. There are advantages and disadvantages to being in tune with your spouse.

"Max, we're fine. Please don't worry."

"Why not?"

"Because we're fine. Mostly tucked up in front of a blazing fire with the dogs, just catching up. That's part of the reason we haven't gotten any work done. It's just too cold in the other rooms."

"So, Tess is hearing this whole conversation?"

"No, I'm wrapped in a giant down comforter in one of the bedrooms."

Max responded with a few phrases that told me he missed me as much as I did him. I blushed. But he quickly turned back to concerned husband mode.

"Look," I said, trying to forestall more worry. "We're safe. We're watching out for the neighbors and they've got their eye on us. The police are taking care of the murder."

"Name?"

"Who?"

"The police chief or detective. I want to run his name past the guys and see what they think."

By "the guys," I knew Max meant Jason Mueller, the marine turned small town chief of police at home in Orchard View, and his husband Stephen Laird, a disabled marine law enforcement officer with mysterious business and social connections that seemed to extend all over the world. Whenever we'd been in any kind of trouble, those two had leaped to our aid.

"Quinn mentioned meeting Jason several years ago," I said. "He's from New Orleans and his last name is Petit. Tess says he makes a mean jambalaya and hosts a neighborhood shrimp fest to celebrate Mardi Gras. But I'm certain he wouldn't appreciate any interference from the outside. He's made that clear enough."

"Let me call him. You got a number?"

I reached for the pocket of my jeans in which I'd stashed Quinn's card, then realized I hadn't ventured out of sweats since just after I'd fallen and found Dev. "Not on me."

"Never mind. Stephen will find it. There's this thing called the Internet." Max sounded a little testy and frustrated, which told me he was very worried.

"Since when have Jason and Stephen needed the Internet to rally their troops? A bat signal or secret ninja telepathy is more their style."

Max laughed, which was the response I'd been going for. "Sure, contact them, couldn't hurt," I said.

We wrapped up the call, and I shuffled back to the living room, still wearing the comforter. Shuffling was my new go-to gait—to avoid falling on ice or stepping on the corners of my elegant poufy train.

Ryan and Tess looked up as I entered the living room. Mozart and Belle accompanied me to my seat like courtiers, banners waving in the form of their tails. "Max." I answered their unspoken question. "Storms are lined up from here to spring with no sign of letting up in time to make a weekend ski trip feasible. Max wants us to pack it in, but in the meantime, he's going to phone the guys to check on Quinn."

"The guys?" Ryan asked.

"Friends from home," Tess explained. "Former armed forces, now law enforcement. It's Maggie's husband's way of reassuring himself that we're being well looked after."

Ryan snorted. "I'm probably the last person you'd expect to be supporting the guy who arrested me, but Quinn's good people. And more than qualified. A doctorate in Criminal Justice and years of experience in New Orleans."

Tess patted Ryan's hand. "You know that. I know that. And Max will be reassured when he hears the same thing from our friends."

I leaned back into the sofa cushions and readjusted the comforter. "It looks like the snow might be lightening up. The dogs are going to need a run. I'm going stir crazy, myself. Should we take a walk? Check out the views from Elisabeth's windows to the mailboxes? Ask her a few pointed questions?"

Tess stood and folded the blanket she'd been wearing. "Let's build up the fire first. I want to check on Leslie too. Maybe the kids can help us run the dogs and Leslie can get some sleep."

"Can I help?" Ryan asked. "Or is the whole neighborhood terrified of me by now?"

"If you're going to terrorize the neighborhood, buddy, you've got a long way to go." Tess gave his arm a gentle punch. "Helping the police with their inquiries just won't cut it. Not around here. Unless you're planning a serial killing or a chainsaw massacre, I think your reputation is safe."

Ryan laughed with patently fake menace and reached for his backpack. He waggled his eyebrows, hummed some scary music, thrust his hand into the depths of his pack…and pulled out another thermal carafe. "I'll win them over with my coffee, *bwahaha*."

Tess threw one of his leather mittens at him and we began the long and increasingly tedious process of donning our many protective layers.

By the time we finally ventured out with the dogs, the snow had reduced itself to flurries, and the wind had died to a soft breeze with occasional gusts. Puffy white clouds raced across the sky chased by ominous gray ones far to the west. The sun bounced off every snow covered surface, blinding us. "I'm going back for sunglasses," Tess said. "I'll grab yours too, Maggie."

Ryan pulled a pair from an inside pocket of his parka. They fogged up immediately. "Never mind," he said. "They'll clear."

He touched the rough plywood covering the hole in the garage door. "Old Jens really did a number on this."

"Is he having trouble driving?" I asked, thinking about my grandfather's battle with dementia years ago, and our family's traumatic efforts to yank his license.

"Not so as you'd notice. I'll check with Klaus and Han though."

"So, I should knock him off my list of possible murderers, despite his ongoing feud with Dev Bailey?"

"Jens is a curmudgeon on the outside, a real 'Kids today! Get off my lawn!' grouch. But on the inside? Pure marshmallow. Soft and sweet." Ryan stopped in his tracks and touched my arm for emphasis. "Don't tell him I told you that though. He'd kill *me*."

I shuddered. It was entirely too much talk about death, too soon after Dev's demise. I changed the subject. "What are our objectives at Elisabeth's?"

"Bring in more wood," Tess said. "Check for wind damage."

"Deliver coffee and walk that silly little Duke," Ryan said.

"Check sight lines to see what she might have witnessed the night Dev died," I added.

"She's got a bathroom off the kitchen," Tess said. It sounded like a non sequitur until she added, "If we all burst through her door saying the cold has given us an immediate need for a toilet, two of us can nip upstairs. I want to check the other side of the house to find out how much she can see of what goes on at the Bailey house."

"Good plan," I said. "Was the new mailbox structure built in the same place as the old one?" I briefly wondered why, if that was the case, someone didn't bury Dev in the construction area instead of a snowdrift. Without touching the drainage, the structure wouldn't have required much excavation, but the process of digging new post holes would have torn up the ground. I couldn't imagine the earth hadn't needed to be leveled, and that would have meant disturbing the soil. After it had been dug up, but before it had a chance to refreeze, there was a small window of time. Small, but maybe just big enough to dig a shallow grave under the cover of darkness without being obvious.

For that matter, why not just stash the body in the woods and hope nature took care of it before spring? Did the murderer want to make sure Dev's body was found? If so, why? It seemed like every time we gained more information, we also doubled the number of unanswered questions.

We reached Elisabeth's house in record time and found her sweeping snow from her front steps.

"Can I help with the sweeping?" Tess reached for the broom.

Elisabeth pulled it out of Tess's reach. "This is the first outdoor exercise I've had in days. And look at that sun. I think the storm is just taking a breather before catching its second wind. We can't waste a minute." She adjusted her dark glasses and the wide-brimmed flowered sun hat she wore perched atop her warm wool cap.

Remembering our mission, I interrupted with, "I'd like to borrow your bathroom, if you don't mind. Afterwards, we can help you tackle any chores that need doing, bring in more wood, or take Duke for a romp with the other dogs. Whatever you need."

Elisabeth pointed me inside. "There's a powder room off the kitchen."

The others were chatting and had apparently forgotten our plan to create a reason to use the upstairs facilities, but while they held the older woman's attention, I kicked off my boots in the front hallway and dashed quietly up the carpeted stairs. Her front windows gave her a great view of Tess's house with a good angle on the comings and goings of everyone on the street. Out back, she could see a portion of the Bailey's front yard, now filled with tire tracks that led me to think someone had already ventured out this morning. That was odd. We hadn't seen tire tracks on the rest of the street.

To the right, facing the street, Elisabeth had an uninterrupted view of the turn-around circle, the bear-safe garbage bins, and the covered mailboxes. I checked but there were no tire tracks there either. I wondered what kinds of vehicles the Baileys had in their big four-car garage, and whether one of them was capable of going off-road through the resort. If so, they could have gone almost anywhere without anyone else from the neighborhood seeing them.

Tess told me that the fire trails were often used by competitive cross-country teams for training, but surely no one had been breaking trail in this week's deadly storm. With the high winds and low temperatures, Tess had warned me that the woods were dangerous. Limbs ripped from the trees could become spears known as widow-makers or fool-killers and were the cause of a significant percentage of forestry fatalities every year. My fingers itched to write a note on my yellow legal pad so I'd remember to ask Quinn whether Dev's injuries were consistent with those caused by a falling branch.

One dark thought led to another. I wondered if someone could have tried to fake a back-country accident by clobbering Dev with a thick branch. Television characters often grabbed a handy baseball bat when defending their homes from possible intruders. Branches of similar size and shape could be found throughout the forest and, once discarded, would have easily blended in and been overlooked.

I made another mental note to check with Quinn on whether anyone had examined the dumpster and surrounding areas for blunt objects following Dev's disappearance. I was sure they had, but hearing Quinn's reassuring voice confirm my assumption might help me keep from worrying about it in the middle of the night.

I clutched my arms, shivering at the thought of the cold calculating vengeance that could have made someone want to do away with Dev. Though I hadn't met him, I hadn't heard anyone say a word against him.

Except maybe Jens.

Chapter 17

Things are in the saddle, and ride mankind.
—**Ralph Waldo Emerson**, American writer. 1803-1882

Saturday, February 20, Morning

The sound of feet stomping on Elisabeth's front porch mat made me run back down the stairs to avoid having my snooping discovered. By the time Elisabeth opened the front door carrying a snow-covered "pupsicle," I was slipping my feet into my boots. Ryan and Tess were carrying armloads of wood. Tess raised her eyebrows. I nodded, assuming she wanted to know if I'd had time to explore Elisabeth's vantage points from the upstairs windows.

"Where to, Mrs. Roche?" Ryan asked. "By the fire?"

"Just drop them here, dear," Elisabeth said. "That way you don't need to take your boots and coats off. Are you sure you won't stay for a coffee break? I thawed a frozen blackberry pie by the fire last night. Duke ate some of it, but the rest is fine."

Behind Elisabeth's back, Tess vehemently shook her head. Dropping her armload of wood on the floor beside the front door, she said, "That's so sweet of you, Elisabeth, but we said we'd check on the Baileys today. Maybe see if we can help the kids run off some steam."

I took Duke from Elisabeth's arms and wrapped him in a towel I'd plucked from a nearby hook. He growled softly, which I hoped was a doggy sound of contentment rather than an expression of suppressed rage. I returned the wrapped up dog to the safety of Elisabeth's arms.

"You should have seen him out there with Mozart and Belle," Elisabeth said, rubbing his ears. "I knew they wouldn't lose him in a drift, so the little dear had more freedom than usual. He was chasing them as though he thought he was the big dog, jumping up to nip at their ears."

Tess and Ryan had left our dogs outside, but I'd have to be sure to reward Belle with an extra-large treat for tolerating Duke. She was friendly with most dogs, but small ones tended to make her nervous, as though she feared stepping on or tripping over them.

We said our goodbyes, reminded Elisabeth to phone us if she needed anything, and set off down the long dark driveway to the Bailey's house. "I didn't get a chance to look out the windows on this side of the house," I told Tess and Ryan. "But the back windows look out on the end of the Bailey's driveway near the front porch. It looked like someone had taken out a vehicle of some kind this morning. A big one."

Tess furrowed her brows and squinted sideways at the snowy surface of the drive, pockmarked by clumps that had fallen from the overhanging trees. "There are no tracks here. Where could they have gone?"

"The old fire roads?" I suggested. "Breaking trail for cross-country skis?"

Ryan shook his head. "If Dev were home, maybe. But Leslie and Amrita don't ski cross country."

"Could someone from the resort have gone to the maintenance sheds and then come down to check on them?" I asked.

Ryan tapped his chin. "Maybe, but not likely. Dev was friends with some of those guys, but Leslie didn't spend time with any of the back-country people. She's much more of an urban gal—a foodie. She's more likely to know the chefs, bartenders, and event planners than the guys from the maintenance barn."

I turned toward Tess trying to get a better sense of Leslie. "A snob?"

"Not at all," Tess said. "Just different interests. Dev and Leslie seemed to love each other and their family life together, but I know that Dev wondered if he was the right guy for Leslie. He thrived on all the outdoorsy wilderness aspects of life in the mountains. Leslie was more into the après ski scene."

"Ski bunny?" I asked.

Ryan stepped back and wrinkled his forehead. "Whoa. That's kinda judgy and sexist don't you think?"

My face flamed. He was right. "Sorry. Sounds like it came straight out of a 1960s Bond movie, doesn't it?"

"Depends on your definition, I guess. In this century, there's an escort service that uses the term, and Leslie definitely wasn't a prostitute." Ryan turned to Tess, apparently looking for confirmation.

"Leslie always wore expensive ski clothes that looked like they came off the cover of a ski fashion magazine," Tess said. "But she could ski any of the terrain out there. And she was never trolling for dates."

I kicked up a cloud of powder and wished I could disappear within it. I'd just been trying to flesh out my portrait of Leslie, but I'd accidently insulted a real person who was a friend of both Tess and Ryan.

Tess grinned. "She was, however, typically looking for business connections among those with power, wealth, and influence. She worked for Walter and that was her job."

"She was what exactly?" I asked. "His employee? Business partner? Friend? Could it have been more than that?"

Ryan and Tess considered my question, but looked skeptical. "I think they were genuinely friends," Ryan said. "And had similar interests regarding the future of the resort."

"Expansion? Didn't that conflict with what Dev wanted? I asked.

Tess laughed. I turned my head at the sound to gauge the expression on her face. There was a sharp note to her amusement. I wasn't sure whether it was pointed at me, my idea, or Dev.

"Sorry, Maggie. Don't mind me. It's just that Dev's group of activists were more active on the ski slopes and summer trails than they were in the voting booth, at fundraising events, or meetings with state and national politicians. Walter and Leslie know all the mucky-mucks by first name. I doubt they considered Dev any competition at all. If anything, they humored him."

I looked away, a little embarrassed by my naïve question. We were approaching the large turn-around area in front of the Baileys' porch. "Tire tracks." I pointed at the ground ahead. Shadows in the imprinted tracks made them appear pale blue against the white of the snow. We emerged from the dim light among the trees and squinted in the sunlight. Winston barked a greeting from inside the house and a black nose pushed aside the sheer curtains covering the sidelights of the front door.

The door burst open and Winston bounded out, launching himself off the porch, sailing over the front steps and into the clearing, then dropping into a play bow, tail wagging. The trio chased each other in large loops crisscrossing the snow and obliterating any evidence the tire tracks may have offered.

It didn't matter. Our primary objective at the Bailey house was to help out pregnant, grieving, and exhausted Leslie. And I, at least, needed to make amends for my inadvertent attack on her character. We knocked and let ourselves into a room covered in toys, fireplace ash, dirty dishes, and piles of blankets that showed the family had been living and sleeping before the fire, much as Tess and I had done.

"Hello," I called out. "Leslie? Amrita?"

No one answered. It must have been hard to hear over the whining and crying of children who'd been cooped up too long and who must have picked up on the grief and tension expressed by the remaining adults in their lives; Amrita and their mom. I kicked off my boots and padded down the hall in my stocking feet in search of the source of the noise. I found it in the kitchen and suddenly wished I'd kept shoes on to protect my feet. Leslie picked broken glass off the floor. Her once shining brown bob was dull, greasy, and splotched with pancake batter.

I took charge. "Leslie, do you have a generator? Or can we heat water for a bath for you? Followed by a nap? Ryan and Tess are outside playing with the dogs and said they would love to be joined by a big boy and girl with tons of energy and imagination."

Harry and Naomi wiped their tears and sat up straight.

I spoke to them directly. "You two are grown-up enough to dress yourselves, right? With a little help from Amrita?" Leslie sniffed but Naomi left the kitchen in a streak of red flannel nightgown while Harry held up his hands asking to be released from the bonds of his highchair. I helped detangle him from his restraints and he toddled after Naomi crying "Wait Nomy. Wait for Harry."

Amrita entered the kitchen as soon as they'd left the room. She stopped drying her hair with a towel long enough to lift the hem of her robe to avoid the broken glass and spilled pancake batter before plopping herself at the table and pouring a glass of orange juice. She neither greeted nor aided Leslie.

"Nice shower, Amrita?" Leslie asked with more than a hint of sarcasm.

"Oh yes. Thanks. I'm not sure how much hot water is left, though. Once I got in there it was heaven—really hard to step out again."

"Can you run upstairs and help the kids get dressed? The neighbors have volunteered to run them around outside and tire them out in the snow. But they can't go out half-dressed."

Amrita sighed. "They can dress themselves."

Leslie sat back on her heels. Her shoulders rose and fell as she closed her eyes and took a big breath in and out. "Left to their own devices, Naomi's likely to wear a swimsuit and tutu. Harry will need his heavy sweater today and doesn't like the color. Amrita, they're little kids."

"After breakfast," Amrita said, looking as though she was awaiting a menu and fresh coffee.

Leslie remained outwardly patient, but I'd had enough. "The kitchen is closed for cleaning and repairs," I announced. "If you don't want to help the kids upstairs, you can take over sweeping up the glass." I handed her a wrapped granola bar and squashed juice box. "That'll hold you."

After she'd flounced out, I extended my hand to help Leslie up off the floor. Her pregnancy wasn't yet visible, but I sensed she was at the early awkward stage as her body shifted tasks to make a baby. Muscles stretching, hormones raging, and a general sense of imbalance, both literally and figuratively. I had no idea what stage of grief she was in, nor how she'd refrained from killing her supposed mother's helper, Amrita. Based on what Tess had told me earlier about Amrita's interest in social justice issues and her future plans, I was shocked by the surly teenager mode she was in this morning. Was Tess wrong about the girl? Or was it just her way of expressing her grief? It was hard to be sure, since everyone seemed to know a different side of Amrita.

I cleared dishes and wiped layers of stickiness off the table and a chair, then bowed to Leslie like a courtier and invited her to sit. "Would madam prefer herbal tea or decaf coffee?"

"Either, thanks. Use the electric kettle." She shook her head. "We have the most massive whole-house generator money can buy. Dev insisted we install it during our remodel so the kids and I would be safe, whatever the weather. But he hated to break down and use it. Thought it was a sign of environmentally unsound weakness and an inability to adapt to the mountain habitat." She sighed. "But it was either turn it on or lose my sanity this morning."

"I get it," I assured her. "When they say it takes a village, they're not accounting for the energy of smart, healthy, active children who've been cooped up by a storm. That takes a mob or megalopolis—something bigger than a village, anyway." Leslie laughed as my metaphor disintegrated.

"You're a breath of fresh air," she said.

"What's the story with the princess?" I asked.

Leslie bristled. "Naomi?"

"Of course not! She's five years old. She's entitled to act entitled. I meant Amrita. Forgive me, but she seems to have mistaken her employer for the kitchen help at a swanky bed and breakfast."

I extracted a tea kettle from the clutter, filled it, and plugged it into the outlet on the electric range, which was the only clear surface. While the water heated, I found a dirty mug, washed it, and located a box of chamomile tea.

Leslie sighed. "I need to vent."

"Carry on," I said. "I'm listening."

"Dev was her only sibling. I get that. She's grieving. But so are we. Naomi and Harry have lost their dad, and I—" Her voice broke and her eyes teared. I stopped loading dirty dishes in the washer and ran a fresh dishcloth under warm water from the tap, wrung it out, and handed it to Leslie.

She took it and wiped her face. "If you're a figment of my imagination, please don't disappear just yet." Her voice was audible but garbled by the cloth.

"It's more satisfying to clean someone else's kitchen," I said. "It's easy to imagine that, unlike your own, it will stay clean forever."

"Yeah, like that's going to happen." Leslie used the cloth to wipe up a milk spill that may have dated from a day or two earlier. This woman needed help. Amrita certainly wasn't it. At least not today.

"Tell me more about your sister-in-law," I said, handing her the mug of tea. I continued to wipe spills, clear counters, scrape plates, and fill the dishwasher while we chatted. "Is there enough hot water and power to run the dishwasher? If not, they're out of the way for now. I'll wash them after the pots."

"Maggie, you don't have to do all this."

"That's what neighbors are for," I said. "At least until the interstate over Donner Pass is clear, I'm your neighbor."

Before Leslie could list the failings of her sister-in-law, Naomi appeared in a purple sparkling tunic and leggings, accessorized by butterfly wings. "Wow, you're speedy," I said. "Where do you keep your outdoor clothes?" She pointed toward the mudroom off the kitchen.

"Well, I won't be able to tell the difference between your coat and your mom's, but if you go grab what's yours, I'll help you get into them."

Naomi shook her head. "I don't need help. I'm big."

"Of course," I said. I grabbed a box of dog treats off the counter and shook it. "Once you get your mittens on, I'll give you some treats for the dogs. You'll need to make Belle and Mozart sit to earn their treats. Can you do that?"

Her eyes lit up and she hopped on one foot around the kitchen.

"Coat," I reminded her.

Naomi disappeared into the mudroom, where she sat on the floor to pull on her pink polka dot boots.

Leslie smiled. "Why is it that the traits that we want to see in strong adult women are the ones that make them so unruly as children?"

"If you figure that out, let me know. It's the same with boys."

"As I'm discovering. I thought I knew all about parenting, but it's a whole new ball game with Harry."

"The things they don't tell you."

I made room for one last glass in the dishwasher, found soap under the sink, and tossed in a detergent pod. Closing the door, I turned to Leslie.

"Go ahead and run it," she said. "It has its own heater."

She sipped her tea and closed her eyes. Her head drooped and I feared she'd fall asleep with her face stuck to the spilled jam and toast crumbs.

Naomi skipped out of the laundry room with her boots on the wrong feet, struggling with the zipper on her jacket. I tucked her butterfly wings into the roomy garment, and zipped her up. Standing, I pulled three dog biscuits from my pocket and transferred them to her tiny palm. Naomi barely had time to shout "Bye Mom" over her shoulder before she was gone.

Leslie smiled. "Thanks so much, Maggie. I really was near the end of my rope. How long can you guys stay?"

"Can you sleep with the vacuum on? The washer-dryer?"

"Dev would kill me," she said. "He hated to resort to the generator."

"If he were here, we could fend him off together. As it is, you're trying to do your job, his job, and apparently, Amrita's. I think it's okay if we resort to modern conveniences to save your sanity. Without you, where would those kids be?"

"You're right. We've yet to discover a new normal without Dev. I kept thinking he'll come back, apologizing for abandoning us." She cried softly and wiped her eyes. "That's the worst, I think. Knowing I cursed him so unfairly for leaving us when the poor guy was lying frozen—" Whatever else she'd been going to say was lost in a sob. I cleaned the table in front of her and put down a clean and crumb-free placemat. She buried her head in her arms.

I pulled what looked like a small boy's jacket and boots from the piles of clothes on the floor of the laundry room and called up the stairs. "Harry, the dogs are waiting for you."

The dishwasher had started its rinse cycle by the time Amrita appeared, carrying a squirming Harry. He extracted himself from her clutches and ran to put on his boots. I convinced him to remove the boots just long enough to don his snowsuit, then tossed a faded denim coat to Amrita.

It fell to the floor in front of her. "That's not mine," she said.

I didn't even try to hide my contempt. "Then pick it up and find yours. Take Harry outside. I'll clean up in here. The kids need to get out and Leslie needs a shower and a nap. Then you can catch up on some of your neglected chores around here." I employed my strongest "mom face" and Amrita got the message. She grabbed her own coat and chased Harry, giggling, toward the front door with his red wool cap in her hands. Somewhere under her lazy, slovenly housekeeping skills there lurked a good heart.

Chapter 18

Give me six hours to chop down a tree and I will spend the first four
sharpening the axe.
—**Abraham Lincoln,** American President 1809-1865

Saturday, February 20, Late morning

We could hear muffled barking as Amrita and Harry joined the others out
front. "If Tess and Ryan can't keep them entertained, the dogs will," I said.

"I can't decide whether she means well and is incompetent or if she's just
hopelessly out of her depth, or if she doesn't care about us at all," Leslie said.

"It's likely all three, at different times."

Leslie nodded.

"How long has Amrita worked for you?"

"Six months. She wasn't getting along with her parents in Los Angeles.
Her family says she was disrespectful and lazy. Amrita's version is that
her career ambitions were different from what her mom and dad wanted
for her. Dev suggested she could act as our nanny. We didn't need one
then, but I could use a real one now."

I nodded.

Leslie continued. "She says she's interested in environmental activism,
but she's afraid of mud and spiders and puddles, and almost everything
else that lives outside that door." Leslie pointed toward the front of the
house. "An environmentalist she is not. Unless it's the environment of a
hard-drinking party."

"Isn't that what you do? Parties, I mean?"

Leslie looked baffled by my question.

"Siobhan said you ordered food from her."

"Right. For Walter Raleigh. I organize fundraising events with fancy food and drink. But no one gets too wild. They're more glorified business meetings than they are parties." She pushed back lank strands of hair, leaving a fashionable streak of raspberry that owed itself to a blob of jam rather than a trendy dye.

"Amrita and her friends on the other hand…Dev's had to pick her up on more than one occasion when she'd had too much to drink, after hanging out with some of the older kids around here. The last time was the worst. The bartender from a local sports bar–hamburger joint gave Dev a call and they both had to help her to the car. It was like she'd been given a drug."

"What did Dev do?"

"Took her to Alison at the clinic."

"It was that bad?"

Leslie shrugged. "I stayed with Naomi and Harry, so I didn't see her until she'd sobered up. Dev was concerned, but I think he also wanted to shock some sense into her."

"Did Alison test her for drugs?"

"I'm not sure. She's over eighteen, so there's a limit to what Alison could tell us. I know they gave her Narcan, pumped her stomach, and set up an IV…" Leslie's voice trailed off and she appeared to be lost in a memory. "Wait. No. You're right. Dev said they tested her for ketamine, one of the date rape drugs, but the results hadn't come back by the time they left the clinic."

She *tsked*. "It didn't matter in the long run I guess. At least not to us. We had a talk with her about date rape, underage drinking, and safety. Quinn did too. She was embarrassed, but she listened and I don't think she's been out with those particular kids since."

She clenched her jaw and stood, pacing. "Ben, Alison, and Quinn keep talking about an increase in crime and violence around here. Everything from smuggling drugs and cigarettes to sex trafficking. Dev was furious that illegal drugs had touched our family and put Amrita at risk. He was going to look into it."

"Did he?"

Leslie clenched her fists. "It wasn't long after that incident that Dev disappeared. I've told Quinn to look at Dev's business files and records. His officers took Dev's laptop. My husband was an accountant for folks all over the Tahoe Basin. For all I know, somewhere among his clients was a business that was a cover for these crooks. I think Dev found something incriminating, confronted whoever was responsible, and they killed him."

"Wouldn't Dev have gone to Quinn?" If Leslie was right, Dev's behavior had been reckless in the extreme.

Leslie rested her head on her hand and closed her eyes. "You never met Dev. When his family was threatened, he took immediate action. If he'd had evidence, he might have contacted Quinn and confronted the criminals, but not necessarily in that order. He always tried to get people to do the right thing. And he'd have wanted solid proof before alerting Quinn. We all know how overworked our chief is. Dev may have been digging so deep for evidence that he alerted the bad guys and they came after him." She shuddered. "I hate to think what someone desperate might have done to him."

They were all bigger problems than I could solve today. I stepped into the mudroom and pulled a fluffy warm flannel nightgown from the dryer. Folding it into a neat square, I returned to the kitchen and handed it to Leslie. She took it and held it against her face, looking relaxed for a fleeting moment.

But then she continued to pace, breathing hard. "Or maybe Amrita knew too much after her brush with the vile creature that slipped her the ketamine, and Dev died trying to protect her and the rest of our family. It's all been too much."

I struggled to shift the subject back to something less worrisome and focused on learning more about Amrita.

"Did she finish high school?" I asked.

"Last spring. We all went to the ceremony. She's taking a gap year."

"Did she work with Dev?"

"No more than she works as a nanny." Leslie hugged the nightgown like a lifeline and appeared to calm down at least a little. "You sure you won't be insulted if I leave you here on your own?"

I turned her gently toward the front stairs and gave her a little push. "Sleep as long as you can. We'll look after the kids. There are three of us. We should be able to keep them from burning down the house."

Leslie had tears in her eyes. "They're good kids."

"I know. And you're a good mom. But they're also smart, healthy, and active. That's exhausting, particularly when the new one you have on board demands all your energy."

Leslie touched her belly and started to respond, but I gave her another little shove. "Quick, before they come back inside demanding hot chocolate and lunch."

She disappeared up the stairs and within minutes I heard the shower running. I ran upstairs to locate a linen closet and start changing the beds. I wanted to help out. But I also wanted to uncover any secrets Amrita or Leslie might be hiding in their closets, sock drawers, or under the bathroom sinks.

I'd changed the sheets on Leslie's bed and tidied up a little before she stepped out of the bathroom. "Maggie, your help is without measure," she said, yawning. "There's no way I can pay you back."

"I don't keep score. Nap now and we'll keep the kids as quiet as we can." Though she made a token show of protest, she was nearly dead on her feet. I changed the kids' beds then checked back on Leslie and found her sound asleep.

I gathered up the laundry to throw in the washer, grateful that Leslie was running her generator. With any luck, the power would be back on within days or even hours, and she'd be able to keep on top of everything herself.

I cobbled together meals while cleaning out Leslie's fridge. Casseroles dropped off by concerned neighbors looked close to spoiling. I rescued, chopped, and sautéed some tired vegetables, added a can of tomatoes, leftover vegetable soup, and a quart of chicken stock. I sniffed at the drying remains of a rotisserie chicken, and tossed that in the stock pot along with the rest. So far, the concoction smelled edible. I wiped down the now nearly empty shelves of the fridge.

I unloaded the dishwasher and while searching for places for the clean dishes, I stumbled on a bread maker. Like the simmering soup pot, the smell of hot yeasty bread was comforting and cozy and would make a perfect easy dinner with simple clean up.

For lunch, I pulled packages of food from the laundry room freezer, which wasn't hooked up to the generator. The frozen items were starting to thaw, but still firm. I deemed them safe. But would the kids eat them? I rummaged in the cupboards a little more and located cupcake tins. In an upper cupboard, behind the spices, I found some old cupcake liners. Perfect. I lined the tins and had finished reheating the frozen food just as the kids, dogs, and two adults burst through the door.

"No Ryan?" I asked Tess as she helped a red-cheeked Harry and Naomi off with their gear.

"He was called back by the snowplow crew," Tess said. "We're getting more snow tonight—a normal storm, couple inches—but they want to get the old stuff off the roads as much as they can before then." Every time someone mentioned the weather report, it changed. Typically for the worse. But that was the nature of California winter storms in the High Sierra.

"Have you heard anything about the power?" I asked Tess. Spending the day in a house with all the modern conveniences had spoiled me, and I wasn't keen to return to the tiny circle of warmth surrounding Tess's fireplace. Tess must have read my guilty thoughts.

"You're not the only one," she said. "I got a text message from the power company that said they were hoping to restore electricity to most of the Tahoe basin by six p.m.—maybe earlier."

I glanced at the wall clock. Could we hold out for six more hours? Of course we could. Although if the power didn't kick back on, I'd lobby Tess to get back on the road before the new storm began.

"What's for lunch?" Naomi asked, sniffing the air.

"Spear fishing."

"I don't like fish."

"You'll like this kind. It's kinda tricky, though. Get your hands washed and I'll show you how it works."

The kids raced to do my bidding. Tess looked intrigued. Amrita sneered. She opened a high cupboard, grabbed a handful of granola bars and a room temperature soda and was about to disappear upstairs when Tess said. "Wait up," From the tone of my friend's voice and the look on her face, I was glad I wasn't Amrita. Tess ushered Amrita from the kitchen into the hall.

Though their voices were muffled, I could hear firm, whispered, declarative sentences from Tess, and did my best to distract the children. Harry and Naomi hopped up in their seats, and I pretended not to notice that Harry chose a grown-up chair rather than his highchair. I handed them each a fork, warning them to be careful of the dangerous spears. Their eyes grew wide as they accepted the challenge and the powerful imagination of childhood transformed their ordinary forks into deadly fishing gear.

"Okay," I said. "Listen closely. You're going to be catching six different kinds of fish." I placed the muffin tins in front of them filled with cut grapes, Tater Tots, carrot coins, sliced string cheese, blanched green beans, and a dollop of ketchup in the sixth cup. "Some of them are tricky to catch. Others, you'll be able to catch with your fingers." I pointed toward the ketchup. "You might want to dip some of them in this magic sauce. It keeps them quiet and makes them easier to handle.

The kids were entranced by the game, as I'd hoped, and ready to dig in. "Oh, wait," I said. "Last rule. You need to fish with your eyes closed." I'd first made sure the kids were seated far enough apart to keep them from "accidently" spearing each other. Both kids slammed their eyes shut. Harry kept his entire face scrunched up but quickly abandoned his fork in favor of his fingers. When Tess returned, she picked up the ketchup bottle and spoke into it as though it were a microphone and she was providing color commentary at a sporting event. Naomi cheated, peeking through the fingers of the hand she'd slapped over her eyes, but did use her fork.

Both kids ate more than I thought they would. I was dying to ask Tess what she'd said to Amrita and what, if anything, she and Ryan had learned from her and the kids and their investigation outside. But it would have to wait.

Chapter 19

We are happy in proportion to the things we can do without.
—**Henry David Thoreau**, American writer. 1817-1862

Saturday, February 21, Afternoon

We still had the two children to look after. I was out of practice and so was Tess, but we scrambled for ways to help Leslie, entertain the kids, and get to know Amrita better. Something told me she might hold the keys to all the mysteries.

I announced our next event: a treasure hunt for socks. We washed lunch off the kids and left the table to clear up later. "Amrita will take care of that," Tess said confidently, though she mouthed "I hope" to me.

I gave the kids the rules for the "treasure hunt." Hidden inside the great laundry mountain on their sofa were socks. The sock children had been on a school trip and each had a buddy, but they'd gotten separated in a storm. Every time Naomi and Harry found a sock, they could say *alakazam* and spin around once before they put the sock on the coffee table. If they found a sock that matched one already on the coffee table, they got to say *Jabberwocky* and growl like a horrible monster. If they didn't want to play the game, they could be a gargoyle on the couch. Belle and Mozart retreated under the coffee table to avoid any stray spells or spinning preschoolers. Winston had crashed out in the laundry room with his nose buried in the pile of sheets still awaiting their turn in the washer.

Naomi and Harry lost interest in the game at almost the same time Tess and I finished folding up the tiniest clothes either of us had seen in years.

We all pretended to be gargoyles on the couch while I explained what they were in my most hypnotic voice. The kids zonked out. We tucked them in snugly, left Belle and Winston to watch over them, and returned to the kitchen where we could sip hot coffee and chat without disturbing anyone.

The clothes dryer chimed the signal that another batch was done, and Tess went to shift the loads again.

"Excuse me, Winston," I heard her say, followed by *alakazam* as she closed the door on the front loading washer and started it up. I was with Tess. After days without power, almost anything that ran on electricity seemed like magic.

"So, what did you learn while Ryan and I were outside?" Tess asked as she returned from the laundry room. "I assume you snooped?"

"You first. Did you discover who made those tire tracks?"

"You'll never guess. The reason they went nowhere beyond the front of the house is that the vehicle stayed in that area. Leslie didn't want to get stuck."

"Driving it up and back in front of the house? Why do that?"

"Leslie was running out of ways to entertain the kids. She told Harry and Naomi that if they climbed the stairs ten times, she'd let them drive their old Land Rover." There'd been a time, apparently, when every family in the area needed one for plowing through the winter weather.

"Points for creativity. Could they even see over the steering wheel?"

"They stood on her lap."

"Before you know it, they'll be drag racing around the neighborhood."

"I think she put the fear of Quinn into them." Tess made a stern face, lowered her voice, and sounded remarkably like the police chief, saying "Never ever touch the keys without a grownup's okay."

"Anything else?"

"Harry wanted to show Ryan the truck he drove, so we peeked inside the garage. It's a banged-up old thing. According to the pint-sized expert, it's 'indy-trucked-able.'"

I fought to keep from spurting my coffee all over the clean kitchen while Tess continued. "Harry also wanted Ryan to see snowcats—the giant grooming machines. The maintenance barn is only a few hundred feet behind Elisabeth's house."

"Is the barn locked? What else do they keep in there?"

"I glanced in the windows and saw all sorts of maintenance gear used by the ski patrol and the snowcat drivers—shovels, snow blowers, stretchers, first-aid kits, etc."

"I'd think they'd keep all that at the lodges in the village and at the summit—closer to the center of activity where access is easier."

"I wondered about that, but Ryan said they stock equipment in both spots. This building is easier to reach via the fire road when the snow is not so deep. You'd have to know it was there to find it, though. It's mostly hidden by the trees."

I tapped the table with my fingernails. "Is it remote enough that they'd leave it unlocked?"

"No way. One stray candy wrapper and you'd have bears in there. It's locked up tight with big garage bay doors. Those snowcats are huge—bigger than the plows that clear two lanes in one go."

I thought of the cross-country path we'd skied the day before. "That track we were on yesterday had been groomed by a snowcat. But there's no way a beast that wide could make it through the trees."

"They come in different sizes for different jobs. The big monsters live in the barn behind Elisabeth's."

"Rats," I said, frowning. "I'd hoped one of those snow groomers could explain how Dev's body was moved."

Tess glanced toward the front room where Dev's children were sleeping and held a finger to her lips. "Don't use his name." She scooted her chair closer to the table and leaned in, lowering her voice. "You're right. But even if it could maneuver, it would leave an unmistakable track and create a horrific noise. We would have assumed something was wrong and gone to investigate."

"What about a plow?" I asked. "The little ones they use for driveways and paths? Would their scoops be strong enough to move a body?"

"I assume that's one of the reasons Quinn was talking to Ryan," Tess said. "That and trying to determine whether some vehicle hit him, and if so, what kind."

I sighed and pushed my hair off my forehead. All our theories were growing tangled in my head. I tried to outline my frustration for Tess. "We need to talk to Quinn again. We're assuming someone killed Dev at the mailboxes on the night he went missing and found a way to move him to the snowdrift where we found him. But without confirmation from Quinn, that's a pretty big assumption."

Tess scoffed. "It's so easy to go galloping ahead of the facts. You're right. Without hearing from Quinn we have no way of knowing when he was killed."

"Still," I said. "Let's look at the snowplow angle. Chances are, whenever he was killed, wherever he was killed, someone needed to move him. That means someone needed to be pretty darn strong or they needed mechanical help. I know the Zimmers have a blade on their pick-up truck. So does Quinn. Who else plows out driveways for people?"

Tess thought for a moment. "I suppose anyone with a decent-sized pickup could have a plow stashed in their garage or barn." She picked up her mug and mine, clearing the table. The bread machine's timer went off and I removed the pan containing a mouth-watering golden loaf that would be difficult to resist.

Tess wiped down the table. "The only way to be sure who has snow removal equipment is to break into their garages. And if it's snowing, anyone with a blower or plow is apt to be out clearing driveways with it, not leaving it behind for us to find." She rinsed out the cloth and draped it over the dish drainer. "We're supposed to have more snow tonight."

I glanced at my watch. "I don't suppose we could sneak out of town before the storm starts? Head back to the Bay Area and throw in the towel on your moving project and the murder?"

Tess brightened up a bit. She checked the weather app on her phone, looked disgusted, then turned the screen so I could see it.

"What am I looking at?" I asked, squinting at the screen.

"Sorry!" Tess tapped at the screen a few times and then turned it again. "The Doppler radar image of the storm." She pointed at the tiny map. "There's the storm. Here's Donner Pass. This dot is us."

"Okay..."

"We leave now and we're toast," she said. "The storm's coming in fast and is nearly to Donner summit already. If we left right this minute, we'd be stuck in a drift at seven thousand feet."

I deflated, realizing how much I'd hoped to put Tahoe behind me. Tess was running out of steam, too. If we couldn't go home to Orchard View, at least we could go home to Tess's cabin.

* * * *

Leslie and the children woke up within moments of each other. We said goodbye to them, leashed up our dogs, and set out. The wind had come up in advance of the approaching storm, but the sky was the clear steel blue of winter mountain twilight.

"So, spill," said Tess. "What did Leslie say? What did your snooping reveal? You've found the murderer right? All we have to do is phone Quinn?"

"Just before Dev disappeared, Amrita was taken to the hospital under the influence of alcohol and what Alison suspected was a date rape drug."

Tess's jaw dropped open. "But she's underage. What was she doing drinking?"

"Apparently, it wasn't the first time she and her friends were involved in risky behavior involving older guys and too much alcohol. Leslie said the area's been suffering from a local crime wave that includes underage drinking, drugs, and sex crimes."

"Yikes," Tess said. "Sounds like Amrita was lucky not to have been raped or abducted. But is Leslie seriously thinking she was the target of a gang involved in sexual trafficking?"

"That was the impression I got from Leslie. She said Dev was looking into it when he disappeared."

"Amrita is definitely hiding something," I said.

I filled Tess in on the rest as we made our way back to the house. Within steps of Tess's front porch, a gust hit us, causing us to lurch across the road like we were under the influence. But the lights popped on as I touched the front door knob, restoring my faith in my magical powers. In the light, nothing looked as bad as it had during the darkest hours of the howling blizzard.

The wall phone in the kitchen rang as we climbed the stairs. Tess rushed to answer it. "It's Koko, from the garage. About your car."

I rolled my eyes and felt the back of my neck tense as I moved in slow motion toward the kitchen. While most of the jobs in our household weren't assigned on the basis of gender, my husband Max generally took care of all car-related maintenance, checkups, and other decisions. Today it was my job. I didn't like it. Was the car totaled? Would I have to pull the plug on life-support? Would repairs approach the cost of a new car?

"Hello?" I answered the phone with false cheer that made Tess crack up. Trying and failing to control her laughter, she found something to do in the back of the house.

"This is Maggie. How's my car? Is it bad news? How terrible is it?" Whenever I was under strain, I fired off way too many questions in a row.

"There's good news and bad news," Koko said. I wondered if his parents had attached that name to him at birth or if Koko earned the name from his cohorts growing up. Tess would know.

"Good news first," I said, wincing at the whiny tone in my voice.

"The damage is superficial," Koko said, in a distinguished deep bass voice incongruous with my stereotype of a garage owner—a stereotype I wasn't aware I had until Koko spoke. "The axle and frame are fine."

"So it's drivable?"

"Not yet, I'm afraid. You need new lights, front and back, new front bumper, possibly a whole new back gate and window assembly. That's why I'm calling. It's going to cost you, and I'll need to order the parts from Reno. There are trucks backed up all along the interstate due to the storm, and I'm not sure when I'll get delivery. You may want to tow the car to a dealership closer to home instead of having me take care of it."

"Can you send me an estimate?"

Koko took down my email address and my cell phone pinged almost immediately in a pocket muffled by my storm parka. "You'll need that for your damage claim. We're an approved body shop for most insurance companies, but some folks feel more comfortable with their hometown mechanics or the dealer. I can help with whatever arrangements you need."

Taking a deep breath, I decided to come clean and admit to Koko how little I knew. "I'm going to forward the estimate to my husband in the Bay Area. I'm a delegator and he's my go-to car guy."

"We can't all be experts in everything," Koko said. "Tell your husband to call my cell with whatever he needs. Whatever will help him make a decision."

"Do I need to come down?"

"Not tonight. That storm's about to give us another wallop. It won't matter whether I order the parts tonight or tomorrow or the next day. I'll need a deposit though, before I arrange for delivery."

"Of course," I said. "Thank you." And I meant it. Koko had treated me respectfully without a hint of condescension.

We ended the call after I verified that Koko would take electronic payments so that he could order whatever parts he needed without waiting for the roads to clear so I could stop by with a check. I was dialing Max when Tess appeared in the hallway. She checked the thermostat, and reentered the big front room.

"Update?" she asked, after I'd left a message. "Is the car on life-support?"

I scratched my chin and stared at my phone. "Koko says the damage is superficial, but the repair estimate makes it look pretty major. He'll need to order a slew of parts from Reno and that will take days."

"If you want to abandon it, we can probably make it home in my mountain clunker. It's not pretty, and the tires are shot, but it runs."

"I may take you up on that, but first I need to talk to Max and the insurance company. Or, rather, have Max talk to our agent. My brain hears words that sound like car parts and skitters off in any other direction."

"Do you want me to talk to Koko or check out the car? I speak gearhead."

"How did he get that name? And that voice. He sounds like a British opera singer."

"You'll see when we go to the shop."

"No hints?"

"You'll see. It's a visual thing."

"Koko says we can go see the car tomorrow, or the next day if the weather is still bad."

"That's how things work around here," Tess said. "Everything hangs on the weather."

"Vacuuming, wash, dinner, or dishes?" I asked. With the power back on, there were a ton of deferred chores we needed to tackle quickly, before we lost the electricity again in the next blizzard.

But before we could get started, the doorbell chimed. And despite all the warnings from Ben, Alison, Quinn, and Leslie, neither Tess nor I thought twice about opening the door.

Chapter 20

Simplicity is making the journey of this life with just baggage enough.
—**Charles Dudley Warner**, American writer. 1829-1900

Saturday, February 20, Early evening

Luckily, it was Quinn who waited on the doorstep when Tess opened the door. He greeted the dogs and Tess cajoled him into staying for a hot meal.

We chatted and folded sheets while Tess threw together an Italian soup made from a partially thawed frozen lasagna, chicken broth, sautéed frozen vegetables, and generous helpings of oregano and other herbs.

Quinn cleared his throat. "So, Maggie, I took a call from your pal Jason Mueller in Orchard View..." He did that sneaky cop trick of saying nothing and hoping I'd fill in the blanks. I didn't bite.

"And?" I asked.

He pressed his fist to his lips then smiled openly. "Jason said I wouldn't be able to fool you into revealing more than you wanted to. He told me that you and Tess were extremely observant and had a way of encouraging people to share information they might keep from the police."

"He did, did he?" Tess joined us at the table.

"Jason said my best bet was to throw myself on your mercy, tell you everything we've discovered so far, and encourage you to share any little anecdotes you've picked up that might blow the case wide open."

"And what's in it for us?" I asked.

Quinn didn't answer directly. "Be careful. Violent crimes around here have ramped up recently. We're after the guy responsible, but we haven't been able to pin anything on him. If we're right, he and his gang are everywhere, doing bad by blending in."

His descriptions were dark. Rather than elaborate, he shifted gears. "According to your pal Jason, I'll be hard pressed to keep you two from snooping, unless I lock you up myself."

Tess snorted. "Maggie likes to think of 'snooping' as restoring order to the universe. She's a professional organizer."

"Yeah? Like that 'Life-changing magic' gal?"

I hedged. "Maybe not so rigid but we have the same goals." Far be it from me to comment on another organizer's methods, particularly ones that were so different from mine.

"So, you might be able to help me get my desk and storerooms in order down at the station?"

"If you felt like letting a civilian into the inner sanctum...yes."

"Without putting everything on computer?"

"If that's what you want...or we could research software specifically designed for small town law enforcement."

"Pricey?"

I grabbed my backpack off a nearby chair, pulled one of my business cards from a front pocket, and handed it to Quinn. "I can give you an estimate and we can go from there," I said. "Or we can tailor a project to your budget."

"Enough with the marketing, Mags," Tess said over her shoulder as she dashed to turn down the heat under the stew pot. "Quinn, what can you tell us about Dev's death? Did the autopsy results come in?"

"You want those over dinner?" Quinn shrugged, took a seat, and updated us, hitting the high points, which confirmed the bits and pieces we'd picked up from others in the neighborhood. "Dev sustained a knockout blow to the head that would have left him dazed, but alive. He had some other major injuries including two broken legs that we believe were caused by a vehicle running him over, maybe more than once."

"What was cause of death?" I asked.

Quinn tilted his head. "Despite all those injuries doc says she thinks he'd have survived if he'd had immediate medical attention. Instead, someone left him somewhere cold enough to sustain frostbite and cause death from exposure. But he was dead before he went into the snowdrift."

"He didn't die there." I said, nodding.

"How'd you know that?" Quinn asked.

"Not much blood in that drift," I said. "In my experience growing up with four older brothers and raising two active boys, head wounds are usually a bloody mess."

Tess filled soup bowls and brought them to the table one by one. The lights flickered and we all froze, smiling sheepishly when they stayed on.

"At least we've already got our hot meal," Tess said. "But I really could use a solid night's sleep without getting up to fuel the fire."

"And crash on a real bed instead of sharing the sofa with the dogs," I added.

Quinn nodded. "I won't keep you much longer. But can you tell me what, if anything you've learned? Run it all through from the beginning as though you've told me nothing. When there's a big event that everyone's talking about, it's hard to remember who you've told what. Leave nothing out."

* * * *

Tess and I reviewed what we knew about Dev's movements the night he disappeared and then how we stumbled upon him. We ran through what we'd learned from Ryan and recounted Elisabeth's fear that she had killed Dev at the mailboxes. When I came to the part about Leslie's suspicions, he rolled his eyes, suggesting he'd heard it all before.

In the end, I threw my hands in the air. "It's looking like *Murder on the Orient Express*—everyone could be guilty. Or maybe no one…"

Tess finished my thought. "…But if two or more of them were working together, the whole thing becomes more plausible."

"If they're covering for each other, we can't trust anything anyone says."

"*Whoa*," said Quinn. "We have a few facts that are indisputable." He counted them off on his fingers. "The autopsy report. That makes Dev himself our most important witness. I'm sending my officers door to door or garage door to garage door to be exact, to examine every car, truck, plow, ATV, and snowmobile."

"What about the county snow plows, the guys that clear the driveways, and the smaller groomers?" I asked, knowing that Ryan, who drove one of the snowplows, had been questioned.

"It couldn't have been the groomers," Tess said. "The first time you saw one operating on the hillside at night, you thought it was an alien invasion. If one had ventured down here in the turnaround circle in daylight, we all would have noticed. They're huge and they're loud. Besides, there were no grooming tracks on the road."

"I'll concede that it's unlikely," I said. "But remember how quickly the tire tracks filled on the first night of this latest storm? By the time anyone realized Dev was missing and set out to look for him, Mother Nature could have obliterated the evidence."

I thought for a moment about the neighbors we'd met. "Have you looked at Siobhan? She seems to have a truck that can battle tough weather, and her hours mean she's out and about when others aren't. If I saw her in the middle of the night, I'd assume she was on her way to or from the bakery. I probably wouldn't even remember it. And most of the trucks belonging to residents are old and banged up. If they had new dings, like from running into someone, how would anyone prove when the dents were made? Most are too old to have GPS units that would tell us who was where and when."

"Experts can glean a remarkable amount of information from trace evidence," said Quinn. "But I take your point."

This case was falling apart before it had ever come together. I wished that Tess and I could dash back to the Bay Area, immerse ourselves in our ordinary lives, leave the investigation to Quinn, and forget any of this had ever happened.

But then I was shrouded in guilt. Dev was dead. Tess needed to sell the house to make her dreams, and those of her orphaned son, come true. We had to do better. I vowed that I'd do what I could to lessen the strain and grief left behind from an untimely and violent death from the neighborhood.

* * * *

The next morning, I awoke to the sound of Tess moving around in the kitchen, buried myself deeper into the puffy down comforter, and relished the luxury of sleeping on a real mattress in a real bedroom—until Belle touched my cheek with her cold nose, insisting that it was time to get up, get moving, and feed the dogs.

I shuffled out to the kitchen, poured kibble and refreshed the dogs' water bowl.

Tess handed me a steaming mug of coffee, waiting until I'd finished half of it to speak. The perfect friend.

When I reached for a package of bagels, selected one, and popped it into the toaster, she must have decided it was safe to speak. "Plans?"

Still groggy from sleep, my brain felt as though it was filled with sawdust. There were ideas in there, but it was difficult for me to locate and organize them. I tried anyway.

"It looks like the storm may have fizzled a bit, but we offered to help Leslie with a grocery run."

"And she said she'd call it in and get Amrita to pick it up."

"Can that tiny teen drive that huge Land Rover?"

"*Harry* can apparently handle the thing," Tess said. I smiled at the image her words drew in my mind, complete with a little boy's truck noise sound effects.

I caught my bagel as it popped from the toaster, juggling it in my hands before transferring it to a plate. Tess looked at me expectantly. I bought time by taking a big bite of my breakfast, enjoying the crispness of the outside and the softness of the inside. Warm food was so much more satisfying than a cold meal in the winter.

"Do I need to leave you two alone?" Tess asked, inclining her head toward the bagel.

"Sorry. A plan. We were making a plan." I scanned the table for a yellow pad and a pen. Tess nudged them toward me. I glanced at the calendar on the wall. It was Sunday. Tomorrow was Presidents' Day. A big weekend for a ski resort.

I missed my family. I ached for the predictability of life in Orchard View. It was time to face facts and review my promise to help my friend.

"Tess." Though there was no one else in the room, I felt the need to focus her attention. "I promised I'd help you clear out and get the house ready for staging and repairs. But we've spent five days here and nothing has gone according to plan."

"Right, so?"

"It doesn't seem to bother you much. I have to ask. Are you sure you want to sell?"

She looked into her coffee mug for the answer, then scrunched up her nose. "I'm really not. There are a lot of memories here of Patrick. They're bittersweet. Teddy needs time to process them. Me too. I'd like to carry the Olmos family holiday traditions into the next generation—and they all center around this cabin."

I nodded.

"But I have no choice. Not if Teddy wants to go to college and I want to change careers. That's really important to me, Maggie. The only way I've been able to cope with Patrick's death was hanging on to the idea that if I studied criminal justice and worked in law enforcement, I could make a significant contribution to keeping other families safe."

I knew Tess's ideas on the subject like I knew my own thoughts, but reciting her goals seemed to give her more confidence and strengthen her sense of purpose.

"But does it have to be now?" I asked. "Could you delay the sale by renting?"

Tess sighed and pushed her hair back. Her normally velvety black hair looked as if it had thrown a wild party while she'd been sleeping.

"I know delaying action after you've made a decision isn't your thing," I told her. "But I can't help feeling that part of the reason we've accomplished so little is that it's just too soon."

I scooted my chair forward and grabbed her hand. "It's been eighteen months. Every self-help book and pop-culture TV talk-show host would tell you to wait at least a year or two—or as long as it takes."

Tess rolled her eyes and pulled back her hand, drawing her baggy sweater closely and hugging herself tight. "Like I care what they think." She had no patience with pop psychology. Not now. Not ever.

"I know how you feel about those shows," I said. "But sometimes the conventional wisdom is actually right."

Tess tilted her head. "I can't, Maggie."

"Can't what?"

"Shift gears. This decision was so hard to make, I'm afraid my whole world will fall apart if I change my mind."

I frowned, uncertain how to tell Tess that her fears seemed a clear indication that now was not the time to plow forward. But she came to the same conclusion on her own.

"I guess terror isn't a very good foundation on which to take life-altering action," she said, sounding very much like Winnie-the-Pooh's friend Eeyore.

I swept the crumbs from my placemat into my hand and tipped them onto my plate. "How much time do you think you can give yourself? We can still work on the clutter while we're here. Maybe taking some of the pressure off will make it easier to make those millions of micro-decisions about what to keep and what to discard."

Tess slid the pad of paper back toward her side of the table and clicked the pen. "I need to figure that out."

"A plan!" I said, standing up to clear the table. "Now you're talking. Do you want more coffee?"

Tess didn't answer but handed me her mug.

"A refill it is. I'll work on the guest bedroom closets. Even if you decide to keep everything, it will be easier to see what's in there if it's a little more organized."

Mary Feliz

Tess bit her bottom lip and didn't respond. As a Realtor, she was comfortable juggling money, making tricky financial decisions, and helping people consider their options. But as is the case for most professionals, she was finding herself an extraordinarily difficult client.

Chapter 21

It is always the simple that produces the marvelous.
—**Amelia Barr**, British novelist. 1831-1919

Sunday, February 21, Morning

While Tess crunched numbers, I pulled everything out of the guest bedroom closet and lined up all the shoes against one wall in order of how much I thought Tess might want to hang on to them. The array of footwear included toddler-sized ski boots and ancient adult tie-up ones. They represented a retrospective of the Olmos family's winter sport fashions. Clothing ranged from serviceable to hilarious as I pulled out decades-old winter jackets. The worst were the itchy moth-eaten wool ski skirts of the 1930s. *What were they thinking?*

By time I had everything neatly folded or securely zipped onto hangers, Tess appeared in the doorway holding the yellow pad aloft. She looked weary but triumphant. "This looks like a museum of winter fashion," she said. "There are some costumes here I swear I've never seen before." She put the pad down on the Tyrolean dresser next to the door and picked up one of the long itchy skirts and matching jackets. "They must have really wanted to ski," she said. "Can you imagine enduring this? Fabrics with no stretch, lace-up boots, and long, heavy, unwieldy, and unforgiving skis. It was a different world."

"You look like you've discovered a life-giving elixir," I told her. "Spill."

Tess picked up the pad and pushed the pen behind her ear. "I need to check these figures with my accountant. The tax and estate issues are complicated, but I realized I'd overlooked Patrick's apartment in Mountain View. At first it was too painful to think about clearing it out and then other priorities took over. It's downtown, near the Google shuttle stop, Caltrain, and the light rail station. Everything in that area is in high demand. We could rent it to a young tech couple for a fortune."

"Or sell it," I said. "You've got the Orchard View house."

"In any case, Teddy and I have options," she said. "If we can rent the Mountain View place and keep it rented, it could finance the bulk of our schooling." She did a little victory dance. "We might even be able to pay someone to manage it for us instead of renting it out ourselves."

"That's the way to do it," I encouraged her. "If you're both going to school, neither one of you will be able to respond to maintenance emergencies at the drop of a hat."

I held a garish acid-green jumpsuit to my chin. "If Dev had been wearing this, there's no way he could have been hidden in that snowdrift," I said, glancing down and averting my eyes from the glare. "This color could melt snow."

Tess chuckled. "To think that was once the height of fashion."

"Do they have fundraising retrospective fashion shows up here…or costume parties?"

"I could offer them to Leslie for her events. I doubt very much Teddy will be interested."

I looked skeptically at the skiwear and agreed with her. "Though it would make for a wild afternoon of dress up on a day the lifts are closed. Maybe Naomi would have fun with them." I plucked a neon orange and pink striped stocking cap with a turquoise bobble on the end, and modeled it for Tess. "I'll give you fifty cents for this one."

She ignored my antics. "Let me make a few preliminary phone calls about renting the apartment. Then we need to get to the store. Can you start a grocery list?"

Within forty-five minutes, Tess was ready to go. We hopped into the rusty but trusty Land Rover with the dogs in the back seat. "The tires are worn," she said. "But they should be reasonably safe. Maybe once we get your car fixed I'll have Koko put new tires on the Rover."

The engine growled confidently, but every joint rattled when we hit a bump. The heater could barely defrost the windshield, let alone warm my frozen toes. Either the ice on the road was exceptionally slippery or Tess had underestimated the tire wear.

The storm had blown itself out overnight, and though the skies were still overcast, patches of bright blue sky poked through.

Tess depressed the clutch and wrestled with the shift lever as the gears briefly ground together. "The clutch is mostly theoretical," Tess said. "We've all learned to double-clutch and shift by sound. Teddy loves it. So few kids know how to drive a manual transmission, let alone one with a dying clutch." She braked gently as a car approached from the opposite direction. Turning the wheel hand-over-hand, she edged the Rover close to the snow wall at the side of the road. The other car passed so closely, I felt Tess could have high-fived the driver as we inched by.

"The plow crews work all night to widen these main arteries," Tess said. "Some of the side streets in town may not be open yet at all."

"I had no idea the roads took so long to clear. I figured folks up here would have it down to a science."

"We do, mostly. But when we get so much snow at once, there's nowhere to put it. The roads become open-roofed tunnels through the snow and it's impossible to shove all that onto the shoulder."

I eyed the snow walls on either side of the main road, which towered above the Rover's roof. The unchanging view was hypnotic and made me feel claustrophobic. I put my sunglasses on and took them off again, not sure they did anything to improve my vision.

"Where to first?" I asked in an effort to distract myself.

"Koko's. I want to introduce you. After that, we'll have lunch at Siobhan's and return her coffee and soup containers. Then head to the grocery store."

We drove several miles without passing more than a handful of cars. It was hard to judge how far we'd gone with so few landmarks. Most of the road signs were buried in the snow, though someone had made an effort to dig out fire hydrants and mailboxes. Tess turned at a break in the wall of snow into a large cleared parking lot in front of a strip mall. A tow truck was parked at the far end in front of a garishly painted building set apart from the rest of the shops. "Welcome to the fanciest garage on the planet," Tess said. "Owned by Koko, the Rococo mechanic."

"*Wow.*" There was no other word. Sweeping curves of Baroque letters announced the name of the garage. Pink walls adorned with elaborate white trim boasted murals of cherubs, minstrels, and mythical creatures all sharing the same cozy clearings in dark forests. "Was this a brothel before it was a garage?"

Tess laughed. "Aren't you glad your car needed repairs? I would never have thought to bring you here otherwise. The building started as a garage. At some point in the early sixties it was converted to a restaurant. The owner went a little overboard trying to create a luxurious setting."

I opened the car door and got out to examine the murals. Up close, they revealed an amateur's technique. But someone knew their art history. Elements of some of the most famous paintings of the late Baroque period were combined randomly in each scene.

"It's even better inside. Don't miss the ceiling." The large garage bay doors were closed. Tess opened a smaller, human-sized, door. It too was decorated with painted curtains.

We stepped inside and I was immediately disappointed by the plain off-white walls of a nondescript office-waiting room that smelled of motor oil and rust. An oil-stained phone rang several times and stopped. After a moment it rang again. A tall man without an ounce of fat on his large frame ducked through the doorway, picked up the receiver, listened for a moment, and dropped it back in its cradle. He frowned and I assumed the line was dead.

But then he spotted Tess and beamed. "Tess," he said, like a man in love.

"I had to bring my friend Maggie in," Tess said. "She wouldn't have believed this place otherwise."

Koko wiped his hands on a towel and then reached out to shake mine. "Right. The crashed SUV."

"It was crashed *into*," I clarified. "I didn't crash it."

"Right. I knew that. I can tell by its injuries. I chatted with your husband and got the okay to order the parts. I'll call you when they come in. Now that Interstate 80 is open down into Reno, it shouldn't be too long."

I peered through the doorway into the maintenance bays, spotted my car, and gasped. The damage looked extensive, with the quarter panel dragging and the hood crumpled like a discarded ball of paper.

"It's not as bad as it looks," Koko said. "The frame and axles are solid—much better than the other way around, when the car looks fine but the expensive parts are damaged past saving. My labor costs and overhead up here are going to run you less than in Mountain View."

I wondered how he'd figured out where I was from, until he handed me the broken license plate frame celebrating the Mountain View high school band. "This looked like it might have some sentimental value," Koko said.

I took it from him and brushed the dirt from the faded letters. "My boys sold them as a fundraiser. You're right, it's worth far more to me than what I paid for it, but I think I can get another one."

"Look up," Tess said, pointing. Koko flicked on a bank of lights illuminating the coved ceiling covered with gilt-edged paintings more reminiscent of a European palace than a mountain garage. Ribbons, exaggerated blooms, cherubs, full-skirted women, and their foppish swains filled every inch.

"Is your name really Koko?" I asked the mechanic. "Or did the nickname come after you bought the garage?"

"It's a childhood nickname. Something my older brothers saddled me with thanks to my long arms and devotion to a pet kitten. They dubbed me 'Koko the gorilla.' This wild rococo paint job was just a bonus."

"There's no forgetting it," I said.

Tess scanned the more prosaic working floor of the room with its lifts, tires, dangling hoses and massive tool chests. "Where's the rest of the crew?"

"Up the mountain. Most of 'em are on the ski patrol. The resort called in everyone they could to help with avalanche control."

"I'd think that would be a specialized job requiring lots of training." I said.

"It's potentially very dangerous," Koko said. "But most of the guys that live here year 'round take the courses. Testosterone, youth, danger, and explosives. It's a heady combo."

I looked at Tess for confirmation. She nodded. "He's right. Patrick did it, and so did most of the guys you've met. Not Quinn, but Ryan, the Zimmers, Dev—all of them."

Something tickled the back of my brain, telling me this was critical information. But the more I chased the thought, the more elusive it seemed. If it was important, I needed a few more links in the chain to connect it to the rest of the facts we had at our disposal.

I thanked Koko for the work he'd begin soon on my car. He and Tess made arrangements to replace her tires later in the week. Vehicular chores accomplished, we were off to Flour Power in the village for lunch. The approach to the resort was stunning. Above us, rising thousands of feet into the sky, were the snow-covered spires of the Sierra Nevada. In front of us, the pseudo-Tyrolean village sprawled with hotel, restaurants, shops, and rental agencies, and far more cars and people than we'd seen in several days.

"I expect everyone who works at the resort has been called in. Hordes of skiers will descend as soon as Donner Pass reopens." Tess said, reiterating what Koko had said earlier.

"The mountain isn't open to the public yet?" I pointed to the big white tram exiting its cave-like boarding area and chugging up the mountain against a backdrop of increasingly blue sky.

"That runs in all but the worst weather," Tess said. "Today it's probably mostly taking ski patrol and service workers up to the summit. Maybe some of the skaters who use the rink at the top." She pointed behind us toward a lift where broad seats dangled empty. "If the slopes were open, that one would be working." No sooner than she'd said the words, the chairs began moving. A cheer went from the first chair filled with people, six across.

"Still not open," Tess explained. "That's ski patrol and avalanche safety. They'll set off charges and check out the terrain. Once they okay it, civilians can go up. We might be able to go for a run tomorrow if you want. I've got discount passes."

"Are you giving up on the decluttering?"

"Spoil sport."

"It's my job," I reminded her. "But for now, I'm starving."

We ordered food and carried our trays across the room to a table near the hearth. Today, the internal patio was open. A few hardy souls ate their lunch at tables that had been cleared of snow. A gas firepit and propane patio heaters had warmed the area enough that the diners had removed hats and gloves and unzipped their jackets.

The village looked picture perfect, like a photo taken to advertise an idyllic winter get-away. But, like a retouched brochure image, the cozy scene masked dangers and flaws.

Chapter 22

Housekeeping ain't no joke.
— Hannah Mullet, *Little Women*
Louisa May Alcott, American writer 1832-1888

Sunday, February 21, Afternoon

On our previous visit, some of the village shops had been closed. Today, every security gate was up and each store was busy with employees. A maintenance team trudged past our table lugging heavy tool kits. They were part of the storm-damage containment crew—the least glamorous but most important team among the hardworking resort support staff.

I swiveled my head toward the rental shop, where Jens and Klaus stacked skis, boots, and poles on custom-built racks. A young employee straightened and refreshed displays of rental jackets, pants, and helmets.

Among this crowd, Jens and Klaus both looked like old men. Tess and I were old ladies. The average age of the employees was mid-twenties. They all seemed incredibly fit. Bundled up, they'd be impossible to tell apart. Even without their layers of storm gear, their youth, energy and athletic hipster clothing and hair styles made them all look remarkably similar.

Most of the unskilled minimum-wage positions were staffed only half the year. I wondered what became of the crews in the off season. Did they all decamp for the slopes of South America? Or were the jobs a planned ski break from school and careers?

"Nice to see you again ladies," said Sam Stillwell, joining us at our table.

I tucked my legs under my chair and scooted it back an inch. Last time I'd seen him, the pretzel shop counter had been between us, and while I'd still been a little creeped out by his slimy personality, this time was worse. I glanced around the table to determine if I was the only one feeling this way.

Tess leaned away from Sam. It wasn't so much what he said or did, but the nebulous feeling of discomfort that surrounded him. Tess began to pack up her lunch. I followed suit.

"You're welcome to the table," Tess said. "We'll be leaving soon."

Sam waved to Han, who approached from Flour Power carrying a tray that held three paper coffee cups. "Stay, please. I ordered coffee. I haven't talked to anyone much since the storm began. Let's catch up." He leaned forward and waggled his eyebrows.

All my flight or fight panic reactions kicked in. My hands grew clammy and my leg muscles tightened. I plucked a napkin from the dispenser on the table and pleated it like a fan.

"Thanks," Tess said, reluctantly taking the coffee Han indicated was hers.

"I ordered three black, but Han said he knew what you liked." The words, in Sam's mouth, sounded dirty. I wished I knew how to surreptitiously activate the recording device on my phone. I knew I was safe, in a public place, surrounded by people. But every word Sam uttered made me feel increasingly uncomfortable. I would have liked to have an FBI profiler analyze his body language and micro-expressions to help me understand why, since I couldn't put my finger on any one thing that provoked me. I fought to tamp the feelings down.

"What's new with you?" I asked Sam. "Any storm damage? Did your supply orders come through? Are you expecting a crowd of tourists? Have you tried the new powder?"

Tess's foot swiped at mine under the table, and I brought my barrage of questions to a halt.

Sam draped himself across his chair, taking up as much room as possible. "Look at all the busy shop owners," he said. "I've got my business down to a science. My delivery guy has a key to the freezer. All I need to do is turn on the machines and apply heat to the merchandise. At the end of the day, I empty the till."

I glanced over my shoulder toward his shop. "It's okay to leave it unattended like that?"

"Locals are health nuts," Sam said. "No hot dogs or cotton candy for them, and no ice cream, either."

I wondered if it was the snack food they were avoiding or Sam himself, but I said nothing. Sam nudged Tess. "Any more neighbors of yours keel over? Is that lazy cop still looking at my cousin? I hate the way they wanna pin stuff on Ryan. It's like they picked his name out of a hat and are tossing out any evidence that points to anyone else." There was a whiny yet threatening note in Sam's voice that reminded me of a crook in an old noir film. And, since Ryan had been released after questioning, Sam's continuing focus on his cousin's brush with law enforcement seemed like a lame bid for attention.

Tess sat up straight in her chair as if she was preparing to leave.

I got ready to follow her, but she shook her head ever so lightly. I tried to relax.

"Who do you think the cops should be looking at?" she asked Sam.

"Better Ryan than me," Sam said with an unpleasant chuckle. "But seriously, I dunno. That old bat, maybe? Mrs. Roche? Elisabeth? She was always yelling at the maintenance guys to make less noise." He scoffed. "Like those slope groomers have a silent switch or something."

"Who knew how to drive those rigs?" I asked. "Did you? Did Dev?"

Tess kicked me under the table again, but I ignored her. And Sam didn't seem to notice that I was trying to prove he'd had an excuse to lurk around the maintenance shed and an opportunity to have killed Dev.

Sam picked at the plastic lid of his coffee cup. "I don't know that Dev ever drove 'em, but he was on ski patrol. And avalanche control. We all were. It's the only sure way to be first up the mountain."

"How does that work?" I asked.

"Huh?"

"Avalanche duty. Do you show up in some office or at the bottom of the lifts to volunteer and they take you all? Are you on call or are you scheduled for preset shifts? Do you bring your own equipment or check it out from somewhere? Does anyone monitor to make sure you've done the work?"

"Depends."

"On what?"

"The day, I guess. Some guys get a salary—ones who go up first thing, set the explosives, run the guns."

"Is there a lot of training required?"

Sam shrugged. "Sure, I guess. Outdoor rescue, EMT certification, firearms safety..." His tone was patronizing, as though this was all stuff I should already know.

"And the volunteers? Can anyone do it? Could I?"

Sam looked me up and down and sneered. "If you had first-responder certification, maybe. But you gotta be able to ski all the terrain, for one."

"I mean, what if I'm one of those hot-dogging ski demons that shoots down beginner slopes at top speed? They wouldn't let me do ski patrol, would they?"

Sam bristled, his back stiffened, and his face reddened. If my guess was right, I'd nailed his on-slope behavior.

Tess pushed back her chair. The legs screeched as they dragged across the floor. I popped up before she could change her mind about leaving. "You're right, Maggie," Tess said. "Even the volunteers need tons of training. Some of them are doctors. Most have completed at least the three-week first-responder training. But part of the job is to prevent accidents and set a good example. Wearing the jacket is a privilege. If you don't follow the rules, they kick you off."

A muscle in Sam's cheek twitched as he clenched his teeth, but he didn't respond. We said our goodbyes as we pulled on our coats and moved quickly through the crowd to the exit. As we stepped outside, I whispered to Tess.

"So, Sam was kicked off ski patrol for hot dogging?"

"Several times. Why?"

I shrugged. "Curiosity?" It was as good an explanation as any. I was wondering how easy it would have been for someone with a grudge against the ski patrol to have used their knowledge of the team's procedures to have gained access to explosives and pain killers, both of which I suspected might have a high street value. I wasn't sure if it really mattered though. Impersonating a ski patroller was problematic. With the team's swift response time, real patrollers would be on the scene to identify fake ones almost immediately. And it sounded as though most of our suspects were on ski patrol, slope maintenance, or avalanche control, anyway.

Tess summed up my thoughts as if reading my mind. "Why would anyone want to pretend to be ski patrol if they weren't? The real team is protected by millions of dollars of liability coverage. A fake one would get slapped with a lawsuit so fast..." Tess shook her head.

"But aren't ordinary skiers supposed to help out if someone gets hurt?"

"Sure. But they don't provide medical care—just basic courtesy like shielding the injured from other skiers, keeping them company, rounding up their skis—that kind of thing."

"Got it. Did you want to talk to anyone else here in the village before we go to the store? It seems like there must be things we could ask the Zimmers."

Tess frowned and pulled on her hat and mittens. "I don't think so. They deal more with the guests. Locals usually own their own gear."

"But the Zimmers have lived here for generations, right?"

"Jens's dad established the business. But I don't think we're looking back that far for our culprit, do you?"

I tugged my hat down over my ears and trudged toward the parking lot, disappointed. I enjoyed talking to the crusty old Jens who uttered every sentence that entered his head. I didn't want him to be guilty. But, even if he weren't guilty, could he know something important? Probably. In our previous investigations it had helped to talk to old timers familiar with the lay of the land. But in this case, any disputes that had contributed to Dev's body ending up in the drift were likely to be more recent. Dev and his family hadn't lived here for generations like the Zimmers had on the mountain or the Olmos clan had in Orchard View.

"Who could tell us about current feuds?" I asked. "Arguments about land use? Development? Property boundaries?"

"So, you're not going to stick with the tried and true motives?"

I raised my eyebrows.

"Lust and greed?" said Tess.

"Or love and money."

"Same thing."

I wasn't winning any arguments this morning and so said nothing more until we reached the grocery store. Tess pointed out local landmarks like the emergency clinic, the fire station, the road to the dump, and Quinn's offices. I responded with grunts, wiggled my toes in my boots to keep them from freezing, and wished I'd never agreed to drive up here with Tess.

In the parking lot at the grocery store, we circled twice before nabbing a space from someone who was pulling out. Taking advantage of the break in the storm cycle, everyone was stocking up on food and stopping by the hardware next door to buy items they needed to repair storm damage.

Inside, the store was equally packed. It looked like the day before Thanksgiving or Christmas. The festival-like atmosphere was similar too. Neighbors were greeting neighbors and catching up on the events of the storm. The mother of a friend of Teddy's reported that a tree had fallen on their garage, smashing their car. They fixed the roof up with a tarp, wrote off the car, removed the debris, and would wait until spring to do repairs.

I drove the cart through the aisles while Tess darted around the store. I was in charge of restocking staples—things like rice and paper goods that every home needs and lots of cookies. Tess was buying perishables based on the meals she'd planned for the next few days.

We'd end up with too much stuff, no question. But we moved efficiently around the store and we could take the extras with us when we returned to the Bay Area.

Every checkout lane was working. Lines snaked to the butcher's department at the back. Shoppers and their carts were sardined in every aisle.

"Maggie," called a voice from behind me as I reached on tiptoe for coffee. "It's Klaus Zimmer, I'm a few carts back."

Tess had just arrived and plopped three loaves of bread into the basket. She directed traffic so that Klaus could move up closer to us. The maneuvers took every ounce of Tess's command presence and her people skills. I'd feared folks would think we were cutting in line or otherwise gaming the system, but the neighbors all seemed willing to help facilitate a conversation—especially one on which they could eavesdrop

"Maggie," Klaus said once he'd caught up. "I wanted to thank you for being so patient with my dad. We're trying to get him to cut back his hours. He's working too hard, stressing about the future of the store, and he's cranky. And taking it out on whoever is nearby."

"I like Jens," I said, surprised that Klaus felt the need to apologize for his father's behavior. "He's direct. No hidden agenda. You always know where you stand with him."

"Even if where you stand is at the mechanic's paying for your car?"

"That's what insurance is for," I said, but then shifted topics. "Tess took me to Koko's. It's unbelievable."

"My dad can be equally over the top," said Klaus. "You'll be glad to know you're one of the few neighbors he hasn't accused of murdering Dev."

"Should I be flattered or offended?" I asked wondering if I'd wriggled off the hook because I was a visitor, or because he didn't think I had it in me to take charge of a situation.

Klaus laughed. "You've got my dad's number, all right. He thinks you're smart enough to figure out a tidier solution than murder."

"Then I am flattered." I lowered my voice and looked up and down the aisle. "Who's leading his list at the moment?" I wondered how Jens's suspect inventory might differ from mine.

"Anyone he has a grievance against," Klaus said.

"Who else does he have in his sights?"

"Walter Raleigh."

"The businessman? In the slippery Italian shoes?" I was flabbergasted. I couldn't imagine Walter carrying anything as heavy as a weapon, let alone using it. Violent movements on icy surfaces would have sent him sprawling. Killing someone might have splashed blood on his swanky clothes.

"The same." Klaus pressed his lips together as though trying to keep further speculation from escaping.

I wondered if I'd extracted all the information from him that I could. I tried to glean more. "But why?"

"Leslie'd worked closely with Walter and was putting in long hours on a new project. She was frequently seen walking home from the mansion at night. Dad thinks Walter had designs on Leslie that went far beyond the business."

I reviewed the other information we'd gathered about Walter and Leslie and realized we didn't have much dirt on either one of them. Was that because there was none to be found or because we'd overlooked them as serious suspects?

Klaus's voice dragged me out of my thoughts and back into the here and now.

"...boarding school, if you can believe it," he said.

"Sorry, can you back up? I lost the thread."

"Dad is sure Leslie and Walter are having an affair, but Leslie has two kids, soon to be three, and a dog. Walter prizes his independence and has opposed all dog-related proposals by the town council."

"What proposals are you talking about?" In Orchard View, tempers flared over any changes considered by the council. I imagined the neighborhoods of the Tahoe Basin had similar problems.

"A dog park, more flexible leash laws, even a doggy swim area in the summer."

"Belle would go for that."

"But Walter was strongly opposed."

"So, what did your dad say?"

Klaus leaned in and lowered his voice to a barely audible whisper. "That he'd heard from one of the delivery guys that Leslie was ordering wedding cake and signing the kids up for boarding school."

"Boarding school? She can't be. They're preschoolers."

Klaus shrugged. "According to Dad, that's what the delivery guy said."

"But she'd still have Winston. Sounds like a dog would be a deal breaker for Walter."

"Not for long, I don't think. The poor thing's twelve and slowing down. Had a bad health scare just after Christmas. They're still monitoring his kidneys, I think."

"And this happened right after Christmas? Around the time that Dev went missing?" I wondered if Winston's illness had been caused by a deliberate poisoning that Dev had tried to stop or retaliate against.

Klaus tilted his head and consulted his memory. "I think so." He scratched his head. "Yes, it was definitely at the same time. Part of the reason that Leslie waited to call the police about Dev was because Winston was so sick. She had to wrangle the kids and the dog and get him to the vet. He was on an IV for days."

"Poison?" I suggested.

Klaus blanched, and would have backed up if it hadn't meant banging into the cart of the person immediately behind him. "You mean, something deliberate? You're as bad as my dad with all his conspiracy theories. He's seeing evil criminal cabals everywhere these days."

"I'm just trying to create an accurate picture," I said. "Remember, I don't know everyone who lives here, and I haven't spent the weeks since Christmas rehashing every supposed slight or feud. I'm not accusing anyone."

"No one has mentioned poison," Klaus said. "But there are dozens of cleaning products and foods that are bad for dogs. It wouldn't be hard to make a deliberate attempt look like an accident." He picked up a jar of peanut butter and scanned the label. "Every day my social media pages are filled with something new that can hurt family pets. This is one of them."

He tapped the side of the jar and made a face as though he'd just sucked on a lemon. "I don't know why peanut butter needs to be sweetened at all, let alone with something artificial." He shook his head in disgust. "Our food isn't food anymore."

The woman behind Klaus must have overheard him and they launched into a discussion about the dangers of various additives in food and other household items. It gave me a chance to think. Could Walter really have wanted to take Dev's place in Leslie's life? If that was the case, had he sped Dev's demise or just begun looking at Leslie in a new light now that she was, theoretically, available. But just because Walter was interested in Leslie didn't mean his feelings were reciprocated. Unrequited love, like the songs it spawned, was universal.

Tess reappeared with her face just visible over an armful of groceries. "That's the last of it," she said. "We're ready to check out."

* * * *

When we were back on the road, I updated Tess on Klaus's suspicions.

"I can't decide whether we've got too many suspects or not enough," I told her, summing up my difficulty in keeping all the players straight.

"Hang tough. Something always bursts through just when we're ready to give up. The guilty parties must be under a lot of pressure at this point."

"So we wait for them to slip up? What if they hurt someone else?

Before Tess could answer, an enormous *boom* rent the air. I grabbed the door handle and hung on tight, instinctively reacting to what I feared was an avalanche-triggering earthquake. We'd had a series of tremors in the Bay Area recently, and any instability in the ground under my feet shook me up.

Chapter 23

Have nothing in your houses that you do not know to be useful or believe to be beautiful.
—**William Morris,** British designer. 1834-1896

Sunday, February 21, Afternoon

Tess slammed on the brakes. The car skidded and rocked, making me vaguely seasick.

"Is your house okay?" I asked. It was a stupid question. There was no way Tess could know until we were closer to the house.

Tess floored the accelerator. The car lurched forward and fishtailed up the hill. At first glance, Tess's house was fine. But we both had lived in quake-prone areas long enough to know that appearances weren't much to go on. Tess parked the car in front of the house. I opened my door and the dogs rocketed out with their tails between their legs, sniffing and jumping to lick our faces in ways they were both too well trained to do under normal circumstances. We calmed them and ourselves simultaneously.

"Do you think it's safe to go inside?" I asked.

Tess pursed her lips. "If we had a child upstairs we needed to rescue, definitely. As it is, let's wait until someone a little more knowledgeable checks it out."

In the Bay Area, we all knew to look at the foundation of the house for cracks, bulges, or places where the building had moved in one direction while the foundation slewed in another. But here in the high country, following a series of intense storms, the foundation was concealed deep under the snow. Some of the neighbors' houses boasted drifts that covered the ground floor window sills. I frowned.

"Whoa!" Tess said, after she'd seen my face. "If a disappointed mom look could make a house shape up in a hurry, we'd be safe now."

"I don't think it works on houses."

Tess unlocked the front door. It opened easily, which meant the framing probably hadn't shifted. She flipped open the cover on a keypad positioned at the top of the still-intact garage door. She pushed a series of buttons and the door chugged open, sliding easily on the undamaged track. "If the garage door was off the track or misaligned so it wouldn't open, we'd be wise to stay out."

"Should we unload the groceries?" Once again, my Flatlander experiences weren't up to deciphering the protocol of a mountain emergency.

"They'll keep for a few minutes. Let's check on Elisabeth. Tess pointed toward the house in front of which Leslie and Amrita trudged through the snow, each carrying a small child. Belle and Mozart surged forward to compare notes with Winston. As we neared the little cluster of people, a second explosion threw me off balance.

"That was no earthquake," Tess said.

"It came from Elisabeth's backyard," added Leslie.

Two fire trucks with lights flashing and sirens blaring squeezed past Tess's car, scraping the wall of snow and ice on the opposite side of the road. They parked in the turnaround circle near a hydrant. Firefighters jumped out as an ambulance arrived, parking in front of Elisabeth's house. Two of the emergency workers asked us if anyone was injured. Two more powered through the snow to the back of the house. Another pair pounded on the front door before breaking it open.

A firefighter quickly emerged carrying Elisabeth wrapped in a blanket. A second one carried a snapping and growling Duke. I stepped forward to take charge of the dog.

"Hang on," the firefighter said. "I've got an emergency leash in the truck." He pulled out a coiled blue plastic rope, threaded one end through a loop on the other, and fixed it around Duke's neck. "He's upset. That'll keep him from running off."

I held the shivering dog, but he strained to reach his person. Elisabeth sat in the back of the ambulance. Her teeth chattered as an EMT checked her vitals. I held up Duke so she could see him. "I'm fine," she protested, swatting at the first-responder's hands. "I could have walked out on my own. I was about to. I just couldn't get my coat on soon enough."

A firefighter emerged from the house carrying her coat, boots, and hat. Elisabeth shed the blanket and wriggled into her own clothes.

"Did a gas line blow?" I asked

The EMT examining Elisabeth pronounced her reasonably healthy. "Your heart rate and blood pressure are both higher than we like to see, but not bad given the fright you just experienced," she said. "Is there a neighbor's home you can go to and get warm? Spend some time snuggling with your dog? Nothing returns blood pressure to normal faster than that."

She looked at me with her eyebrows raised. I turned to Tess who nodded rapidly and stepped forward. "Of course. Assuming whatever just rocked our world didn't damage my house."

An older woman with a take-charge posture appeared around the side of the firetruck. Her communication device squawked unintelligibly, but it must have been a language she was used to translating because she replied quickly, barking orders I couldn't make sense of.

She approached Tess and shook her hand. I didn't catch her name, but Tess appeared to know her and called her chief. The way things were going, I assumed she was another neighbor I hadn't yet met.

"Can you stay with Mrs. Roche?" the EMT asked me. "She's fine, but a tad wobbly. We don't need her losing her balance on the ice and getting some other injury."

I handed Duke and his makeshift leash to Elisabeth, who cooed to Duke. His tiny tail wagged as he licked her face. It was a miniature version of the same reassuring motions Belle and Mozart had gone through after the first explosion. I was in the habit, rightly or wrongly, of thinking that tiny dogs were some species *similar* to the larger canines, but different. Duke was changing my mind. Yes, he was loud and obnoxious. But maybe he was just demanding that he not be overlooked, insisting that his role as Elisabeth's protector be recognized and respected.

"Though he be but little, he is fierce," said Elisabeth, misquoting Shakespeare while petting Duke. I nodded agreement.

Tess thanked the fire chief and then turned toward us. "It looks like some kind of explosive devices, two of them, were set on Elisabeth's back porch. The steps are destroyed and firefighters are checking the house for damage. Gas and electricity have both been turned off, so it's not safe for you to stay there tonight." Tess placed a hand on Elisabeth's shoulder. "Will you and Duke join us? I've got a spare bedroom and bath with fresh sheets ready and waiting."

"Did the chief say that *your* house was safe?" I asked, wondering if the wisest course would be to leave the neighborhood entirely.

"She did. We were shaken up by the explosions, not an earthquake. I told her my garage doors were working, so nothing could be too off kilter. She urged the Baileys to go home too."

I glanced at the small family clustered around the big hook and ladder. "They won't go easily," I said. "Harry's mesmerized by the firefighters and their trucks." Someone had given both children tot-sized helmets they wore proudly over their ski hats.

Tess touched Elisabeth's arm. "Say you'll join us? The Baileys offered too, but Leslie's got her hands full."

"As soon as they cut me loose," Elisabeth agreed, tilting her head and raising her eyebrows as if daring the EMT to keep her longer.

"One more heart rate and BP." Elisabeth's attendant transferred Duke back to me then pumped up the blood pressure cuff. The EMT's words sounded as though she was bargaining, but her tone brooked no argument. She completed her tasks quickly, made notes in her tablet, and pronounced Elisabeth fit. "If anything changes or you're worried, give us a buzz," she said, handing the older woman a business card. "Someone's on call 24/7." She leaned down and said softly to Elisabeth, "Some people have a delayed reaction to a shock like this. No shame in that. You call us. Promise?"

Elisabeth nodded but then snapped "I'm tougher than I look."

"No doubt," agreed the EMT.

While the EMT finished with Elisabeth, Tess got the car to transport the older woman the few hundred feet between their homes. Everyone treated Elisabeth like precious cargo. The fire chief helped her into the passenger seat, took Duke from my arms, and plopped him on her lap. "You two look after each other," she said. "You've had a fright. I'll talk to my team and to Quinn later. We'll both have questions for you, but we should also be able to tell you when you can get back into the house." She and Tess shared a look I'd have to ask about later.

Was Elisabeth's house more severely damaged than they were letting on? Had they found evidence, beyond the explosion itself that told them Elisabeth was in serious danger?

Back at Tess's house, we settled Duke and Elisabeth in front of the fire with a cup of tea and a plate of cookies. Belle and Mozart supervised. Duke fell asleep on the sofa, curled up next to Elisabeth.

The older woman's wrinkled hand dwarfed Duke's head as she massaged his ears. "He hates comings and goings," she said. "But as soon as I've made it clear I'm going to stay put, he's fine." She looked from the dog to me. "I'm afraid visitors to the house don't see the real Duke. He makes a terrible first impression."

"I like this Duke," I said. Belle must have agreed. She sniffed the little dog's head without waking him up. Her tail wagged.

We lingered over our tea until it was time to start dinner. While Tess whipped up smoked salmon with lemon dill Alfredo sauce to pour over shell pasta, I took Elisabeth and Duke to their first floor accommodations. I turned down the bed and showed Elisabeth the choice of evening wear Tess had selected for her—nightgown, robe, and a thick pair of wooly socks in lieu of slippers. "I put fresh towels in the bathroom. Everything else you need should be in the closet in there."

Elisabeth sighed contentedly. "I may retire right after dinner," she said. "Especially if Tess can loan me a good murder mystery. There's something about knowing detectives will set the world right in 300 pages that is so comforting when everything turns upside down."

"Or when your back porch stairs have gone missing."

Elisabeth's eyes sparkled. "Little does our local delinquent know, he saved me the cost of demolishing the porch. It was *riddled* with termite damage. I haven't felt safe using those steps for months. The same fellow who built the new mailbox structure is going to build a deck in the back."

"Good idea."

We headed back upstairs. Duke led the way, bouncing up the steps with his tiny tail held erect like a drum major's baton.

* * * *

Approximately an hour later, as we were polishing off dessert, a young officer from Quinn's team stopped by.

"Officer Zack Tanner," he said, showing us his badge. Then he knelt and spoke softly to Elisabeth. "Mrs. Roche, the arson team and their engineers have checked out your house, as have our crime scene techs. Your house is habitable, as long as you don't use your back door." He removed his hat and spun it between his fingers. "We'd like you to stay here for the night, though. In case the culprit comes back. We'll get the gas and power back on by midmorning tomorrow."

"She's absolutely staying with us," Tess said. "As long as she needs to." The second half of her sentence was less enthusiastic than the first. Tess was a good neighbor, but she valued her privacy and her sanity. Elisabeth and Duke were both challenging personalities best tolerated in small doses.

"Chief Quinn said I should tell you he'll be by in the morning to give you a report on what our team has discovered so far," Zack said.

We offered him dessert and coffee. He blushed and declined, though he'd looked longingly at the plate of cookies and the ice cream dishes. I wrapped up a cookie in a napkin and handed it to him as I walked him out. Duke followed on our heels, yapping and threatening to trip us up on the stairs.

I opened the door for Zack, and stepped back, my mouth agape. Our friend Stephen Laird from Orchard View was outside with his hand raised to knock.

"Sorry to startle you," Stephen said. "I've got Paolo and Munchkin here too, along with someone new you need to meet."

Quinn's officer stepped in front of me. "Sir," he said formally, straightening his spine and squaring his shoulders to appear as large as possible. "May I help you?"

I peered over Zack's shoulder, past Stephen.

Paolo stepped forward, stomped to shake an accumulation of snow off his boots and jacket, and displayed his shiny new detective's badge, the result of a recent promotion. I relaxed, but Zack didn't let them in until I'd confirmed they were friends.

Zack touched his hat brim and disappeared into the night.

"Where did you come from?" I asked Stephen, cringing as I listened to my not-very-welcoming words. "What are you doing here?"

Tess leaned over the railing at the top of the stairs. "For heaven's sake, Maggie! Let them in. Are you hungry? I can heat up dinner or you can join us for dessert. And who's your new friend?"

I wrinkled my forehead and turned to see what or who Tess was referring to. I half-expected that Paolo or Stephen had rescued a new dog. My mouth dropped open when a young woman in a heavy down coat stepped out from behind Paolo. "Welcome," I said, to fill the silence. "Let me take your coat."

She unzipped the coat, stashed her mittens and hat in the pockets, and shrugged out of it. "Thanks," she said. "I'm Peggy. Peggy Salisbury." She flipped two long thick chestnut braids over her shoulders. Instead of handing me her jacket, she turned and lifted it onto one of the hooks behind her. Kicking off her boots, she revealed neon wool socks in mismatched prints.

Munchkin, Stephen's enormous mastiff, woofed once, silencing Duke who shivered behind me. Finally, a voice of reason that could quiet the yappy pup. But Belle and Mozart replied immediately to the big dog's greeting and barreled down the stairs in a flurry of wagging tails and bouncing feet. I placed Duke on the third stair up, and he dashed upward. With four people, three sets of puffy outdoor gear, and three normally well-behaved but excited dogs, there was little room to maneuver in Tess's entryway. Stephen knocked over a rack of skis, grabbing them before they clattered to the floor.

"Go on up, Peggy," I said, waving and hoping she could hear me over the din. "Introduce yourself."

Behind her back, I raised my eyebrows. Stephen saw me, smiled, and shook his head. Paolo blushed and followed Peggy up the steps.

"Relax," Stephen said. "We'll tell you everything. But only in exchange for the details about the trouble you and Tess have run into. It's not safe to send you anywhere."

Chapter 24

The secret of getting ahead is getting started.
—**Mark Twain,** American writer. 1835-1910

Sunday, February 21, Evening

It took a while to introduce and update everyone. Stephen spoke first. "I hitched a ride up with Paolo and Peggy. Max asked me if there was anything I could do to help you solve your case and get back home faster." He patted my knee. "I figured I could do a better job if I showed up in person. Your husband misses you, Maggie, but I think those three boys are running him ragged."

"But Donner Pass is still closed," I said, wondering how they'd made it through.

"To all but emergency personnel." Stephen's crystal blue eyes twinkled.

I stared at him with what my kids called my "mom face." "And you're emergency personnel?"

"Paolo flashed his shiny new badge," Stephen said. "Besides, Max said it was an emergency. Who am I to doubt your husband?"

"Where are you staying?" Tess asked. "Our bunk room is pretty spartan, but it's yours if you want it." I knew the room she referred to. A cavernous room that was part ski storage and maintenance and part family room, but also boasted four pairs of bunk beds and a pull out sofa, a widescreen television, and online gaming gear. The beds and workbench dated back before Patrick's time. The electronics had been added for Teddy and his friends.

"Peggy and I are staying at the resort," said Paolo. A muscle in his cheek twitched as though he was trying to coerce his skin not to blush. He failed.

He reached an arm around Peggy's back. "A getaway week," he explained. "Peggy here is an avid skier."

"I'm here on business, too," she said. "But that's a small part of our plans."

"Peggy works at the farm at Rancho San Antonio," Paolo said, puffing with pride. "She's got an equine rescue plan underway and wanted to visit a farm here in the valley that's already got a great program."

Stephen warmed his hands over a steaming mug of hot chocolate. "That bunk room sounds perfect for me. And Munchkin." The big dog stirred lazily, as he drifted to sleep under the table with Belle and Mozart.

Stephen reached into his backpack, which he'd slung over the back of the chair, and pulled out a sheaf of papers. "I did background checks on all the people Max told me you'd talked to, along with anyone owning homes in the neighborhood," he said. "I've got maps of the property boundaries. I can get more if there are other suspects you've uncovered since you last talked to your beloved." While the hard-copy printouts would come in handy should we suffer another power outage, I knew that Stephen preferred reference materials he could touch to records stored on a tablet, computer, or in the cloud.

Retired from the Marine Corps, Stephen was married to the drop-dead gorgeous Orchard View police chief, Jason Mueller. He never ever used profanity and employed a formal language all his own that included disused but elegant descriptive words like 'beloved.' A long battle with PTSD meant he didn't always sleep well, but he controlled his demons with lots of exercise and by helping fellow sufferers in the veteran community. In Stephen's heart, that group included returned soldiers of both the human and the canine varieties Thanks to his uncanny ability to appear, out of nowhere, when people needed help, Max had dubbed him the ninja marine. It was very much in keeping with Stephen's legend that he'd found a way through a roadblock that had stopped everyone else.

Elisabeth levered herself out of her chair, her joints creaking. "Very nice to meet you all," she said. "But I'm afraid I'm headed to bed. Too much excitement in one day for me and my chatty dog." Stephen stood in an old-fashioned show of respect for the older woman.

"Oh, hang on," Tess said. "I'm afraid the bunk room is reached through your room, Elisabeth. Do you two mind sharing such close quarters?"

Elisabeth looked from Tess to Stephen. "I don't. Not at all," she said. "And don't worry about waking me. I take my hearing aids out at night so you'd have to work very hard to disturb my sleep.

"And what about your valiant protector?" Stephen asked, nodding toward Duke, who sat in a sphinxlike position eyeing Munchkin and growling softly.

Elisabeth laughed. "Never mind him. He sleeps at my feet, under the covers. After trying to supervise the entire neighborhood over the last few days, he'll be out all night. You won't know he's there."

Elisabeth and Duke descended the stairs to the ground floor. Stephen sat and scooted his chair forward. "I think I'm up to speed on the discovery of Dev's body and the mysteries surrounding his disappearance," he said. "But something else must have happened today or we wouldn't have been greeted upon our arrival by the earnest young Officer Zack Tanner and you wouldn't be housing the neighbors. My brain needs something new to noodle over in the wee hours. Give me the abridged version."

Tess and I took turns telling the story and Stephen made notes, asking questions from time to time as we mentioned unfamiliar names.

Against my will, I yawned. A big audible rhino yawn that allowed everyone to check my dental work and tonsils. It broke up the party.

Paolo and Peggy excused themselves to head back to their hotel in the resort complex. Stephen gathered up his papers. "I'll update my notes tonight and make a list of questions for tomorrow," he said. "We can work out our plan of attack in the morning."

"I'm glad you're here," I said, stifling another yawn.

"We make a good team." He patted my shoulder. "But not unless you get enough sleep."

Stephen was right. We'd solved a number of tricky mysteries together, solidifying our friendship. He had a sharp mind and extraordinary powers of observation. His time in the military had given him stealth surveillance abilities and access to veteran experts in a variety of law enforcement fields. Between his nighttime wakefulness and my daytime connections in the information-sharing parent network in a small town, there was little that escaped us. Add Tess to the mix, with her fierce work ethic and connections throughout the Silicon Valley business community, and we were unstoppable. But there was one problem. We weren't in the Bay Area anymore. I wondered if our partnership would flourish or flounder at the heady altitude of the Sierra. Time would tell.

* * * *

The next morning, Elisabeth appeared for breakfast wearing the borrowed robe with its length trailing behind her like an evening gown. Seated, it pooled around her, creating what Duke thought was the perfect bed for a small dog. As Stephen emerged with Munchkin and Tess with Mozart, each of the bigger dogs greeted tiny Duke. After all the sniffing was finished and we'd let the dogs outside, it was apparent that Duke had accepted the larger dogs as part of his pack. The aggressive stance typical of his breed still made him appear slightly on edge, but after they'd all reentered the house, slurped up water and kibble, and collapsed in front of the refueled fire, Duke positioned himself next to Munchkin's snout, within snacking distance were the mastiff so inclined.

Tess announced that breakfast was self-serve only, and that everyone needed to bus their dishes straight into the dishwasher. Hearty oatmeal with dried fruit and nuts bubbled on the stove and we each fixed our own coffee, tea, or hot chocolate.

"Plans?" Tess asked succinctly when we were all seated. "No, wait. First things first." She leaned forward and peered at Stephen. "What's the story on Paolo and Peggy?"

Stephen leaned back in his chair and held up his hands. "You'll have to ask them."

Tess tilted her head and adopted a wheedling tone. "Give us a hint. A crumb. Are they an item?"

"I haven't asked and they haven't offered. That's their business. All I know is what you've already heard—she's the head honcho at the educational farm at Rancho San Antonio in Mountain View."

"But how did Paolo meet her?"

Stephen sighed. "You won't let up, will you?"

Tess pressed her lips together and crossed her arms.

"If I've got the story right, a miniature donkey introduced them." Stephen fought to keep his face straight.

I snorted, nearly spilling my coffee. "A donkey?

Stephen took a long sip from his mug. Then he lowered his voice and spoke in a conspiratorial whisper. "Don't let on that I told you. Make them tell you the story. But during a big storm a year, year-and-a-half ago, a tree blew down on the barn where Peggy works. Several animals escaped. Local law enforcement was called to help round them up and keep hikers and mountain bikers off the trails. Paolo volunteered to handle crowd control 'cause he doesn't know much about horses and such." Stephen drew out the story, taking another drag on his coffee, smoothing his beard, and pulling at the cuffs of his flannel shirt.

"Go on," Tess urged.

"On his way to the farm, Paolo found the donkey caught in a blackberry thicket. He freed the animal and the little guy trotted behind him all the way back to the barn, head butting him most of the way. Peggy says the donkey had been a rescue whose previous owner had died. The newcomer hadn't been eating properly. She had her hands full wrangling a momma cow that wouldn't let anyone near her newborn twins, so she asked Paolo to get the creature settled and try him on some feed. When she checked later, Paolo had named the donkey "Hotay" and had him literally eating out of his hand."

"Hotay? Is that donkey in Spanish or something?" Elisabeth asked.

"Donkey Hotay...after Don Quixote." Stephen didn't try to hide his amusement over the groan-worthy play on words.

"So, I'm guessing that Peggy laughed at the pun and Paolo was instantly in love," I said.

"Something like that," Stephen said. "But ask them. It's an even cuter story when one of them tells it."

Tess stared at me, her mouth agape. "How did we miss this?"

I shook my head. "We're slipping." But then I remembered Paolo being cagey about a date he'd had around the time that Patrick died. That date could have been Peggy. The timing was right. I smiled. There was something delightfully infectious about the joy of a young couple in love.

Stephen moved to the counter to refresh his mug and then held up the carafe. "Anyone else? There's a little left but after that we'll need a new pot."

"I need to get home," said Elisabeth. "Though I slept like the dead last night, it would be nice to get back into my own space and my own clothes." She rolled up a bathrobe sleeve which had drooped perilously close to her oatmeal.

"I'd like to walk down there with you," said Stephen. "To familiarize myself with the neighborhood and reassure all of us that there's nothing in your house that might hurt you or anyone else."

"I'm not particularly worried," Elisabeth said. "The kind of people that would set off a bomb on my back steps and run away aren't the sort that would stand their ground in broad daylight, but ..."

"Better safe than sorry," I finished for her.

"I was going to say that discretion is the better part of valor."

"Same thing," I said. "Though the Shakespearean version sounds more dignified."

"Any idea who could have planted that explosive?" Stephen asked. "Someone with a grudge?"

Elisabeth, Tess, and I checked silently with each other before I spoke, "We've been over that same territory for everyone in the immediate neighborhood," I said. "We've come up with a pretty tame list of minor tiffs. Access to explosives is another story."

Stephen raised his eyebrows over the top of his coffee mug.

Tess continued. "We'll need to check with Quinn to verify this, but the most likely source is the Ski Patrol maintenance shed and the devices they use for avalanche control."

"What do those charges look like?" asked Stephen. I had the sense he already knew but was evaluating Elisabeth's familiarity with the equipment.

Elisabeth tilted her head to one side then the other as if weighing the options and the explosives. "One of them is a time-delayed grenade-type thing a little bigger than a soup can. Given the size of the blast, I'm guessing that's what they used at my house."

"And all of those munitions are stored in a maintenance shed near here?" Stephen asked.

"Most of them are locked up in ski patrol headquarters in the village," Tess explained. "It's where they meet before going up the mountain in the morning, but they keep some of the charges in the shed here, directly behind Elisabeth's back yard, for the groomers to use if they spot a problem."

Stephen frowned. "I'm no avalanche or explosives expert, but is that unusual? Can you get a grooming machine into those high peaks where the risk is greatest?"

"You're right, for the most part," Tess said. "But after a wild series of storms and high winds like we've had over the past few days, you never know. You wouldn't want one of those expensive snowcats buried under a collapsed cornice."

"So, who knows where the explosives are kept? And who has access?" Stephen asked.

I stood up, collecting empty oatmeal bowls and taking them to the sink. Self-serve breakfast or not, I felt antsy and needed to move. "As far as we can tell, everyone knows they're stored there and quite a few people have access," I said.

"They aren't locked?" Stephen's brow furrowed and he appeared angry about the possible lack of appropriate security for potentially deadly munitions.

"They are, but every male over the age of twenty-one has been or still is on the avalanche crew and uses all the necessary firearms."

"Firearms?"

"Big guns, literally," said Elisabeth. "Army surplus. Howitzers."

"Okay..." Stephen's voice trailed off. He doodled spirals in his notebook, thinking, then pushed back his chair and stood. "Let's get ready to take Elisabeth back. I want to see all this for myself.

We tidied up the kitchen and then vanished to get dressed. Elisabeth emerged last, looking more comfortable in her own clothes. "Tess, thank you so much for everything," she said. "If I can ever return the favor..."

Tess embraced her. "It's not necessary..."

"...But if you need anything, you'll ask?" Elisabeth said.

"You got it," Tess said. She was staying home this time, hoping to catch up on a few chores.

"I'm right behind you." I called to them, clipping leashes on Mozart and Belle. Stephen followed with Munchkin, unleashed but under voice control. Elisabeth uncharacteristically overlooked the breach of local leash laws, perhaps because she had Duke secured in her arms without his temporary leash, which Elisabeth had deemed too ordinary for the tiny dog's taste.

Stepping outside, I squinted in the bright sunlight reflecting off every snow-covered surface. "We're headed down the hill," I told Stephen, pointing left toward Elisabeth's. "That's her house there near the bottom."

"And the roof in the trees behind the house?"

"The maintenance shed."

"And way back in the trees?"

"The Bailey family."

"That's Dev?"

I nodded. "And his wife, their two kids, and a kinda bratty teenaged sister-in-law named Amrita."

"Dev's sister or Leslie's?"

I explained all the relationships and pointed out the other houses. Siobhan's, where car tracks in the snow indicated she'd already left for work. And Quinn Petit's, where the driveway and front walk were freshly shoveled.

"And that structure in the turn-around circle past Elisabeth's house?" Stephen asked. "The mailboxes?"

I nodded. "See that spot where the plowed-up snow is cut out? It's where we found Dev's body. Crime scene techs removed the whole chunk of the drift so they could melt it looking for trace evidence."

The booming sound of automated charges punctuated my statement. The earth beneath our feet shook.

Chapter 25

Having too many things about us is a certain confusion to the intellect.
  —**Oscar C. McCullouch**, American clergyman. 1843-1891

Monday, February 22, Mid-morning (Presidents' Day holiday)

I jumped at the noise and Stephen shuddered, dropping to his knees to comfort Munchkin. Loud noises had terrifying associations for both of them.

Elisabeth didn't blink. "Those are the automated air charges," she said. "They use them in the areas prone to slides."

We waited while Stephen and his pal got it together. After a moment, my friend stood, brushing snow from his knees. "It's a good thing fewer people get murdered in the winter," Stephen said.

"Seriously?" I said, figuring a murderous rage couldn't be easily chilled by cool climate.

"It turns out even bad guys don't like to operate in cold weather," Stephen said. "Major crimes drop off dramatically with the first frost and ramp up again as temperatures climb in the spring."

"I was thinking fresh snowfall would cover up all sorts of crimes," I said.

"Or make it hard for the bad guys to keep from leaving footprints," said Stephen. "It takes special techniques and extra patience to examine a crime scene that turns your toes to ice."

I shielded my eyes from the glare of the sun. "There's less daylight for a search, too, I guess."

We slowed in front of Elisabeth's house and Stephen examined the property as a whole. "The explosion was out back?" he asked.

Elisabeth nodded. "Do you want to come in and take a look from the kitchen, or head straight to the back yard?"

Stephen thought for a moment, rubbing his chin. "If you two could stay here with the dogs, I'll go 'round back and check things out. If it all looks good, I'll head back here right away, otherwise I'll give you a call."

"Give us a call?" I asked.

He held up his cellphone. "If there's anything surrounding the porch that I think Elisabeth should look at."

"Got it," I said, but then movement up the hill near Tess's house caught my attention. I turned and waved. It was Quinn.

"That's Chief Quinn Petit," I told Stephen. "Coming to give us a report on last night's findings, I'm guessing."

Munchkin followed Stephen around the corner of the house while Belle and Mozart bounded up the hill to greet Quinn with their leashes dragging. Elisabeth picked up Duke, who was shivering.

"Find anything?" Quinn asked.

"Our friend Stephen's checking behind the house now." I told him.

"I'm disappointed," Quinn said. "From everything the Orchard View Chief of Police said, you and this Stephen work miracles with minimal evidence. I would have expected you two to have solved the case by now."

Quinn had earlier mentioned that he knew Jason, but now he seemed to be implying he'd talked to our friend recently. "When did you talk to Jason? And why?" I asked.

"Professional courtesy. He called to tell me Paolo and Stephen were coming, vouch for them, and ask whether I minded if they poked around a bit." Quinn pointed toward the house. "For the record, I welcome the help."

We chatted while we waited for Stephen to return. When he did, I introduced the two men and then left them alone to confer while I helped Elisabeth up the walk. Normally, she wouldn't have needed any assistance, but having her home bombed had shaken her up physically, emotionally, and mentally. She seemed fragile this morning and triggered my protective instincts.

"I've got a couple of things I want to go over with Elisabeth," Quinn said loudly enough for all of us to hear. "Maggie, do you and Stephen want to join us?"

"We'll check back later," Stephen said. "I want to take a look at the maintenance shed and meet Leslie Bailey and her family. Unless you've got something specific?"

"My guys have looked over the whole area several times in the last few months and found nothing. I don't know if there's anything there to find, but you're welcome to investigate it yourselves."

Stephen and I set off for the Baileys' house. Belle, Mozart, and Munchkin bounded ahead of us, down the long driveway through the trees to Leslie's front yard. "The easiest way to reach the shed is via an old fire road that branches off from the driveway," I said, pointing to the trail head. "Most of it has been groomed as a cross-country ski trail."

"So who you do you like for this murder, Maggie?" Stephen asked. "Any favorites in the running? Anyone you can rule out?"

A gust of wind rolled through the tree tops, knocking clumps of snow to the ground. The dogs snapped at them as if they were a barrage of tennis balls thrown for their personal enjoyment. I thought for a moment about all the players in this drama, none of whom had set my antenna aquiver for more than a little while.

"I'm not sure," I told Stephen. "Not yet. It seems like everyone might have at least a flimsy reason for wanting Dev dead, but there's nothing, forgive the expression, explosive. No passion or energy."

"What do you mean?" Stephen asked, though I had the sense he knew exactly what I meant.

I stopped in the middle of the road. "I'm not sure. But everything is different up here. In an emergency, the neighbors are dependent on each other for their safety and survival. They have to get along. In Silicon Valley, animosities flare up because people work or live on top of one another. Here? It's tough for anger to build to a homicidal level when anyone can stomp off into the forest to blow off a head of steam."

Stephen made a noise to indicate he was listening and thinking. "Just because someone can hike their way out of a temper tantrum doesn't mean they will," he said.

"Excellent point. As usual. But see what you think when you meet Amrita. We'll stop by the house first. She's hiding something—angry and afraid. Some of the locals have told me she's wonderful, but I've only seen a surly teen. And I haven't discovered the source or target of her emotions."

"Couldn't her anger just be part of the grieving process and being a teenager?"

"Maybe," I said. "Talk to her and tell me what you think."

We trudged toward the house through the trees, listening to the birds, and watching the dogs. All the typical sounds of civilization—cars, planes, mechanical equipment, were muffled to the point of silence. It was unusual to experience such relative quiet and I appreciated being in the company of someone who was as unwilling as I was to shatter it.

We entered the clearing in front of the house just as Leslie and her two children, led by Winston, barreled out of the door, across the porch, and down the steps. Harry looked from his mom to the tire tracks and back at us. The tire tracks won. He ran off, as fast as he could in his voluminous snow pants, making race car noises while gripping an invisible steering wheel.

I waved to Naomi and she danced toward me, twirling. Halfway, she flung herself into the snow to make a snow angel. Belle, Mozart, and Munchkin raced to "help." Gray-snouted Winston bounded forward like a puppy.

"Pull up a step," Leslie said after I introduced Stephen with a brief summary of his background and his interest in Dev's case. I hesitated before sitting on the icy stone steps, but I could barely detect a temperature difference through my insulated pants. Sheltered from the wind, in air warmed by the sun, I could easily imagine myself in much cushier surroundings.

Stephen's first objective was to learn more about the explosion at Elisabeth's and verify the safety of Leslie and her kids. He asked a number of questions without uncovering new information.

Amrita emerged from the house carrying a basket filled with a flask of coffee, thermal mugs, and a couple of raggedy blankets. "To sit on," Amrita explained. "And keep from freezing your buns off."

We rearranged ourselves quickly. Stephen pulled out a paper bag of cookies from an Orchard View bakery and offered them around, ending with Amrita. When her mouth was full, he turned to face the dogs and children. Without looking directly at her, he delicately questioned Amrita. I knew this trick. I used it whenever I had uncomfortable questions to ask my own children. Talking in the car, where side-by-side seating and a need to watch the road precluded eye contact, made any difficult conversation seem less confrontational.

"Any idea where the explosives came from?" Stephen asked the teen. "The ones that took out Mrs. Roche's porch?" He glanced at Amrita but then turned back to watch the children trying to build a friend for the snowman they'd made the day before.

"Uh…" Amrita said.

"Can you get me into the maintenance shed to look around?"

Amrita didn't answer. She stood, brushed crumbs off the front of her jacket, and went to help the children.

"What do we think?" Stephen asked when she was out of earshot.

"Something's bothering her," Leslie offered. "She's lost weight and isn't sleeping well."

"Grief?" Stephen asked. "Or some other form of trouble? How does she act when Quinn's around?"

Leslie sighed. "I finally asked her directly about pregnancy or an illness yesterday, suggesting she go for a checkup. She stomped upstairs and slammed the door. Some days I think that Harry and Naomi are more mature than Amrita and I are."

"Were she and Dev close?" Stephen asked.

Leslie squinted and looked toward the treetops. "It's hard to say. When she wanted to get away from her parents in Los Angeles, she came straight here, and we took her in without question. It's hard enough for me to examine my relationships with my own siblings, let alone dissect the ups and downs of someone else's family connections."

"Maggie said she'd been in trouble with the police?"

Leslie shook her head. "Not really. Underage drinking. Quinn was called to a local bar to defuse a fight and found her puking in the parking lot. Dev picked her up. There was a second time that was worse and she ended up in the ER. The police questioned her a bit, but no charges were filed."

Stephen tugged on his beard. "How did Dev take it?"

"He administered lots of toast and fluids and ibuprofen, followed by encouraging excessive noise from the children the next morning."

"The classic combo of brotherly care and...natural consequences."

"You have sisters," Leslie said. It wasn't a question.

"But you think she's hiding something?" Stephen probed gently. "So does Maggie."

Leslie nodded. "Definitely."

Stephen whistled and the dogs bounded toward him. I stood and he called to Amrita. "Can you show me the way to the shed?" He turned to me and said quietly, "You come too, Maggie."

We watched as Amrita shepherded the children back toward the porch and their mother. Her body language and facial expression were obscured by her storm gear and the glare, but she seemed less resistant to Stephen and his questions than she'd been when he'd questioned her moments before.

Leslie stepped off the porch to help the kids with their snow friend. Like a small parade, the rest of us trooped toward the cross-country ski trail behind the house.

Stephen was surprisingly chatty on the walk. "Leslie told Maggie and Tess that Winston's been super nervous lately, barking at something out here. She was thinking bears or a prowler. You have a theory?"

Amrita didn't answer. After a few moments of silence, Stephen tried again.

"I'm usually pretty good at mysteries," he said. "But there's one thing I can't figure out about your brother's disappearance..." He let his voice trail off, but his inflection signaled that he hadn't finished his thought. He let the silence drag out until Amrita cleared her throat and looked up.

"Right," he said, as if Amrita had voiced a thought. "He was missing for six weeks. Where was he during that time? If someone killed him close to the time of his disappearance and the investigation didn't turn up anything at the time, why didn't the killer leave Dev's body wherever he'd first stashed it? Why bring the body out of hiding?" He pulled his hat down over his ears. "It makes no sense to move the body to a spot where Maggie would literally trip over it. Someone wanted his body found."

I heard Amrita gasp, but I said nothing. I didn't want to disrupt the delicate connection Stephen was building.

The snow squeaked under our feet and the wind stirred the branches over our heads.

"I—" Amrita began to say something, then stopped.

Stephen turned and looked her in the eye. "Whatever it is, you can tell me, Amrita. I'm here to help and I won't tell the police anything they don't absolutely need to know."

She sank to her knees in the snow. Munchkin moved close to her. She wrapped her arms around his neck, and held on tight, leaning on the enormous dog for support. Her sobs rent the air. Belle and Mozart stopped playing, barked, and came to sit on either side of me. I ruffled their ears and wished there were something similar I could do to help Amrita.

As her sobs wound down, Stephen stepped toward her and offered his bear-paw sized hand to help her up. "Is there somewhere we could sit for a few minutes?" he asked.

"There's a picnic table by the maintenance shed." Amrita said. "They use it like a break room in good weather."

The rest of the path was cleared and packed in a design like corrugated cardboard, thanks to the coming and going of the machines designed to keep the slopes groomed. The barn was in a clearing marked by shadows from the surrounding trees, leaving sharp delineations between light and dark.

"That's not right," Amrita said, slowing and pointing at the building. "The doors should all be locked. Everyone should be out on the slopes working at this time of day."

Stephen moved forward with his arm outstretched to keep us safely behind him. Munchkin joined him, the fur on his spine raised. Stephen's hand went to his belt, as if to unsnap the holster he hadn't worn since leaving active duty.

I pulled Amrita into the shadows. As my eyes adjusted, I could see that while the large garage bay doors on the barn were closed and locked, a smaller door meant for people gaped open. One side of the door jamb lay splintered in the snow. The sun glinted off an oversized metal lock someone had set on the picnic table. It was still connected to a broken hasp.

"Sending the dog in," Stephen called out. "Freeze so he won't bite you."

Chapter 26

Possessions are generally diminished by possession.
—**Friedrich Nietzsche**, German philosopher. 1844-1900

Monday, February 22, Near noon (Presidents' Day holiday)

Munchkin eyed Stephen's face and leaped forward at a silent signal so subtle I must have missed it. Stephen followed the dog into the dark building.

A moment later, the big marine poked his head out the door. "No one's here," he said. "Maggie, call Quinn."

I relayed the request to my phone, which autodialed Quinn. When he answered, I put the call on speaker and told him there was something he needed to see at the maintenance shed.

"Injuries?" he asked. "Ambulance?"

I looked at Stephen, who shook his head.

"No," I told Quinn. "There was a break in and there's more evidence inside."

"What is it?"

"Show you when you get here," Stephen said.

Quinn ended the call without another word.

To avoid disturbing the scene further, Amrita and I perched on a fallen log in the sun. Stephen crouched on the ground in front of Amrita, picked up a small branch, and drew circles in the snow. Amrita examined her boots.

Stephen cleared his throat. Amrita ducked her head, drew her knees up close, and wrapped her arms around them. "You know the schedules for the maintenance workers," Stephen said. "You know about the set up here and where the crew takes breaks." It was a statement of fact, not a question.

I struggled to keep my mouth shut in the silence that followed.

Amrita lifted her head and jutted her jaw, staring Stephen down in a show of defiance. "So?"

Her bravado didn't last. She dropped her gaze, then looked up with a diminished level of confidence. "Everyone does. We hear the snowcats when they arrive and when they leave. Anyone who's been here for more than a few days knows their schedule. Even Winston knows. They give him treats, so he barks to go out whenever he hears that rumble." Her face and voice softened as she appeared to forget that she was in surly defiant teenager mode. "We keep him indoors until we hear the engines turn off. Even though he's a black dog on white snow, it's hard to see all the way to the ground from the cabs of those things. That's partly why the teams usually head out after the slopes are closed—for safety."

I put my hand on Amrita's arm. "Help me understand," I said. "You might have heard my old pal Tess call me a Flatlander. I don't get how any of this mountain stuff works. Do all the locals know when this building will be empty?"

Stephen turned away from Amrita and gazed at the damaged door frame. "The locks seem to be mostly for show," he said. "They wouldn't keep out anyone who really wanted to break in...or needed to." I wasn't sure what he was implying, but I didn't ask.

Amrita reached into her pocket and pulled out a key with a red satin ribbon tied through the hole at the end. "Lots of people have keys," she said. "I don't know anyone who'd have to break in."

"And you have a key because..." Stephen said.

Amrita blushed and ducked her head.

Stephen waited her out. She caved. "It's a boy. From ski patrol."

"He gave you the key?" Stephen asked.

Amrita nodded.

"Why?"

"He wanted me to meet him here."

"And did you?"

She shook her head. "I told him my brother wouldn't let me."

I scooted closer to Amrita on the log and put my arm around her. "Was that true?" I'd told my own boys to invent parental prohibitions at will to dodge peer pressure. Of course, I'd also suggested they tell me what rules they'd invented so I could back them up.

She shook her head again. "I'd seen the guy around the resort with my friends, and he seemed nice. He bought me drinks the time that Dev had to pick me up. But meeting him here, alone? I wasn't ready for that."

"But you didn't want to tell him?"

"I didn't want to seem like a baby. I invited him to come to dinner at the house with some of my friends. You know, meet Dev and Leslie."

"Good idea." I said. "He wouldn't come?"

He said that was too formal for him. That he didn't want to wait for a big occasion to see me. He acted like he thought that would make me feel good, but it just felt weird."

"Good instincts," I told her. "There's something not quite right about any relationship that has to be kept a secret."

"How'd he take that?" Stephen asked.

"He got mad. Like, really angry. I took the key so he'd calm down." She handed the key to Stephen. "Take it. I don't want it. I don't want to see him again. There's something going on here that I don't understand."

Stephen took the key and slipped it into his pocket. "Like what?"

Amrita chewed her lower lip and looked away.

"Are you afraid it's something bad?" I asked.

"It's Winston," Amrita said. "He knows most of the guys on the crew. I've brought Harry and Naomi up to watch them put the snowcats in the barn. It's kinda fun to watch them maneuver those big things. Harry loves it. They wave to him and ham it up, but they get on with the job."

"Go on," Stephen urged when her voice slowed and hesitated.

"Like I said, we know their schedule. It's normal. Winston wouldn't growl at them. He'd bark to be let out and get treats."

"But..."

"Winston's been growling at the back door late at night. Not as if he wants to go out, but more like he wants to keep something...or someone from coming in."

"Do you think it was the boy?" I forced myself to ask the question, but I was starting to feel sick. The only young man I remembered seeing around the neighborhood was Han. Or Ryan Stillwell at a stretch, but I doubted a person Amrita's age would call someone in his midtwenties a boy. I liked them both. Ryan and Amrita had seemed comfortable together yesterday. Even a little flirty. Could the boy she was growing wary about be either of them?

Amrita hesitated to answer my question but then spoke softly. "Maybe. Or some of his friends. Going to or from the shed." My heart ached.

"In the middle of the night?" Stephen asked.

"They work when the lifts are closed," Amrita reminded him in a voice that dripped with impatience. "That means after dark. Or before dawn if there's a heavy snow and they want to get more of the lifts open for the weekend."

Stephen raised his eyebrows and looked at me for confirmation.

"She's right," I told him. "It's a wonder anyone around here gets any sleep at all."

"But that's just it," Amrita said. "Normally, we don't even hear them. Or, if we do, we just roll over and go back to sleep. Even the kids do that. But lately, since before Christmas at least, Winston has been waking up. He's anxious and angry. So he wakes us up too."

I was confused. "But you said Winston is comfortable with the crews. Isn't your friend part of that? What's different about him?"

Amrita frowned. "I hadn't thought...I'm not sure..." Her voice trailed off and Stephen changed tack.

"What happens when Winston barks like that in the middle of the night?" Stephen asked.

"What do you mean?"

"Does Leslie let him out?"

Amrita gasped. "At night? When we don't know what's out there? It could be bears or a mountain lion. Or a skunk we don't want him to tangle with. If he barked at the back door, Dev would turn on the outside lights to scare away any animals and take him on the leash out the front door in case, you know, he had to do his business one more time."

"And?"

"Winston wouldn't go out. At least not in the last few weeks, not when Leslie or I opened the door for him."

"Wouldn't go out? What kind of dog says no to a walk? Ever?"

"Winston *really* didn't want to go. Didn't want us go out either. He stands between me and the door. Won't make eye contact. None of his normal "Ooh, a walk" behavior."

"What did you and Leslie think was going on?"

She shrugged. "Maybe some of the guys were using the shed like a club? Beer and weed after work? And Winston was hyper protective of us because Dev isn't here. Maybe the old dog is just getting senile."

I looked up as Quinn's official vehicle rounded the bend in the fire trail and crunched across the corrugated snow.

While Amrita and I sat with the dogs, Stephen directed Quinn toward the barn. Before they disappeared through the door, I heard Stephen say, "You're going to want to take samples out back." Unintelligible words followed, and a sentence ending with "...blood." My heart stuttered, but I made small talk with Amrita in an attempt to distract both of us from trying to imagine what Stephen had found. It didn't work for me and I doubted it did for Amrita.

After a few moments, the men reappeared and Quinn knelt to examine the remains of the broken door jamb. He plucked his phone from a jacket pocket, took a few pictures, then made a call. He walked away from the barn to pace while he talked.

Stephen pulled up another fallen log and sat on it facing Amrita and me. "Quinn's calling in the crime scene techs."

"What'd you find? Does he need us to stay?" I started to blurt out a third question, but Stephen interrupted me.

"They were planning to come down here anyway, after they finished at Elisabeth's. Quinn has a warrant to collect avalanche explosives so they can determine whether the same devices demolished Elisabeth's porch."

"Is there more damage inside the shed? I heard you say blood. Is someone hurt?" I swallowed hard before adding, "or dead?" But Stephen didn't seem to be listening. He watched Quinn as the chief made a series of calls.

"Sorry, Maggie," Stephen said. "Can you repeat all that? Quinn's going to be a few minutes. He's calling the district attorney or whatever they call that position in this county. He's got a slew of other calls to make before he gets to us." Munchkin whined and nudged his hand.

It was no use being impatient. I stood to throw a stick Belle had brought me. The sun had gone behind a cloud, making me realize how cold I'd grown sitting still. I wriggled my icy toes inside my boots and thick socks. My stomach growled to remind me we'd missed lunch.

"Did Noah do something bad?" Amrita asked in a barely audible voice. Her face was ashen and her hands shook as she rearranged her scarf and zipped her jacket. Louder, she added. "Did he hurt someone?"

I sat next to her again. "Is that the boy's name, Noah? Was he violent with you? Did he lose his temper often?"

Before she could answer, we were interrupted by the arrival of two dark SUVs with county logos on the doors. Quinn emerged from the first one and his feet crunched on the snow as he walked toward us. *Finally!* I waved, but he passed us by with barely a glance and stood in the center of the cross-country track, facing the Bailey house. Three people wearing insulated jumpsuits and heavy boots popped out of the other vehicle. They conferred with Quinn as they shook out enormous disposable white crime scene suits that fit over their puffy winter gear and made them look like snowmen.

They trudged toward us lugging aluminum gear cases and top-heavy lamps mounted on expandable stands.

"There's electricity inside," Quinn told the smallest tech, and she turned, presumably to put a coiled length of orange extension cord back in the SUV. But she must have changed her mind. "No one ever has enough outlets," she said.

The crew passed us, lifting their chins in greeting, and disappeared through the splintered door. I started to shiver and was about to suggest that Quinn could talk to us back at the Baileys' house.

Quinn spoke before I had a chance. "We took samples at Elisabeth's and hope to match them to the explosives here," he said. "We think someone has been living in the maintenance shed, or maybe bunking down there when the weather was too bad to get home. There's a sleeping bag and a bunch of empty food wrappings. Beer cans." He shook his head. "Maybe it was just a party place. The trace evidence will help us decide who to question, but I've already got a list of likely suspects."

Quinn turned toward Amrita. "Is Noah McKane a friend of yours? His name was on the sleeping bag we found."

Amrita's mouth gaped and she took a step back. I put my hand behind her back to steady her and encourage her not to run off. She nodded but then shook her head. "Yes. No. Not really. Maybe." The words tumbled out.

"Which is it? When did you last see him?" Quinn barked the words. I wondered why the normally gentle and quiet man was being so abrupt, but then I noted the dark circles under his blood-shot eyes. Had the man had any sleep in the last seventy-two hours? It seemed unlikely.

"I knew Noah," Amrita said. "He wanted us to be close. But we weren't. I haven't seen him in days."

Stephen pulled Amrita's key from his pocket and smoothed the ribbon on which it was threaded. He handed it to Quinn. "He gave her this key."

Quinn removed his thick gloves and examined the key. "It's just one of what seems like thousands that are floating around. We'll never track them all down. After a series of break-ins a few years ago, they created a system of changing the codes on the big bay doors. At the same time they popped a new padlock on the pedestrian door and handed out a limited number of keys. But that 'limited number' has expanded exponentially over the years. If it weren't for bears wanting to get in and raid their snacks, they could have left the door wide open for all the good that lock did."

"Why tear off the lock then?" I asked.

Quinn and Stephen looked at each other and back at me. "Good question," said Stephen. "Anger maybe. Misplaced frustration."

Quinn shrugged. "Maybe someone forgot their key."

"What was out back?" I asked.

Quinn looked away, not speaking for so long that I feared he'd never answer my question. But then he relented. "We found what looks like blood. Lots of blood."

Amrita gasped, and the gasp turned into a sob. "You think someone was killed back there? By someone on the avalanche squad?" I could feel her shaking and hugged her close. She buried her face in my shoulder. I glared at Quinn over the top of her head.

"Let's take this one step at a time," Quinn said. "All we know at this point is that there's a considerable amount of what looks like blood behind that barn. We don't know yet if it's animal or human."

Quinn counted off the investigative steps on his fingers. "First, the crime scene techs will run a quick test to verify the substance is actually blood. Then they'll run a second test to determine whether it's animal or human. After that, if it is human, it will go to the lab for DNA testing."

Quinn closed his hand. "Even if it turns out to be human blood, it looks to have been from a recent event. We'll check with the ski patrol and with Alison and the other Emergency Room docs to see about injuries reported over the last 24 hours. It's not likely to be Dev's blood." He could have led with that.

I ducked my head and whispered in Amrita's ear. "Did you hear that, hon? It's probably not Dev's blood." My statement was more definitive than Quinn's had been, but it was still mostly true. And it was what Amrita needed to hear. I suspected she was terrified that her connection with Noah had resulted in Dev's death. My thoughts had jumped to the same conclusion. But could it be true? Was Dev held captive and wounded inside the shed with his wife, children, and sister within shouting distance?

I hoped not, for their sake, and struggled to imagine how Dev's disappearance six weeks ago and this latest discovery could be connected.

Chapter 27

To accomplish great things, we must not only act, but also dream; not only
plan, but also believe.
—**Anatole France**, French writer. 1844-1924

Monday, February 22, Afternoon (Presidents' Day holiday)

Thinking can be a dangerous thing. One stray thought leaps to join another.

While I initially thought Ryan and Han were the only young men I'd
met from the neighborhood, I now remembered Han and the other boy
we'd met on Friday when we were helping Siobhan at the bakery back
before the big storm. Noah McKane.

Facing a local emergency, when everyone else was pitching in, Han
had helped out while the other boy thought only of himself. I tilted my
head hoping that one of my loose marbles would roll into its proper spot,
connecting and untangling the jumbled threads of the mystery.

"Amrita, did your friend Noah work at Flour Power?" I asked.

She sniffed and wiped her nose. "Sometimes. When Siobhan was really
desperate. That's how I met him. My friends and I would go there on the
weekends and he'd take his breaks with us. But he stretched out his breaks
and came in late too often. Siobhan cut his hours way back."

If Quinn had been a dog, his ears would have pricked up. "Do you know
where Noah lives? With his parents? On his own? Bunking with friends?"

Amrita thought for a moment. "I was under the impression he was
couch surfing, but I don't think he ever said for sure. He never mentioned
parents, either." She blushed. "And when he wanted to meet me, this was

the place he wanted to come." Amrita's voice squeaked out the last words, as if her throat had tensed up. I hugged her again.

Quinn did something to his posture that made him look shorter, rounder, kinder, and less intimidating. He smiled and spoke softly. "You've been a big help," he told Amrita. "I wonder if you'd be willing to come down to the station tomorrow and go through some mug shots. I know Noah and all the folks who work on the avalanche crew, but we're looking at some other guys in connection with some burglaries, smuggling, and vandalism. Folks you might have seen with Noah."

"I don't really know the dudes Noah hung out with," Amrita said. "When he was with me and my friends, he was really secretive about any other parts of his life. I'm not sure..." her voice trailed off as she furrowed her forehead. "He took calls on his cell phone sometimes that made him really tense. They involved work he was doing for some guy he called BB. I think Noah was afraid of him, but he never said for sure."

"We'll ask Siobhan and some of the other store owners if they've seen him with anyone. And regulars at the road house in Truckee. But we could use your help too," said Quinn.

"You're not just saying that?" Amrita asked.

Quinn scoffed. "It's not really part of my job description to make people feel good. Yes, I need your help." He took off his hat and slapped it against his thigh. "I can use all the help I can get."

"You mentioned smuggling," I said. "What kinds of things do people traffic in an area like this?"

Stephen spoke before Quinn could answer. "Whatever they can get away with. Interstate 80 is so close. Wealthy folks fly in and out with their private planes. All the bad guys need to do is blend into the scenery and make a quick getaway with the goods."

"He's right," said Quinn. "The combination of tourists and money is irresistible to crooks. We see a lot of identity theft, stolen credit cards, cigarettes without tax stamps, and recycling fraud."

"Recycling fraud? Seriously?" I couldn't imagine a more victimless crime and was surprised the offense was even on the radar of a resource-strapped law enforcement operation.

"We work closely with state agencies," Quinn said. "California charged one gang with smuggling hundreds of thousands of pounds of cans and bottles worth more than eighty million dollars across the state border from Nevada."

"Bootleg baby formula is big," Stephen said. "Diapers, baby formula, wild animals, people, you name it."

I felt Amrita shudder. "You think Noah was smuggling *people*?" she asked. "Was he trying to smuggle *me*?"

Quinn was quick to reassure her. "Sex trafficking is an increasing problem everywhere, but particularly in resort areas where there are new people coming and going all the time. But the guys I'm thinking of, the ones we think Noah might have been involved with, are more interested in drugs. They're small time. Too much sampling of the merchandise."

He scratched his chin. "This BB might be someone we've been trying to identify for a long time—someone who seems to be running an operation out near Incline Village. We know he exists, but we've never been able to get a name or a description."

Quinn waved his hand to usher us back toward the house. "Let's head back. There's no reason all of us have to freeze out here while my team does their work."

"Do crooks still traffic in marijuana, now that it's legal?" I asked.

"Illegal sales are still lucrative." Quinn added as he walked with us. "No tax. Same thing with regular cigarettes and booze."

"That's still a thing?" I asked. "I thought rum running went out with the end of Prohibition."

"It's never stopped. Taxes differ by state. On cigarettes, it's about a dollar a pack higher in California than in Nevada. A truckload of cigarettes smuggled across state lines and sold in California—that's real money."

"And here I thought the big business around here was tourism," I said.

"No such luck," Quinn said.

We all walked together back to the Bailey house. Stephen and I waited on the steps outside while Quinn had a few words with Amrita and Leslie. The shadows lengthened and the wind came up. I shivered and rearranged my scarf, looking forward to returning to the cozy warmth of Tess's living room.

Stephen was lost in thought. Belle sat on my foot and leaned her weight against my leg. Munchkin lay on the ground but was alert to Stephen's slightest twitch. Mozart's tongue lolled but his ears perked up as Quinn rejoined us on the porch.

"Thanks for waiting," Quinn said. "Let's walk back."

"But your SUV..." I said, reminding him that he'd driven down.

"One of my guys will drive it back. It's a pool car. I left the keys on the visor."

"Another practice that I was sure had disappeared into the mists of time," I said. "Theft isn't a problem?"

"It's a country thing," Quinn said. "I don't advise it for most folks. But it takes real chutzpah to steal a police vehicle."

"Good point." A gust of wind kicked up snow from the driveway. I ducked my head as the sharp crystals hit my cheeks.

"Did you get anything more on this Noah guy from Amrita?" Quinn asked. "I think she'd confide in you or Leslie before she'd talk to me."

"Unlikely," I said. "Today's the first time I've heard her speak more than a few words. But that Noah is bad news. I gather he was pressuring Amrita for sex and may well have been stalking her. If he sees her going into the station tomorrow..." I frowned, thinking about tragic stalker-turned-murderer plots I'd read about.

"I had a word with Leslie about that," Quinn said. "We'll send a car for her tomorrow. Amrita will wear Leslie's coat, hat, and scarf. We'll bring her in through the underground garage."

I let out a breath, and then sucked it in again. Even the slight uphill slope of the road to Tess's was tough for me. My heart raced and my breath came fast, as though the quiet walk had been far more suspenseful and thrilling than it actually was.

Quinn's next words didn't help. "Make sure your doors are locked tonight. Leave the outside lights on. We'll send a car around to check the neighborhood."

I stopped in my tracks and stared up at Quinn through the fuzzy fake fur that trimmed the jacket of my parka. "You really think we're in danger?"

"Absolutely," said Quinn.

"Get some sleep, man," Stephen said, shaking the chief's hand. "I'll look after them. I've got some guys of my own keeping watch too."

I knew what he meant. Stephen had a secret posse, much like Sherlock Holmes's Baker Street Irregulars. They comprised friends from the Veterans Affairs hospital programs in which Stephen volunteered. We'd met one of them— an elusive retired Special Forces marine called Rocket. Other members of the group remained unseen, at least by me.

Jason must have outlined for Quinn the details of Stephen's qualifications and those of his cohorts. Anyone who wasn't already familiar with them might have looked askance at an unofficial group acting outside the confines of the law but the chief seemed neither surprised nor concerned.

Quinn just lifted his chin in that way men do to communicate with their colleagues, speaking volumes with one tiny micro-expression. Stephen echoed the move.

After Quinn left, Tess offered us her favorite winter warmup, hot apple pie cocktails—apple cider spiked with a citrus and vanilla liqueur topped with a layer of whipped cream pierced with a cinnamon stick.

Though the toddy should have been comforting in every way, I felt restless. Every question we asked seemed to launch two more, and my confusion was escalating.

"Stop fidgeting, Maggie," Tess said with unusual impatience. "I'm going to enjoy this drink and then cocoon into my comforter with a book. It's been too long a day."

I rubbed the back of my neck and stood, walking toward the kitchen. I'd gone ages without food. "I'm making a sandwich," I said. "Anyone else want one?" Stephen nodded. Tess didn't seem to hear me but I decided to make her one anyway.

"We came up here to get your house ready to put on the market," I said as I slathered bread with mayo and mustard.

"But then you helped me figure out that I didn't want to sell and that I don't have to." Tess held her hand to her heart. "That means so much."

"But the house is still full of stuff you and Teddy will never need. Your closets are bulging with things that weigh you down when they could be doing good for someone else."

"Like what?" Tess's words held a note of defensiveness, but she also sounded as though she were humoring me.

"Like that time-traveling wardrobe in the bedroom closet. Where do you and Teddy put the clothes you're wearing in this decade if the closets are full of a fashion retrospective from the last century? How much time do you waste getting ready to come up here because you can't be sure what's already here? Or rushing out to buy some staple you thought was here, but isn't?"

"We'll get to all that. It's not like we've been twiddling our thumbs. Dev's murder—"

I didn't let her finish. "I know. Priorities. But we're not moving forward on any of those projects either. We were going to solve the murder so it wouldn't taint the neighborhood. We haven't done that. If anything, I feel less safe now than I did at the start of the trip. Don't tell me you aren't feeling the same way." I cut the sandwiches, put them on plates and carried them to the coffee table, placing one in front of Tess and handing another to Stephen. I flopped on the sofa.

Tess conceded the point. "But that was only *one* of the reasons we wanted to unlock the secrets surrounding Dev's disappearance. We need to help the neighbors and keep our community safe. It's the right thing to do." She crossed her hands over her chest. "Unless you think that we should throw Elisabeth and Leslie to the wolves so I can tidy up my garage."

My temper rose. I was too tired to keep it completely under control, and my best friend's statement put me on the defensive. I took a too-generous slug of my drink, swallowed wrong and coughed, spraying whipped cream on the coffee table. Stephen brought me some water and wiped up the spill. He was silent, leaving Tess and I to sort things out. By the time I got my coughing under control, I'd cooled off.

"I'm not saying we should abandon Elisabeth and Leslie. Of course not. But are we actually helping?" I looked to Stephen for support. He closed his eyes.

"Stephen's here," I said. "If we need his protection, it means we must be in greater danger now than we've been since we arrived."

"I brought my pal Rocket for backup," Stephen added.

Tess's eyes grew wide and a sheen of sweat coated her forehead. "Rocket's here?"

Stephen nodded. "We're taking this very seriously."

I filled Tess in on what I'd learned from Amrita about Noah and his possible criminal connections. Stephen contributed the details he'd learned from his brief inspection of the maintenance shed and from talking to Quinn.

"Rocket's here to help, but I'm hoping we won't need him." Stephen added.

Tess stood, walked to the window, and peered out through a gap in the closed drapes. "Is he out there now? Will he be safe, with the storm coming?" She turned her back on the window. "He's welcome inside. You know that."

"He's a marine," Stephen said, which in his mind, I knew, was sufficient explanation. But for my sake and Tess's peace of mind, he fleshed out the statement. "He would rather be outside than in, and he knows what he's doing. He's a Red Hat."

"A Red Hat?" Tess said, saving me from asking the question myself.

Stephen gazed at the ceiling in false show of impatience. Tess and I both knew he loved explaining marine operations to uneducated civilians. "Red Hats are instructors at the Mountain Training Center. Rocket teaches winter skills."

"I thought he had done bomb-squad stuff." I must have picked up that impression on one of our earlier encounters with Rocket, or inferred it because of his name.

"That too," Stephen said.

"Nothing changes the fact that time is running out for us," I said. "I've got a new job coming up early next month. If we're not doing any good here,

I'd like to get home and prepare for that. Koko said my car might be ready tomorrow. We could leave as soon as we pick it up. What do you think?"

Stephen drained his drink and set down his mug. He arranged it so the handle and the coaster were parallel to the edge of the coffee table. "Another storm is blowing in. Colder temperatures, more snow, and high winds, but shorter duration. Should be over by noon tomorrow, but I don't know how long it will take to get the roads clear."

I turned to Tess, the local expert. She grimaced. "It's hard to say. But with this storm on top of the earlier ones, skiing conditions will be awesome as soon as the weather clears. We still have three teenaged boys who were promised a ski trip. What if we stayed through next weekend? Max could bring Teddy, Brian, and David. Knowing them, they never unpacked the car."

Before I could mount an argument, my phone rang. I glanced at the screen. "Hey Max," I said. "We were just talking about you." I stood and moved to the kitchen. Max had come to the same conclusion about the weather that Tess had and proposed a similar plan.

"I'm not sure it's safe," I said.

"What do you mean? If it's not safe, you and Tess shouldn't be up there. You need to leave tonight."

I explained why we couldn't. Besides the fact that my car wasn't ready yet, Tess's tires weren't up to the trip. Max suggested that Stephen or Paolo could bring us home.

"I'm sure they could. But leaving now would put us in the middle of the storm. Deliberately heading into blizzard conditions over Donner Pass would be trading one danger for another."

In the silence that followed, I could hear and feel Max's frustration. His macho instincts fired up when his family was in danger. The only surefire antidote was action. But in this case, action wasn't the wisest move.

He let out an audible sigh. "Sit tight then. Call me when the storm's over tomorrow and we'll regroup."

"By then, all the danger will have passed, I'm sure." I spoke with more confidence than I felt.

"Are you and Stephen plotting one of your schemes?"

"It's perfectly safe," I argued, negating my statement to the contrary moments before. Stephen and I had not yet made a plan, but Max's question helped me decide upon my next step. We needed to bring Noah out of hiding.

Before we ended the call, I talked to each of the boys, both of whom seemed to be having a great time with their dad, barely missing me. They each snuck in a pitch for the ski weekend. I finished up the call with Max, promising that we'd keep safe.

I only felt a tiny bit guilty when I returned to the living room and interrupted Tess and Stephen's conversation to formulate a plan that might, truth be told, involve a little more danger than I'd let Max believe.

"This is what we have to do…" I began.

Chapter 28

A good system shortens the road to the goal.
—**Orison Swett Marden**, founder of *Success Magazine*, 1848-1924

Monday, February 22, Evening (Presidents' Day holiday)

My strategy was simple. We needed to lure Noah into the open and expose him for the bad actor he was. But we needed to accomplish that goal without endangering anyone else. The balance would be tricky.

"Why not go straight to the police?" Stephen asked. "Quinn seems like a good cop."

"Amrita is the best weapon there is against Noah, and the person most likely to draw him out. Right now she thinks of herself as a victim. But we can alter that. We have to. She can become the agent of change, the warrior who restores the balance between good and evil."

"You sound like you're pitching a screenplay," Tess said.

I ignored her. "Help me flesh out my plan. Once it's solid, we can bring Quinn in on it. He'll notice any activity going on over here anyway. And Max won't worry as much if I tell him we included the authorities."

"Spill." Tess leaned forward with her elbows on her knees.

"Job one is to keep everyone safe from the storm and the bad guys. Let's invite everyone in the neighborhood here, tomorrow tonight. With everyone in one place, we'll use fewer batteries and candles than we would if we were each holed up in our own homes. And if we need protection, we'll all be easier to keep safe if we're all together."

"Or a bigger target." Tess pursed her lips. "But it could work."

Stephen cleared his throat. "Maggie's right. With everyone here, Quinn will be able to focus his resources in one place to keep everyone safe and nab Noah."

We firmed up the details and phoned Quinn, telling him what we had in mind.

I tapped the speaker button on my phone so everyone could hear. "I've got no problem with getting the neighbors together," Quinn said. "In fact, I've got a massive amount of shrimp I flew in to bring a little New Orleans flavor to the high country. It started to thaw when the power went out, and if I don't use it soon it will go bad."

"That'd be a crime," Stephen said.

Quinn snorted and said he'd bring the shrimp over in the morning and help pin down a few more of the details. In the meantime, I called Leslie to invite her and the kids to the shindig and ask if we could borrow Amrita the next day to assist us with setting up.

"She's on her way back from the grocery store, but I'm sure she'd love to," Leslie said. "But I'll send her over after breakfast tomorrow."

As we called it a night, the storm started again, later than expected and moving slowly. All indications were that it would dump more snow than anticipated, stalling directly over our heads. I was beginning to hate snow and the sound of the wind.

* * * *

The next morning, we were just finishing our coffee and getting ready to start the kitchen cleanup when Quinn arrived lugging a cooler full of shrimp. Stephen took it from him, and Quinn went back for the rest of the barbecue fixings which included pounds of butter and special Cajun seasonings.

Amrita texted "On my way!" and came right over.

"Spread newspaper all over the dining table," Quinn told her when she'd kicked off her boots and shrugged her way out of her coat. "You can help clean the shrimp."

To her credit, Amrita did as she was asked, without whining or launching into further questions. Unloading her secret concerns about Noah seemed to have already lightened her mood.

While we worked, we outlined the scheme for the neighborhood gathering. Amrita was excited and eager to help. We'd bring the neighbors together so we'd be sure everyone was safe. Amrita would arrange to meet Noah after midnight when everyone else would supposedly be asleep. No matter where Noah suggested they go, Amrita would insist he pick her up at Tess's, where they could get together in the garage and then figure out where to go from there.

It wasn't a plan that would have worked for capturing a sensible adult, but we were confident Noah's interest in Amrita would override any suspicions he might have about the meeting place or other arrangements. He'd been trying to lure her to the shed, so meeting in the garage wasn't too much of departure from someplace he'd suggest on his own.

But when we launched into the details for phase two, the part that hinged on Amrita's participation, she wasn't immediately on board. Quinn backed her up. "Unless Amrita is completely confident, I'll shut down this escapade. We'll just have a great party while the storm rages. Nothing like some Louisiana Zydeco tunes to keep everyone on their feet and toasty warm on a cold night."

"Noah has it coming to him," Amrita said, cleaning shrimp and placing them in flat pans. "I just don't want anyone around here knowing how stupid I was, believing that he cared for me."

"You're not a victim," I told Amrita. "And tonight we're going to prove it."

Amrita nodded, but she wasn't convinced. She looked at Quinn. "Do people need to know I thought that creep was my friend?"

Quinn rubbed his chin. "How 'bout we make sure all the key players are on the same page? Everyone else will know eventually. It's a small town. But by the time the whole story gets out, we can focus on how you helped us shut down a crime ring. You'll be the warrior hero. Deal?"

"Deal," said Amrita. She still appeared twitchy and anxious, but she was all in.

"We'll wire you up," Quinn said. "Listen in and keep you safe."

I shook my head. "I don't want to embarrass anyone, but Noah has been pressuring Amrita for sex. What are the chances that Noah would find a wire?"

Amrita's face flushed. "Dead certain."

"We'll go old school," said Tess, disappearing down the hall toward the back bedrooms. A few moments later she returned, holding aloft something that looked like a big white plastic radio. "Baby monitor." She sidled up next to me and nudged me in the ribs. "Sometimes clutter can be a good thing."

I rolled my eyes. "I'm never going to be able to convince you to toss anything after this."

* * * *

We spent the rest of the day prepping for the party, inviting Tess's local friends to a shrimp feed and sleepover to wait out the storm. Amrita, Stephen, and Quinn rehearsed the teen's confrontation with Noah.

During a brief evening lull in the storm, the guests started to arrive, carrying an odd assortment of sleeping bags, board games, and contributions for the feast.

Siobhan brought desserts and improved the efficiency of the food service operation we'd cobbled together. She roped the Zimmers into transporting some of her catering tables and chairs to augment the seating. Tess's cupboards held the variety of dinnerware any family-owned vacation cabin accumulates after several generations. Ryan busied himself carrying armloads of wood to stoke the fire, but body heat and the propane oven warmed the room quickly and kept it toasty.

Elisabeth brought Duke, who commanded attention with his constant yapping. Tess suggested we put all the dogs together in the game room downstairs, push back the living room furniture, and dance. Quinn hooked his Louisiana play list to the speakers and my anxiety fled. After hours of supervising the party preparations, the dogs put up only a halfhearted resistance to being banished to the ground floor.

I escorted the animals downstairs, filled water bowls, and turned up the heat. Munchkin claimed one of the beds while Mozart and Winston settled on opposite ends of the sofa. Belle turned her woeful brown eyes my way and tilted her head.

"I'm onto your Jedi golden retriever tricks," I told her. "Be good. Keep your friends company." I still felt a little bit guilty as I closed the door. Duke put up a few token yaps but calmed quickly.

I returned to the living-room-turned-dance-hall where enthusiasm and energy outpaced style and coordination. Harry and Naomi entertained everyone with frenetic and inventive dance moves that were difficult for anyone else to duplicate.

By eleven o'clock, Elisabeth was clearly fading. "I'm headed downstairs," she told me. "I'm going to see if I can interest the kids in checking on the dogs and keeping them company."

Our plan had included the extra safety measure of keeping the children and the dogs as far away from Noah as possible. Elisabeth would take them all into the bunk room. With any luck, they'd sleep through whatever happened.

"Do we have to go to bed?" Naomi whined as Harry rubbed his eyes.

"Absolutely not," Leslie answered. "But you have to be quiet so the dogs can sleep."

Naomi and Harry consulted each other.

Naomi was silently appointed chief negotiator. "And we can sleep in our own sleeping bags?" she asked.

"Of course," Elisabeth said.

"Did you bring yours?"

I knew that Elisabeth had planned to curl up in the bed she'd slept in during her earlier visit, and would have preferred the comfort of real sheets and a down comforter, but she took one for the team. "I'm hoping Tess has one I can borrow."

"In the cupboard under the stairs," Tess said. "There's a purple one that would be perfect for you. But take whatever you find. They're all clean."

Loud conspiratorial whispers and giggles accompanied Elisabeth and the children down the stairs and provided narration for the selection of a sleeping bag fit for a queen.

Everyone who remained upstairs seemed to know how we hoped the rest of the night would unfold. Among friends Amrita had lost her shyness and found her courage. As the dancing wound down, everyone pitched in to restore order, allowing Tess to advise them on the proper location for the sofas. Siobhan directed the kitchen detail.

Ryan set up a board game on the coffee table and walked the gang through the many convoluted rules. Amrita, Quinn, Stephen, and I sat on the stairs, reviewing the details of the plan one last time.

"Everyone up here is going to be as quiet as possible," I said. "Since Noah thinks you're sneaking out to see him while everyone is asleep."

"I warned him to be super quiet. I said that if Leslie finds us she'll be furious."

Quinn fiddled with the baby monitors. He'd agreed to use them for back up, but Paolo had brought over more high-tech police-issue microphones and recording devices, set them up, and tested them. He and Quinn would listen in on headsets.

"I'll need to get Noah to tell me who he works for and what happened to Dev." Amrita checked her watch. "I better get down to the garage. It's almost midnight."

I hugged her and kissed the top of her head. "We've got your back. If you're in trouble, just say *ice dancing*." We'd struggled to create a code word that Amrita wouldn't use in ordinary conversation with Noah, but that she could utter reasonably if she needed to alert us to a problem.

Stephen clapped her on the back. "You've got this," he told her. "Try to keep him near the door to the house."

"I'll take him a plate of food and put it on top of the counter next to the door," Amrita said. "But why do you want us there, exactly?"

"Tactical concerns," Stephen said, which didn't really answer the question.

A muffled woof from Munchkin and a light tapping at the front door told us Noah had arrived. It was 12:15 a.m. "Unusually prompt," Amrita muttered as she tiptoed down the stairs.

The rest of us surrounded the baby monitor, which had earned pride of place in the center of the dining table. Stephen switched it on as we heard the connecting door to the garage open and then *snick* shut.

Chapter 29

A man's brain originally is like a little empty attic...the skillful workman is very careful indeed as to what he takes into his brain-attic. He will have nothing but the tools which may help him in doing his work...all in the most perfect order.

—Sherlock Holmes, *A Study in Scarlet*
Sir Arthur Conan Doyle, British writer. 1859-1930

Wednesday, February 24, Just after midnight

I shuddered as Noah's oily voice filled the room. "It's cold, babe. Let me warm you up."

"You're late." Amrita spoke with a tiny quaver in her voice that could have been the fault of bad reception.

"If you ran away with me, we wouldn't have to worry about meeting up like this." Noah's voice rose and fell in volume. Either the monitor was faulty or he was exploring the garage. I clenched my fists, hoping he wouldn't spot the listening devices. Tess grabbed my hand and held on tight.

"I told you, I can't leave," Amrita said. "I have responsibilities here. Leslie needs me."

"I can get rid of Leslie. No problem," Noah said.

"What? No. What are you talking about?"

Noah mumbled something and we heard the sound of rustling clothing.

"What does that even mean? 'Get rid of Leslie?'" Amrita's voice rose. "Is that what you did to Dev? Are you the reason my brother is dead?" She choked back a sob.

"No. Course not. I saw him that night though."

"What night? How are you mixed up in all this?"

"The night he disappeared. I saw him at the mailbox walking that dog—Winston, the slobbering poop machine."

"You never said. Do the police know?"

"Why would I be talking to them?"

"To help them find my brother."

"Too late for that."

I marveled at how well Amrita seemed to be doing—holding on to her temper and keeping Noah talking.

"Did you kill him? Do you know what happened?"

"I didn't kill no one. Saw him at the mailbox, like I said. Dev told me to stay away from you. Like that was going to happen." An ugly slurpy kissing sound followed, with more rustling. "Come on, babe. Do you need all these layers?" Noah's voice dripped with frustration and anger.

"It's freezing." Amrita brought the conversation back to the night Dev had disappeared. "Did you argue?"

"He took a swing at me." I imagined Noah pantomiming a fistfight. "I fought back."

The quaver in Amrita's voice grew more audible. "And then?"

"Dev blocked my punch and slipped on the ice. Banged his head on the back of my truck."

"And?" Amrita prompted.

Noah's voice increased in speed and volume. "He was out cold. Blood all over the snow. I thought I'd killed him. I panicked. Jumped back in the truck. Tried to drive off, but I threw the stupid thing in reverse and backed over Dev's legs. Lucky he was knocked out."

"Lucky." said Amrita, her voice low and cold. "Did you call for help?"

"Course I did. Called my boss."

"Who's he?"

"You don't need to know that. I told you. You don't need to know anything about my job. That's a separate part of my life."

"Were you scared?"

"Nah. But the snowplow was coming. I could hear it at the bottom of the hill. I needed to bounce."

"The big plow or the little ones that clear driveways?"

"The big one. That dude Ryan was driving. Good thing. He's zoned out half the time."

Amrita said something we couldn't quite hear. A lull in the conversation and a rustling of clothing followed. I released Tess's hand and pulled my sweater more tightly around me, forcing myself to sit still and keep from flying downstairs and bursting in on the young couple. Amrita was doing fine. I needed to trust her.

"But how did Dev end up in the snowdrift?" Amrita asked. "We searched for days."

"I wrestled Dev into the truck. Kicked fresh snow over the blood. Didn't cover it all, but I made it less obvious. Like I said, Ryan doesn't notice details. And the storm that night must have covered it quick."

"Ryan said he didn't see any cars that night."

Noah laughed. "Parked in the driveway of that empty house next door. Figured if Ryan gave it any thought, he'd figure me for a guest or a renter."

Ryan buried his head in his hands but didn't speak. It would be hard to mistake Noah's old truck for one of the upscale late-model cars the weekenders usually drove. But it had been dark, and Ryan's job was to keep the roads clear of snowfall, not entertain suspicions about every vehicle in every driveway. I couldn't fault him.

"I was afraid the plow would block me in but I got out okay. It's not like I needed to protect the paint job on my truck, so I just rammed it through."

"Did you take Dev to the hospital? Was he still unconscious?"

Noah sputtered, as though it had never occurred to him to take an injured man to the hospital. "Called my boss in Incline. Like I said." A hint of annoyance tinged his speech. I wasn't sure how much more time Amrita had. But she didn't utter the code word. She plunged on. "You drove over there in a blizzard?"

"My boss said to leave it with him. That's exactly what he said. Word for word. *Leave it with me.* Or maybe it was leave it to me."

"What did he mean?"

"You know, that he'd take care of it."

Amrita scoffed. "You idiot. Everyone knows that 'leave it to me' means something bad is going to happen."

My mouth was dry and I had trouble swallowing. Amrita pressed on. "Never mind, babe, I'm sorry. What happened next?"

"I left the truck in the clearing at Big Boss's compound with Dev in it."

"Does Big Boss have a name?"

"BB or just Big Boss. I never heard a name. What you wanna know that for?" Noah sounded suspicious.

Amrita distracted him. "All that time Dev was missing and I was so worried, you knew where he was? You knew BB had him?"

"I thought everything was fine. BB said he'd take care of it. He says something like that, it's gonna happen."

Amrita was silent. My muscles strained as I fought the urge to fly to her aid. I used every ounce of self-control to stay glued to my seat and to the baby monitor.

"I didn't think about it," Noah said. "I couch surfed at BB's for a day or so and then drove one of his trucks back here." If Amrita hadn't already been disgusted with Noah, that statement alone would have done the trick. If he had a brain, he hadn't engaged it. If he had a heart…well, I was pretty sure he didn't."

"But you got the truck back," Amrita prompted.

"Like weeks later. One of BB's guys asked me when I was gonna move the truck with the body."

"They just left Dev alone in the car all that time?"

"Exactly. That's what I said. Like, what body?"

"And then?"

"He's all like 'Your old junker is taking up space. Bringin' down the neighborhood. It's cold, but that dude still stinks to high heaven.'"

Amrita gasped. Upstairs, hearing it on the baby monitor, so did Leslie.

My heart broke for Dev and his family. I chewed my knuckles, ready to shove my fist in my face to keep the slightest sound from escaping.

"I was shocked too," Noah said. "What a wasted opportunity. No ransom? No blackmail? No medical care? BB said he was going to take care of it."

"What did BB's guy say?"

"The jerk laughed at me. Said they weren't running a spa." He mimicked a gruff voice. "We told you to leave the truck here, like overnight, not dump it on us for weeks. You know BB. He expects you to clean up your own messes."

"So you drove back to Incline to pick Dev up?"

"What else could I do? I drove BB's truck back, dropped it off, and got my pickup. It was hard to start 'cause it'd been sitting there so long. But I don't know why they were complaining about the smell. It's been so cold everything was frozen." Noah seemed to have lost sight of the fact that the body he'd found so inconvenient was Amrita's beloved brother. I probably would have decked the kid at that point, but Amrita held herself together.

Stephen's thoughts must have been similar to mine. He clasped his hands and pushed them to his lips, as if fighting to control his fists and his rage.

"…took the body and left it in the snowdrift. With all the snow from a three-day blizzard, it buried itself pretty quick."

Amrita let out a soft sob. "I can't believe this. You killed him. You tossed him by the side of the road like rubbish. And you lied to me."

I bolted down the stairs, unable to wait any longer.

"Maggie, wait," Stephen called out behind me. I ignored him.

I grabbed the first heavy jacket I found, not knowing or caring who it belonged to. I shoved my stocking feet into a pair of enormous insulated boots that nearly tripped me up as I dashed out the door. I made no effort to conceal the noise.

Outside, I scanned the area, looking for something, anything I could use to defend Amrita. Later, I wondered why I'd jumped to the immediate conclusion that Amrita was in physical danger. The best answer I came up with was that there had been something horribly alarming about Noah's voice. I didn't know for certain that he had a weapon, but I was convinced he would hurt her.

Noah's truck was parked illegally in the road out front where it would block any snow removal activity. It was locked, but the window was open. I jumped in and hunted behind the visor for the keys, hoping that Noah adhered to the same old country custom Quinn did. My hands closed over a small key ring. I prayed the truck would start, though I still hadn't formulated a complete scheme for Amrita's rescue. I also had no way of knowing what, exactly was going on in the garage. But I trusted my gut. I had to stop whatever was happening between Noah and Amrita before it turned deadly.

I glanced at the ring, which held three keys. I selected the most likely one and inserted it in the ignition. I held my breath and turned it, pressing gently on the gas. "Please work," I whispered. "Please, if you've got any life left in you, now's the time to show it. Be a hero."

After a tiny cough and a moment's hesitation, the pickup roared to a start, spewing a cloud of blue smoke.

I backed up, shifted into drive, and floored the accelerator.

I closed my eyes and braced my body.

The element of surprise was my only advantage.

I crashed through the mended garage door and slammed my foot on the brake. The tires squealed on the garage floor. The truck lurched to a stop. It was still rocking when I opened my eyes. The bumper was inches from Noah. His left arm held Amrita in a rough approximation of a choke hold. In his right was an enormous fishing knife that was way too close to Amrita's throat.

Before I could open the driver's door, Rocket burst into the garage from somewhere behind me. With some quick ninja-like moves, he freed Amrita, disarmed Noah, and dropped him to the floor. Quinn and Stephen barreled through the connecting door to the house. Rocket transferred custody to

Quinn, who subdued Noah with a death grip to his shoulder. Judging by Noah's grimace, the chief wasn't overly gentle.

I grabbed Amrita and held her tight, backing away from Noah. She sobbed into my shoulder.

I froze, my eyes scanning the room as if daring anyone to move. If I'd expected Noah to be ashamed, guilty, sorrowful, or angry at his capture, the failure of his plan to seduce Amrita, or his role in Dev's death, I'd guessed wrong. If anything, he looked jubilant. A satisfied grin split his face. He held up his cell phone.

"Too late," he said. "I've got Armageddon on speed dial. You're all toast." He held the phone close to his face. "Siri, Judgment Day."

Chapter 30

Do other people, I wonder, find the same keen pleasure that I do in periodically undertaking a pilgrimage all over the house to wage a war of extermination upon its accumulations of rubbish?
—**Chiffon**, *To-Day*, London weekly magazine. 1898

Wednesday, February 24, Very early morning

With no time to take cover, I tensed every muscle in my body, awaiting a blast. But nothing happened.

Noah repeated the instruction. "Siri, Judgment Day!"

Siri didn't respond.

Rocket reached into the front seat of Tess's Land Rover and pulled out a spaghetti-like tangle of wires connected to what looked like dangling soup cans. He held them up in a gesture that echoed Noah's posture with his phone. "Looking for these?" Rocket asked. "Siri can't reach them anymore. I took the liberty of removing them from your truck and disabling them all. Not sure they would have worked anyway. Can't trust the Internet, kid. You want to learn to make bombs, join the service and defuse 'em for a living."

I took a deep breath.

It was over.

* * * *

My original scheme had been to have everyone 'sleep over' and wait out the storm. It had been a fake plan, but in the end, that's exactly what we did. Late night adventures require rehashing and we compared our versions of the story into the wee hours.

Before Noah was taken away in handcuffs, Amrita asked him if he'd bombed Elisabeth's house.

"I needed to test my bombs," he said, as if it were a logical explanation for employing deadly explosives. "Besides, she was always spying on us out her windows. It was creepy."

It's hard to fathom the mind of a psychopath, and harder still to shake off the feeling of terror and filth his actions had left behind. But we all worked together to mend the damage, one step at a time.

The children had slept through the excitement, which meant they'd stayed safe. It also meant they were up and raring to go shortly after dawn while the rest of us were still bleary-eyed. Our guests downed quick gulps of coffee, gathered up their belongings, and set out into lingering snow flurries to prepare for the onslaught of tourists at the end of the week.

I'd nearly fallen asleep at the table when my phone rang. It was Max. I assured him we were all safe, recounted the capture of Noah, and supported my husband's decision to pick up the kids immediately after school on Friday and head to Tahoe to beat the heavy weekend 'get away' traffic from the Bay Area. We both predicted at least four hours of travel time, plus whatever stops they needed to make for food, gas, and bathrooms. I pegged their arrival time at seven o'clock or eight.

I ended the call. Paolo came upstairs from the garage, where he'd volunteered as an adjunct to Quinn's crime scene team. "Tow truck's here," he said, pouring himself a second or third mug of black coffee. "They're taking Noah's truck to the state police impound yard for further testing. We've got what's probably Dev's blood all over the passenger seat."

I shoved away my plate of toast.

"They want to know if Tess wants a tow for her Land Rover. Those tires are shot."

"We'll drop the Rover off when we pick up my car later today. After the storm, the tow guys will be busy pulling cars out of the ditches on the interstate."

"Just make sure Tess's car doesn't end up off the road or in the Truckee River."

I gave him a thumbs up. Paolo had a reputation for being unemotional and reserved. Now that I knew him better, his friendship and caring came through in his statements more than they did in gestures or the empty platitudes most of us use to solidify our relationships. While he had a reputation for being socially awkward, there was something endearingly, undeniably, and refreshingly authentic about the way he expressed his feelings.

"We found a large stash of date rape drugs in a concealed compartment in Noah's truck, and more materials to make bombs," Paolo said.

"Was he going to use the drugs on Amrita?" I asked. "Was he supplying all the slimy low-life rapists in the county or was he trafficking women for BB?"

Paolo's eyebrows shot up. "Did Quinn get Noah to admit to any of that? It wasn't in the transcript."

I shook my head. "No, sorry." I tapped my fingers on the table, thinking. "I made a leap. Drugs and BB the crime lord plus slimy Noah added to a known trafficking problem in the area and Amrita's experience at the bar equals Noah supplying young transients for BB's schemes."

"Quinn's made the same connections, along with the state troopers and the FBI," Paolo said. "They've been trying to identify BB for years, but only managed to nab the lowest tier of his worker bees. With information provided by Noah, the FBI was able to get a warrant to raid BB's house near Incline. They have enough evidence now to put him in prison."

Paolo zipped and unzipped his fleece jacket. "Federal, state, and local authorities are all hoping to turn several of the underlings—Noah plus some other low-level guys they picked up last night. Together, they should provide enough evidence to shutter his operation and take him to court."

"Can the Feds keep Noah and the others safe if they turn on BB?" I asked.

"I think you watch too many cop shows," Paolo said.

"Fair point. More coffee?"

He shook his head and put his heavier jacket on over his fleece.

"Max and the kids will be here for dinner on Friday," I said. "Are you staying through the weekend? Would you and Peggy like to join us? We'd love to have you, but I hate to intrude on your vacation." I was tempted to waggle my eyebrows, but I refrained. Their relationship was new and teasing wasn't appropriate.

He hesitated to answer, so I helped him out. "Talk it over with Peg and let me know. Or just show up. We'll have plenty of food."

"Chili?" he asked.

I laughed. "You know me too well." Chili, crusty sourdough bread, an assortment of condiments, and a fresh green salad comprised my go-to meal for large crowds.

"My favorite," he assured me. "I'm off to the police station to see what more I can do for Quinn. Need anything in town?"

I shook my head. "We'll get it when we drop off Tess's truck." Paolo tapped the corner of the table and headed downstairs.

I heard him talking to Tess outside where, with the "help" of Munchkin, Belle, and Mozart, she was shoveling the berm of snow pushed up against the garage door by the snowplows so we could get her Rover out.

Minutes later, I heard the dogs bound up the stairs while Tess stomped her feet on the doormat. She arrived upstairs still unzipping her coat, but left it on while she grabbed a mug and poured the last of the coffee.

"Ready to go?" she asked.

We loaded up the Rover with our entourage—hundreds of pounds of wriggling dogs.

Tess backed her aging vehicle out of the garage. Snow crunched under the bald tires. "Take it easy," I said. "The tires."

"Did Paolo tell you what Noah said?" Tess asked, driving slowly and braking early. "We have to remember to tell Amrita."

"I'm hoping she never has to give another thought to what that slimy jerk thinks or says."

"No, but this is good. Down at the station, in an official interview, Noah told Quinn that knowing Amrita made him realize that the people BB was preying on weren't 'low-life foreigners, barely human.'" Her hands never left the wheel but she used her pointer fingers to make air quotes. "Amrita showed him they were real people with plans for the future and families who would miss them. According to Noah, he's been trying to get out of the gang ever since."

"Was he saying that to earn points with the district attorney?" I asked. "It seems to me that if he'd truly been trying to get out, he'd have severed ties by now."

"I hear you. But he's not the sharpest ski on the slope. Maybe we should give him a break."

I thought for a moment, then shook my head. "Nah. It's not like he got rid of the drugs."

"Or stopped stalking Amrita," Tess said.

"I talked to her before she left this morning. She seemed stronger and noted that if Noah had done the right thing at any point after Dev fell on the icy street, her brother would still be alive. Noah could have phoned her, the ski patrol, Alison, 911, or Quinn. Or even the anonymous crime tip hotline. If he'd just shouted for help, Elisabeth would have come running. And no one would have blamed him for anything."

"He panicked," Tess said.

"That's no excuse. Dev didn't die right away. Noah could have told anyone over the course of the next day or two. And changed the outcome completely."

"But he was all about saving himself, instead of doing the right thing," Tess said.

"The irony of it—the tragedy—is that doing the right thing should have been its own reward. Dev would be alive. BB would be taken down. Noah would have been safe and in no trouble." I shook my head.

"And, if he hadn't broken Dev's legs, but instead called for help, Amrita would probably have adored Noah for saving her brother." Tess said.

"Instead, she despises him more than ever for his cowardice and neglect."

We drove in morose silence through the snow-covered landscape until Tess flicked her turn signal and made a left into the parking lot at Koko's. She turned into a marked spot, applied the brake, and skidded perilously close to a very expensive black sports car. I gasped, grabbed the dashboard, and let out a sigh of relief. Tess glanced at me, then at the black car and shrugged. "It's a summer car. Only an idiot drives one of those in a blizzard. Twenty bucks says it's here 'cause it's got a broken axle."

We shuffled carefully across the icy parking lot toward the door. Bells jangled as we pushed it open and walked inside. Koko wiped his hands on a rag and joined us at the counter. Tess pointed over her shoulder. "The black racer car. Totaled?"

"Yup." Koko answered. "He'll live to tell the tale, but his car bit the dust."

"Expensive lesson. Anyone else hurt?"

"Could have been worse. We'll pull more off the road today."

While their words sounded cold, Koko's tone and Tess's expression told me they had more sympathy for the stranger's plight than their words implied.

Koko was busy. He pulled my keys from a rack behind him, and placed them on top of an invoice he shoved in my direction. I tried not to gasp, but I failed.

"Sorry," Koko said. "Your insurance will cover most of it."

Embarrassed, I explained the source of my shock. "In the Bay Area, the same work would have cost two or three times that much."

"Less overhead up here," Koko said, neither impressed nor particularly interested. We wrapped up payment and paperwork. Koko confirmed that the tires Tess wanted were in stock and her car would be ready in an hour or two.

"But you're so busy." Tess turned to look at the rest of the noisy shop, where every bay held a car on a lift with at least one mechanic catering to its needs.

Koko pointed to a raised lift in the last bay. "That Jeep on the end is almost finished. Tires go fast. I'll take care of them myself while the guys are at lunch. No problem. You'll be doing me a favor if you can pick it up right away. I'll need the space this weekend."

Tess nodded. It seemed that everyone in the Tahoe Basin was focused on getting as much routine work out of the way as they could before the influx of skiers this weekend. My friend had been right. This world marched to a different rhythm—music a Flatlander like me might never understand.

We took my car to the resort for lunch at Flour Power.

* * * *

We plopped our trays at the table that I now considered "ours" in the cavernous fireplace hall. An army of uniformed workers polished floors and glass, cleaned bathrooms, and emptied garbage and recycling bins. Tess opened her mouth to explain, but I beat her to it. "Getting ready for the weekend."

Ryan joined us. "Your garage door is almost finished," he told Tess, pulling a tiny brown paper bag out of his parka pocket. "I just picked up a couple of extra screws I needed. Take your time here. Give me a head start when you leave, and I'll have it all wrapped up before you get home."

"Thanks," Tess said. "That poor garage door. The whole house has taken such a beating over the last few days. If your grandfather hadn't framed it so well when he built it, our cabin would probably be in ruins. I'll be glad to have it patched up. We can handle the rest of the repairs come spring."

Ryan clarified. "I took down all the protective plywood and put up a new garage door."

Tess sputtered. "But how? When? I didn't hire you. How much?"

"It's a door the empty-house people ordered. It wasn't fancy enough for them but it matches all the other doors in the neighborhood and the second bay in your garage. The color is a little off, but if it hasn't faded a bit by spring, we'll paint them both to match in May."

"How much do I owe you?"

Again, Ryan shook his head. "You saved me the trouble and cost of returning the door. The neighbors kicked in to buy it off me. My labor's on the house."

"That's not right," said Tess, pulling out her checkbook. "Let me…"

Ryan flapped his hand. "It's exactly right. It's what neighbors do. Put it away."

Tess made a show of begrudgingly returning her checkbook to its special pocket in her black leather backpack. But she was touched. She reached her hand out to grasp Ryan's arm and nodded, accepting the kindness. "Come to dinner Friday night. Teddy will be up for the weekend, along with Maggie's family. We're having chili."

Gathering up the remains of her meal, she reminded me to buy lift tickets for Max and the boys. "With my season pass, we can get them ahead of time for nearly half what it will cost the folks who have to stand in line over the weekend."

"Count me in for dinner," Ryan said. "And be sure to take your time getting back. Give me a chance to finish up the door. If you've got your remote, you can pull right into the garage and test out my work when you get home. I'll be working to get the lights at the mailboxes back on after that, so give me a shout if anything else comes up."

"Did you figure out why they haven't been working?" I asked.

Ryan looked disgusted. "That little creep, Noah. He told Quinn he'd overheard Elisabeth complaining that rats were chewing the wires. He decided that if it annoyed her, he'd "help" them go off more often. He's admitted to cutting the wires on a regular basis, just for kicks."

We shook our heads, said our goodbyes, and ran our errands. I dropped Tess at Koko's and drove back to the cabin thankful that she'd be driving the Rover home on new tires. The plows had been hard at work on the accumulated snow and ice, but the hill to Tess's was still so slick that I had to back down and try again after skidding the first time. I stopped a moment to hope for safe roads for Max and the boys.

While I waited for Tess to arrive with the remote to open the garage doors so we could both park inside, I turned on the radio. Local news outlets provided more details on the FBI raid on BB's headquarters near Incline Village. Without naming the crimes or criminals, reporters described it as a "joint operation with federal, state, and local law enforcement." Noting that the skirmish occurred on a remote private property adjacent to the fabled Ponderosa Ranch that provided location shots for the television series *Bonanza*, the chirpy newscaster dubbed it "a shoot-out worthy of the Wild West."

The segment included a brief interview with Quinn, thanking locals who'd heeded his team's advice to shelter in place, making it possible for them to pick up the suspects with only minor injuries. "Two of the suspects are in good condition and under guard at the Carson Tahoe Regional Medical Center. A federal law enforcement officer was treated and released."

Chapter 31

Show me a man's tool-box, his bench, or his desk, and I will tell you what manner of man he is. Orderliness and cleanliness are two important factors in efficiency. A disordered desk is an evidence of a disordered brain.
—Editorial in The *Mediator*, a Cleveland, Ohio monthly journal. 1911.

Friday, February 26, Evening

While our chili dinner had evolved of its own accord, it was clear that we should have deliberately planned to get everyone together, even so soon after our shrimp feast-sting operation.

Max, David, Brian, and Teddy arrived on time. Teddy introduced my guys to the neighbors he'd known his entire life. He and my boys rounded up Harry and Naomi and entertained them and the dogs in the game room downstairs.

Paolo and Peggy joined us and were happy to retell the story of how they met. Peggy kept her coat on with her hands in her pockets, saying she'd gotten a chill she couldn't shake. But after they told their "meet cute" tale, she pulled her hand from her pocket and showed off her engagement ring. Paolo had proposed in the middle of the storm, as soon as he returned from helping FBI and state officials capture BB and his cohorts.

"Newscasters overplayed the 'Wild West' angle a bit in their reports," Paolo told us. "But they weren't far off. There's nothing like being shot at to make you focus on who you'd rather be with."

Peggy laughed and kissed his cheek. "So being with me is better than being shot at during a blizzard?" she said. "That's a low bar. You sure you don't want your ring back?"

"Never." He hugged her and held on tight, but looked more secure and happy than I'd ever seen him. For a man who kept his feelings close to the vest, he openly telegraphed his love for Peggy. The message was loud, clear, and beautiful.

"We just need to figure out housing," Peggy said. "We can pretty much bunk down anywhere, but we need to find an apartment that has room for both Paolo and my dogs." She explained that she had two Labradors, chocolate and vanilla. And often brought her work home in the form of small animals that needed overnight intensive care.

Alison Romo, the doc who'd stitched me up, told Peggy she envied her ability to bring her patients home at night. "I have to stay with mine or leave them at the hospital with someone else and spend a restless night worrying. Bringing them home has a certain appeal."

Paolo shook his head. "Orphaned cougar cubs are high maintenance. It's tough to explain the growling to the neighbors."

"But doesn't everyone melt when they see them?" I asked. "They're just big kittens, aren't they?"

"With a purr about twenty times louder. And those needle sharp kitten claws? Imagine them cougar-sized." Pride in his future wife's work rolled off Paolo, who scanned the faces of the rest of the guests to make sure they were suitably impressed.

"Okay, okay," Alison said, holding up her hands in surrender. "Peggy wins. Patients who stay at our clinic are usually too miserable to complain."

"Where will you live?" I asked the young couple. "A house?" I rubbed my itchy stitches. Alison noticed. "Time to get those out," she said, pulling the tools she needed from her well-organized backpack. I continued to focus on Paolo and Peg to distract me from the tugging, but Alison had a deft hand and removed them with little fuss.

Paolo frowned. "We're not sure. You know the Silicon Valley housing market. I think we're destined to make the two-hour commute from the Central Valley. Tracy or Stockton."

I glanced at Max, who nodded. "We might have the perfect place for you and your adopted creatures to live" I said. "We'd love to show it to you when we all get back to the Bay Area."

"Your barn apartment?" Paolo asked. I nodded agreement. Paolo beamed at Peggy. "That could work," he said. "You could probably walk to work across the meadow faster than it would take to drive."

I explained to the still baffled Peggy. "We live adjacent to the Rancho San Antonio land where you work."

Peggy's shoulders relaxed, but she still seemed confused, or wary, about meshing their life as newlyweds with the world of a busy family. I touched her arm and lowered my voice to a conspiratorial whisper. "No pressure. But say you'll at least come and take a look."

"It sounds perfect," Peggy said. "You really wouldn't mind the occasional small mammal guest?"

"I draw the line at skunks or anything too ferocious," I said. "And snakes. No snakes."

"We could rent or sell my condo," Peggy said quietly to Paolo, thinking aloud.

"Tess is a Realtor. She could help you with that," I said.

Tess's eyes grew wide and she leaped up from the table, spilling her wine. "Teddy! I forgot to tell Teddy about the house."

"What's that now?" Teddy said as the teens reached the landing at the top of the stairs. But any answer Tess gave was lost in hilarity. The boys and their young charges, Harry and Naomi, were decked out in the vintage ski gear with a heavy emphasis on the neon outfits popular in the late '80s and early '90s.

"A fashion show," Naomi announced, twirling, so that the tassel on her chartreuse stocking cap circled around her.

The children pranced across the room, each with their own personal interpretation of a supermodel's stride on the catwalk. The show ended when Stephen announced that dinner was ready.

At the table, talk was all over the map, with the teens focused on what we expected to be the next day's stellar ski conditions and the locals strategizing ways to handle the corresponding influx of visitors.

Next to me, Teddy leaned over to talk to his mom. "What's this about the house?"

Tess put her arm around him. "What would you say if I told you we're not selling?"

He beamed and hugged her but then drew back. "This doesn't mean that we have to give up on college or your career plans, does it?"

Tess shook her head. "Not a bit. If we sell or rent your dad's old condo, we'll be able to swing it."

"That could be another option for Peggy and Paolo," I said. "Moving into Patrick's old condo."

"I'm not sure how the high-tech crowd would feel about mountain lions for neighbors," Teddy said. "But I'm glad we're keeping this place. I feel close to Dad here. Good memories."

"Why didn't you tell me?" Tess said.

"I was just figuring it out," Teddy said. "At first, thinking about this place was just too painful. I was going to ask you last week if we could hold off on a decision, but with the storm delay, this was the first chance I've had to mention it. In person, at least. It wasn't something I wanted to talk about over the phone."

Tess grabbed her son in a bear hug. Teddy grabbed her wine glass before it took a header. "Your dad would be pleased, I think," she said.

I turned away from the tiny family to give them a little privacy and moved toward a conversation between Quinn and Max. Though they'd just met, they seemed like old friends. "BB is going down," Quinn said. "Especially with Noah's testimony. He gave us the missing pieces of the puzzle...connected the dots...and completed the picture we were forming of this human trafficking operation."

"Is that a thing?" I asked, laughing. "Puzzle pieces and dots?"

"If we get a conviction and shut down that monster, you can call it whatever you want," Quinn said, raising his beer in my direction. "Noah knew more than he thought he did. That, combined with evidence unearthed by the forensic accountants, should keep BB in prison for life."

I reviewed the status of the rest of the people in the immediate neighborhood, some of whom had been suspects. Ryan was definitely off the hook for any involvement in Dev's death, though he still felt sorry he'd not spotted Noah hiding in plain sight in the empty house's driveway.

Sam Stillwell was still, well, a lazy jerk. And I wasn't sure I'd forgiven him for implying that Jens was losing it. But maybe the suggestion that Stillwell had made with malice had given Klaus and Han the extra ammunition they needed to convince the family patriarch to slow down. Their business still needed Jens's wisdom and expertise, but three days a week Klaus and Han would try to muddle through on their own. After all, Jens was never more than a phone call away.

Most of the forensic evidence related to the case came back quickly, especially the blood evidence. We were all relieved to hear that the blood found behind the maintenance shed was definitely not human. It turned out to be a mixture of animal blood, prey and predator, providing evidence of a violence typical of Mother Nature but a necessary element in the circle of life.

I resolved two lingering questions by asking the parties involved, flat out.

The first was easily resolved to my immediate satisfaction. "Leslie, we found a receipt at Siobhan's for a wedding cake you ordered," I said. "Why on earth would you order a wedding cake right now?"

Leslie laughed. "I can't imagine what you must have thought with all these mysteries flying around. But it was for an event Walter Raleigh was holding, promoting one of his restaurants as a wedding venue."

I blushed, which made Leslie laugh harder. "Nope, this widowed mom of two preschoolers pregnant with her third child does not, in fact, have time for shady affairs or secret elopements. But I guess a wedding cake really does have one specific purpose most of the time." She hugged me. "I forgive you, dear Maggie, for thinking my life is so much more interesting than it actually is."

The second question was left unresolved. Early on, Tess had told me that Dev wasn't the first husband to go missing from the neighborhood. Years ago, Elisabeth's husband Fred Roche had apparently walked out on his wife, and hadn't been seen since. Rather than speculate, I asked Elisabeth if she knew what had happened to her husband or what he was doing now. "Don't know. Don't care," was her entirely unsatisfying answer.

Max glanced at Teddy and Tess, still conspiring to plan their future. "Sounds like their plans are intact, even without the sale of this place," he said. "What about you, Mags? Any chance you'll be rethinking *your* career?"

I tilted my head, uncertain what he meant. I'd not said anything to him about closing my business. My former colleagues from Stockton had expressed some interest in buying me out, but I hadn't been that interested and hadn't mentioned it to Max.

"I'm a little leery of letting you out of my sight," he said softly. "Do all professional organizers spend the bulk of their time stumbling over dead bodies? Who knew that decluttering could be so deadly?"

Max was joking, but there was a hint of earnestness in his voice that told me we'd need to talk later. For now, I smiled and kept my answer light. "Point taken," I replied. "Simplicity Itself… my organizing business…" I added the extended description for the benefit of Tess's neighbors, "has been anything but simple."

As we were all anticipating an early start the following morning, the party wrapped up following another round of Siobhan's rich desserts supplemented with iced gingerbread snowmen. Our friend Elaine Cumberfield from Orchard View had sent a tin of her signature cookies up with the boys.

The rest of the weekend *was* simple, filled with the pleasures of friends, family, and laughter. We skied under the storm-free bluebird skies of the

Sierra with its steeply pointed peaks and expansive vistas of Lake Tahoe. The largest alpine lake in North America, today it was, hands down, the most serene and beautiful.

Hot Apple Pie Toddy

1/2 cup **Apple cider** (heated)
2 oz. **Tuaca** liqueur (citrus, nut, or vanilla flavors substitute well.)

Garnish with **whipped cream** and a **cinnamon stick**.

If serving children or teetotalers, substitute a few drops of **vanilla extract** for the shot of liqueur.

Meet the Author

Photo Credit: Kathleen Dylan

Mary Feliz writes the Maggie McDonald Mysteries featuring a Silicon Valley professional organizer and her sidekick golden retriever. She's worked for Fortune 500 firms and mom and pop enterprises, competed in whale boat races and done synchronized swimming. She attends organizing conferences in her character's stead, but Maggie's skills leave her in the dust.

Visit Mary online at MaryFeliz.com, or follow her on Twitter @ MaryFelizAuthor.

Sneak Peek

Keep reading for a special excerpt of *Cliff Hanger*, one of Suspense Magazine's Best Books of 2019!

CLIFF HANGER
A Maggie McDonald Mystery
by
Mary Feliz

When a hang-gliding stranger is found fatally injured in the cliffs above Monterey Bay, the investigation into his death becomes a cluttered mess. Professional organizer Maggie McDonald must sort the clues to catch a coastal killer before her family becomes a target...

Maggie has her work cut out for her helping Renée Alvarez organize her property management office. Though the condominium complex boasts a prime location on the shores of the Monterey Bay National Marine Sanctuary, aging buildings and the high-maintenance tenants have Renée run ragged. But Maggie's efforts are complicated when her sons attempt to rescue a badly injured man who crashed his ultra-light on the coastal cliffs.

Despite their efforts to save him, the man dies. Maggie's family members become the prime suspects in a murder investigation and the target of a lawsuit. Her instincts say something's out of place, but solving a murder won't be easy. Maggie still needs to manage her business, the pushy press, and unwanted interest from criminal elements. Controlling chaos is her specialty, but with this killer's crime wave, Maggie may be left hanging...

Look for* CLIFF HANGER *on sale now.

Chapter 1

Packing for a vacation on the central California coast means packing for weather extremes. While the average temperature in June ranges from a comfortable sixty-five to seventy-five degrees, summer daytime temperatures can plummet to fifty degrees or climb into triple digits—sometimes within a 24-hour period. On a typical summer day you're less likely to need your bikini than a warm coat.

From the Notebook of Maggie McDonald
Simplicity Itself Organizing Services
Monday, June 17, Late morning

"Mom, you sure those directions are right?" Fourteen-year-old Brian leaned over the back of the front seat. His sixteen-year-old white-knuckled brother David clutched the wheel and peered into the fog bank. "GPS says this road runs straight into the ocean."

David lifted his foot from the accelerator and hovered it over the brake. The car slowed to a creep. "Seriously?" he said with a hint of panic in his voice. "I can't see a thing. Let me know if your feet get wet and I'll start backing up."

"You're doing great, David," I said to my newly permitted driver. "Up here on the right, you'll turn and take a narrow road out to the condos."

"Narrower than this?" David's voice squeaked a tiny bit as he tried to keep an eye on his mirrors, his speed, the fog-obscured road ahead, and the deep drainage ditches on either side of a road barely wide enough for two cars. The speed limit was 40 mph. The speedometer hugged 25.

Luckily, there was no traffic on the rural road flanked by fields growing strawberries, artichokes, lettuce, and Brussels sprouts.

As we approached the turn, the fog lifted. David easily navigated the narrow bridge over the slough.

"Blue heron!" shouted Brian as one launched itself from a dead log partially submerged in the slough. With a few pumps of its massive wings, it disappeared behind the ridge separating the farmland from Monterey Bay.

I rolled down my window to appreciate the cool salt air. We'd left oven-like temperatures behind us when we'd left the Bay Area less than an hour earlier.

Our golden retriever Belle shoved her nose between the headrest and the window frame for a sniff. Santa Cruz County was home to some five hundred species of migratory and resident birds. She appeared to be smelling and identifying each one.

"Ultralight!" shouted Brian again, pointing out the back window.

"That hang-glider thing?" I asked, locating a lime green and shocking pink oversized kite that looked much like a committee had tried to reverse-engineer a dragonfly. It roared above us.

"They're like hang gliders with engines," Brian explained. "You don't need a pilot's license to operate them."

"Don't even think about it," I said in response to the note of anticipatory glee in his voice. "Ultralight aviation is not included in our summer plans."

"It could be…" Brian began.

"Nope. Not while I'm your mother." I squinted at the aircraft. "Is it supposed to fly like that? All wobbly?" A sharp explosive sound echoed through the hills. "Or is there something wrong with the engine?"

David ended our discussion when he pulled the car onto the gravel shoulder immediately after we drove over a second small bridge. Flexing his hands and fingers, he turned to me. "Can you drive? That last bit was nuts."

As we changed seats, I shivered. The condominium resort complex was only three miles from the nearby agricultural town of Watsonville, but I heard no cars or other sounds of people or civilization. Water lapping in the slough, the screech of a red-tailed hawk, and the crashing waves of the still unseen Pacific were the only sounds I could identify. A brisk wind coming from the ocean, refrigerated by the sixty-degree temperature of Monterey Bay made my summer outfit of shorts and a T-shirt seem ridiculous. I grabbed a sweatshirt off the back seat and put it on quickly before taking a deep breath and restarting the car.

There was no going back and no way I wanted to. The boys were looking forward to their summer vacation at a beach resort, days filled with surfing, skimboarding, hiking, and doing odd jobs. I was committed to helping the condo association management through a contentious transition. The new manager, Renée Alvarez, was a cousin of my best friend, Tess Olmos, who had vouched for Renée's honesty and work ethic.

In exchange for the use of a condo and a small stipend, I would use my professional organizing superpowers to help. The plan was to organize office storage and files, and compile a history of the complex. If time allowed, we'd clear out a few neglected units whose owners had long since abandoned them, unable to sell them or keep up with the taxes, mortgages, and association fees following a market downturn.

It was an idyllic proposition, and I'd agreed to it readily. My husband Max planned to join us every weekend. During the week, he'd commute from our home in Orchard View to his engineering job in Santa Clara while juggling the supervision of several home-remodeling projects that would be easier for construction workers to tackle while the boys and I were out of town.

As we approached the visitor gate, the fog rolled back in, a gust of wind shook the car, and Belle growled. I shivered, but this time it was due to trepidation rather than the chill. I eased the car forward, fighting off the sudden sense that I was heading into unknown and possibly dangerous territory. I shook off the feeling. *Nonsense.* Just because a few of my recent jobs had led to serious trouble for my family and friends didn't mean I was the professional organizer's version of Typhoid Mary. Heebie-jeebies aside, I had every reason to believe we were starting our best family vacation ever.

"Good morning," said the guard, leaning through the drive-up window.

"I'm Maggie McDonald," I said. "Renée Alvarez is expecting us. She said she'd leave a key here in the office."

The guard smiled. "Are you an owner?"

"No, no. I'm working for Renée and the homeowner association this summer. She's giving us the use of a three-bedroom condo. She said she'd leave the key and information packet here for me."

"I'm afraid that only owners are allowed to bring dogs, though I can recommend several good local kennels."

Belle snorted, and I couldn't have agreed with her more. Part of the attraction of taking this underpaid job was the prospect of allowing our golden retriever the freedom of swimming in the ocean and chasing waves, tennis balls, and birds she'd never come close to catching.

"I think Renée said she'd asked the association to make an exception. Is she available at the moment? We can check with her."

A pickup truck pulled up behind me, and I became conscious of holding up traffic. The security guard must have felt the same way. "Tell you what. Pull your car around to the parking spaces. Maybe the boys can walk your dog while you and I straighten this out with Renée."

I followed the instructions. Brian and David took turns holding Belle on a leash outside the building while I sorted out our accommodations. The guard, who had introduced himself as Vik Peterson, handed me a dog biscuit bigger than my hand. "You've got a beautiful pup there," he said, nodding toward the door, outside which Belle sniffed bushes and barked at a rabbit. "Please give her this cookie with my apologies for the confusion. I'll give Renée a ring."

Again, I followed instructions, cheered by Vik's upbeat demeanor and attentive customer service.

"What's up, Mom?" Brian asked as I joined the boys outside. Belle snuffled my hand and took the biscuit. "Are they trying to cancel?"

"I don't think so. The guard is calling Renée right now."

"Should we phone Tess?" David asked. "She set this up, right?"

David was correct, as usual, but I wasn't worried. "Working with a new client can be a bumpy road. If they didn't have a few organizational problems, they wouldn't need me, would they?"

I glanced into the guard station, and Vik waved. When I opened the door, he held up a key.

"I've got the key to your unit," he said, looking triumphant. "I still haven't reached Renée, though." He glanced at his watch. "She's usually the first one here, well before seven o'clock. But her chief lieutenant and head of maintenance says you can go ahead and get settled in."

"Great! Thanks. And Belle?"

"Sorry, no. You wouldn't believe the number of complaints I'd get if I admitted a visiting dog without Renée's say-so."

"I guess we could get groceries and come back, but if Belle doesn't have access, it will sink the deal for me."

"Dogs are welcome at the state beach down the road. You passed it on the way in. You could hang out there while you wait to hear from Renée."

I thought for a moment, considering.

Vik barreled on as though I'd already approved the plan. "Do you have a cell number you can give me? I'll get in touch as soon as I hear from her. I hope she's okay. It isn't like her to be even a few minutes late."

"Do you know where she is? I was under the impression she spent more time on site here than she did at home."

Vik checked his watch and frowned. "Could be anything. There's a first time for everything." He pushed a notepad and pen toward me.

I handed Vik my business card and thanked him again. We all climbed back into the car and were about to set off when Vik opened the office door and called out.

"Your unit is in Building F. Fourth building from the north end of the complex. It's a short hike from the state beach if you want to check it out."

I saluted and put the car in reverse. After a small false start, it looked like the tide was starting to turn on our adventure.

* * * *

The boys had changed into their wetsuits in the picnic area of the state beach. Now they were boogie boarding while Belle chased them and tried to catch waves in her teeth. I checked my phone and my watch. If I didn't move I'd be lulled to sleep by the sound of the waves. I told the boys I'd walk down to the Heron Beach Resort property to check out our unit.

Brian and David had been thrilled when I told them they'd each have their own room for the summer. Our typical Spartan vacation budget meant they normally shared a tent or a room—with mixed results. When one wanted to sleep in, the other would be anticipating a dawn fishing trip. I'd enjoyed summers of overhearing laughter as they whispered to each other past lights-out. Rumbling older voices now conversed well into the night, replacing those early giggles. Mostly, they got along. But proximity also brought fights. Hurt feelings erupted regularly, particularly when they were tired. The three-bedroom condo was a luxury we'd all enjoy.

According to Tess, a third-floor ocean-view unit meant we'd wake up to share our breakfast with chance sightings of surfing dolphins, breaching whales, and playful seals and sea otters cavorting in the waves just steps from the building. It was my idea of paradise.

Wooden staircases over the dunes marked the beach-side entrance to each condo building, and I counted them off until I spotted the sign to Building F half-buried in the dune grass. I climbed the steps and looked for our unit. But when I took the stairs to the top level, the numbers were higher than I'd expected. I checked the key and the unit number again. There was no third-floor, ocean-view unit that matched the key Vik had given me.

I trudged down the stairs, discouraged. Had Vik handed me the wrong key? Had Renée misrepresented the promised accommodations? Had a problem developed that she'd neglected to warn me about? Until Renée surfaced, there was no way to know.

Still, while the third floor would have been a dream, all of the condos were steps from the beach and within earshot of the waves. Living on a lower level would make it easier to unload the car, bring groceries in and out, and keep up with Belle's bathroom needs. I tried to stay positive.

I hunted the shaded lower floors for the apartment number and found it on ground level, where the view would offer beach grass instead of open water. Disappointed, I quickly tried to adjust my attitude. Beach access was beach access. And most of the time we were indoors we'd be asleep. On the first floor, I wouldn't have to worry that the boys' clomping feet would disturb downstairs neighbors.

But as I unlocked the deadbolt and pushed open the door, I feared we'd have to contend with something far worse than a second-rate view. The smell alone had me gagging, and that wasn't the worst part.

Printed in the United States
by Baker & Taylor Publisher Services